A Season

Gone

To the

Dogs

JOSH LANGSTON

ISBN 13: 978-1735373317

More books by Josh Langston

Novels:
Resurrection Blues
A Little Primitive
A Little More Primitive
A Primitive In Paradise
Treason, Treason!
The 12,000-year-old Whisper
Oh, Bits!
Voices
Greeley
Zeus's Cookbook
Garden Clubbed!

Novels with Barbara Galler-Smith:
Under St. Owain's Rock
Druids
Captives
Warriors

Short Fiction:
Mysfits
Christmas Beyond the Box
Dancing Among the Stars
Who Put Scoundrels in Charge?

Textbooks on the Craft of Writing:
Write Naked!
The Naked Truth!
The Naked Novelist!
Naked Notes!

Dedication

For all the wonderful folks–and their pets–who have made our retirement lives so complete. You know who you are, and you know you're always welcome to join us on the patio for an adult beverage or two. Come on down, Soleil!

May all your holiday seasons be bright, cheery, and above all else, memorable.

Contents

Acknowledgments

Chapter One   1

Chapter Two   18

Chapter Three   34

Chapter Four   53

Chapter Five   70

Chapter Six   89

Chapter Seven   107

Chapter Eight   125

Chapter Nine   142

Chapter Ten   160

Chapter Eleven   179

Chapter Twelve   198

Chapter Thirteen   217

Chapter Fourteen   236

Chapter Fifteen   253

Epilog   271

About the Author   279

Bonus Chapter from *Garden Clubbed!*   280

Acknowledgments

First Readers are a godsend. They're willing to labor through first manuscripts and root out the inevitable errors that creep into every story. Some are, by nature, capable of the finest editing skills, others simply use an abundance of God-given common sense.

Among those who gave of their time and talent to bring this tale to life are, in no particular order, Ann Langston, Doris Reidy, Pam Olinto, Sonya Braverman Cooper, Barry Womack, Betty Smith, Don and Jan Wolf, Jan Feese, and Jack Bowie.

I'm indebted to all of you for your invaluable assistance. Thank you!

I also want to mention our fantastic neighbors on Windy Ridge Way in Canton, GA who allowed me to write their pets into this story. Thank you Sharon, Carol, Larry and Gail, Mark and Karen, Sandee, Jeri and Barry, Lynn and Bobby, Karen, Jan and Rich, Kathy and Dan, Bonnie, and Judy. Y'all are the best!

Our (mostly) Canine Cast

Augie

Buck and Brandy

Cody and Zoe

J J

[Editor's note: While canine stars Tater and Noël have both been portrayed vividly, they reside solely within the author's fertile, if unconventional, imagination.]

Finley

Foster

MacKenzie

Maggie

Maple

Pinot Noir (Peanut)

Rascal

Rosie

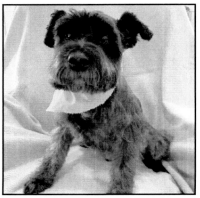

Spike

Chapter One

"Sometimes an itch isn't just an itch. Sometimes, it means something." – Raymond Mays

Lawrence K. "Skeeter" Malone didn't care much for newspapers. Didn't care much for magazines, either. He owned a few comic books, but once he'd struggled through them the first time, a second reading held little appeal. So, it came as quite a shock to his mother, Gloria, when Skeeter brought her an article torn from the Casual Living section of the Sunday paper.

"We should do this, Mom," the ten-year-old announced, presenting the ragged newsprint for her inspection. The headline stood out like a warning beacon:

Pet Auditions Today

She gave him her best puzzled look. "What are the auditions for?"

"TV and movies," Skeeter said. "It doesn't say which ones. They wanna find cool new pets for commercials and stuff. We should take Tater. He could be a star!"

"You actually *read* the paper?" Gloria asked. Though pleased, she remained all too aware of Skeeter's evolving skill as a con artist.

"It's today!" he said eagerly. "Can we go?"

"Do you think Tater's up to it? He's not a puppy anymore." She didn't mention the obvious—Tater's missing leg—and assumed such a handicap would automatically put the aging pooch at a huge disadvantage. The missing limb never seemed to slow him down though. He'd even managed to learn to stand, albeit briefly, on one hind leg.

"Tater knows lots of tricks," Skeeter said. "He can do all kinds of stuff."

"I know. But let me read the article, okay? Then we'll talk about it."

Shaking her head in a mixture of wonder and puzzlement, Gloria quickly absorbed the details. There weren't many. A company called Leon Farms had put out the casting call and said they were interested in seeing any pets with "unusual talents." The article gave no specifics about what programs or films the casting was for, but made it clear that Leon Farms personnel would do any training required. They would need to keep any animals selected for several weeks. The audition was open to all non-aggressive species.

"How carefully did you read this, sweetie?" she asked.

He shrugged. "Pretty good, I guess."

"Would you be willing to give up Tater for a month or two if he's chosen?"

Skeeter's face clouded. "I dunno."

"That's part of the deal."

"Maybe I could visit him."

Gloria held out her hands, palms up. "We'd have to ask. The article doesn't say anything about that." *Or what the job might pay.*

The boy considered the issue for a moment longer. "We should go."

"You sure?"

"Yeah."

"It'll take an hour or so just to drive there, and we might have to stay a long time." She didn't mention that she'd planned to do some Christmas shopping despite the deficit they'd been operating under since the company she worked for had let her go due to budget cuts. This year, Christmas wasn't likely to be terribly jolly.

"It's important," Skeeter said. She wondered where he'd picked up the note of finality in his voice.

"Did Tater tell you that?"

"Aw, Mom." He managed to draw out the "Aw" to thrice its length. "I knew we'd have to talk first."

Gloria squinted at him, but the modified view did nothing to help her decide if the boy was serious or not. They both talked *to* the dog, but Skeeter often seemed to listen to him as well.

~*~

Maeve Blessing exhaled as if she'd finished a month's work and could finally take a much-needed break. "It just makes me angry," she said. "This is the last place in the world I'd expect to find a bully."

Artemis Maker, a co-worker, shook his head. "Don't you think you might be jumping to conclusions?"

"I certainly hope that's all it is." Maeve shook her head and sent a torrent of red curls swirling. "I hate it when things don't work out the way they're supposed to. Of all the auditions we've conducted, we've only found two possible candidates. By this time last year, we had to turn away lots of animals with way above average potential."

"That's a bit of an overstatement." Artemis smiled. "Some years it's easier, that's all. It doesn't mean there's a bully involved."

"You're not outside, meeting and greeting, like me. We made it very clear in the ads that people shouldn't bring mean animals. And yet, they keep showing up."

"Every time?"

"Well, no. Not every time, but often enough." She tried to bring her wild tresses under control. "There was this one lady who brought an alpaca, and—"

"Seriously? An alpaca?"

"Yes! An adorable creature with a smile that'd just melt your heart. It sure melted mine, and it would've made a superb hauler. Anyway, some jerk showed up with a monkey, or maybe it was a chimp. I'm no expert. Anyway, the monkey started throwing stones at the alpaca, and the owner couldn't, or wouldn't, get it to stop. Neither could I. It upset the alpaca so much she ran off. I presume her owner found her in one of the pastures, but she didn't bring her back. She just left. And I can't say I blame her."

"And the monkey?"

Maeve snorted. "Rejected. On the spot. I wouldn't give that little monster an audition if it cost me my job. I told his owner to leave and not come back. Ever."

"That sort of thing is bound to happen from time to time," Artemis said. "You can't always tell how an animal will react before it's been trained. And you shouldn't assume there's a bully to blame."

"Well, that monkey was certainly a bully."

"Perhaps. But you know what I meant. Bullies come in a variety of forms, and just because some critter acts like one—"

"Doesn't mean it is one, or worse, was sent by one. Yes, I know. I know. Still, it makes me wonder."

~*~

Leon Farms occupied several acres of rural land, most of it in pasture. In addition to a modest, one-story, wooden farmhouse, the property boasted several additional buildings. Of those, only a barn and a stable had obvious functions.

"Oh, cool!" Skeeter said when they arrived. He pointed at a swimming pool and some other equipment Gloria guessed was used for agility training—ladders, ramps, plastic tunnels, and jumps. She couldn't help but wonder how Tater would fare on such apparatus. Skeeter's enthusiasm only grew, while hers had rapidly begun to ebb.

"Hey there," said a smiling young woman with bright red hair. It contrasted well with the worn denim she'd dressed in from head to toe. The name tag on her shirt said, "Maeve." She held out a clipboard and pen for Gloria, then knelt to get acquainted with Skeeter and Tater.

"What kind of dog is he?" she asked.

"The best," Skeeter said without hesitation.

"Obviously," Maeve said. "And how old is he?"

"Ten. We're the same age."

Gloria couldn't help but frown. "Is that a problem?"

"Not necessarily," the girl replied. "We've taught new tricks to lots of old dogs."

"Tater's not old," Skeeter said, his tone adamant.

The girl merely smiled. "Once we've got Tater registered, you're free to wander around anywhere, except the barn. There's nothing dangerous or scary in there, but the insurance company says we have to keep it off limits." She stood and rubbed her palms then pointed at a squat, windowless building near the farmhouse. "We'll call you from over there when it's Tater's turn to audition."

"What, exactly, would you like him to do?"

"We'll explain all that inside, but basically, we want to see if he obeys simple commands, and if he's comfortable in an unusual environment."

"He knows tricks," Skeeter said.

"Should we be rehearsing them?" Gloria asked.

"If you'd like," Maeve said. "Just don't wear him out."

For the next hour they wandered around the farm, waiting. A steady stream of pet owners filed into and out of the low building. Most of them brought dogs, but a handful had other animals. In addition to cats and birds, Gloria noticed a rabbit, an iguana, and a goat.

They found a spot of shade to wait in, and Skeeter tried to run Tater through his repertoire of tricks.

"I thought you wanted to do this," Skeeter said after the dog refused to sit, beg, or roll over on command. "We came all this way, and now you won't do anything. I'm disappointed in you."

The words sounded distressingly familiar to Gloria. She gazed at her son and his dog, wondering if the little canine would react like the boy did when he heard those same words.

Instead, Tater licked Skeeter's face.

"Maybe he needs to rest," Gloria said.

Skeeter wiped his face on his sleeve but didn't look convinced. "I just don't want him to mess up!"

Gloria didn't either, especially after reading a note on

the sign-up sheet that said pet owners would receive union scale wages for the entire time a contracted animal remained in the care of Leon Farms, Inc. She didn't know what "union scale" meant in dollars and cents, but whatever the amount, it would be a welcome and much-needed addition to her budget.

~*~

"Was it something I said?" The question Ormsby Ivanov asked hung in the air like the aroma from an overflowing sewer.

"I don't understand. You didn't—"

"Correct me if I'm wrong," Ormsby said from behind his expansive desk, "but I could have sworn I heard you laughing about a monkey and a llama."

"I think it was an alpaca."

"Whatever. The monkey annoyed the animal into running away, which is fine. But how many other pets did you manage to upset?"

The man's mouth opened, but no sounds came out. He cast about Ormsby's oversized office as if seeking an escape route.

Ormsby continued, "Your job was to prevent the best candidates from being selected. Surely the alpaca wasn't the only one in line."

"Well, no," the man began, "but—"

"But you were kicked off the property before you could proceed further, right?"

"I guess, but—"

"Another 'but?' Can't you tell I've heard enough of them?"

7

"I can explain! You don't know how hard it is to tell which ones will be good or bad."

Ormsby crossed his arms on his fat chest. "You said you could tell. Your words, as I recall, offered a guarantee."

"Yes, I know, but—"

"There it is. Another 'but.' Get out! You're done. Don't come back until you're called."

"Bu— Uh... I only did what you told me to do."

Ormsby stared down at the man whose worth paralleled that of some insignificant insect. "You failed."

Somehow the man summoned enough indignation to stiffen his spine. A sneer replaced his snivel, and he squinted back at his employer. "I'll bet the people responsible for that audition would like to know how much you paid me to cause trouble."

Ormsby shook his head and mimed a sad face. "The depth of your stupidity astonishes me. Such a pity. Fortunately, there's a cure." He signaled for Mordecai to take care of the miscreant who quickly backed up against a wall.

"Let's not get carried away," the man said.

"On the contrary," said Ormsby. "That's precisely what's going to happen."

Mordecai yanked the man away from the wall, wrapped his arms around him from behind, and squeezed.

"You won't like doing penance," Ormsby said. "You won't care for the preparation either. Young Mordecai here is quite the wonder. I think of him as part man and part boa constrictor. Wouldn't you agree?"

Mordecai's prey opened his mouth to respond, but with

little air in his lungs, he could only mouth the words. His eyes bulged, and reminded Ormsby of the toads he'd stepped on in his youth.

With one pitiful wheeze, the man went limp in Mordecai's arms.

"You know what to do with him," Ormsby said. "When he wakes up, explain what will happen to him if he says anything to anyone about his employment here."

"Yes, sir. Right away," Mordecai responded. He then hauled the unconscious body away as if it weighed nothing.

~*~

When they called for Tater, Gloria and Skeeter walked directly to the building where the audition would take place. The same smiling girl who had welcomed them to the try-outs met them at the door.

"Which of you will be taking Tater through his paces?" she asked.

"Me," Skeeter said, although his eagerness had clearly peaked a good half hour earlier.

"Great," said the effervescent girl. She smiled brightly at Gloria. "You can wait out here. We won't be long."

"But—"

The girl already had a sheltering arm around Skeeter's shoulders. "He'll be fine. We just need to eliminate as many uncontrollable elements as possible."

Uncontrollable element? "I'm his mother!"

"Indeed, you are," the girl said. "And judging from your son and his dog, an excellent one. We'll see you in a little while."

The door closed quietly but all too quickly, and Gloria

stood on the wrong side of it. She told herself she had nothing to worry about. She had seen other people enter and leave the audition venue without incident. No one wept, or cursed, or in any other way suggested there might be a malevolent angle to the proceedings.

She pressed her ear to the door and strained to make out any voices or activity within the building, but the effort failed. When she stepped a few feet away and gave the structure a slow visual inspection, she decided it had an even uglier, squattier look than she'd previously thought. And, as everyone knew, ugly plus squatty equaled sinister.

Several minutes passed, and no one entered or left. Despite the denim-clad girl's pleasant demeanor and repeated assurances, Gloria's apprehension grew. After all, what did she really know about these people? The world was rife with gracious, friendly, serial killers just waiting for their chance to do unspeakable things to innocent little boys. *And* their dogs!

What was taking so long?

Oh, she ruminated, there was Tater. An outstanding pet, for sure, but that didn't make him much of a guard dog. As far as she knew, he liked everyone. He liked the *mailman* for crying out loud, and she didn't have much use for him at all. The sad truth was, anyone who dared knock on her door stood in far greater danger of being licked than mauled. Fat lot of good Tater would be if anyone tried to do anything to Skeeter. Clearly, he was doomed.

The longer she waited, the more agitated she became.

Suddenly, one short, sharp, bark escaped the squat building. She knew, instantly, that it had come from Tater. *What were they doing in there?*

Finally, she'd had enough. No one had the right to stand between a mother and her child. Pushing her sleeves up past her elbows, Gloria stalked toward the door. She was, by golly, one *uncontrollable element* they'd darn well better accommodate.

As if responding to her rage, the door popped open just before she reached it, and out marched Skeeter, Tater, and the still-smiling, denim-clad Maeve.

Both Skeeter and Tater appeared safe and unharmed. Tater mouthed a dog treat while his ten-year-old "handler" chatted with the ever-cheery redhead who seemed to be the only public face for Leon Farms.

Gloria throttled her apprehension and forced herself to generate a smile at least as wide as the girl's. "How'd it go?"

"They did great," the girl said.

"So, Tater gets the job?" Skeeter asked.

Not surprisingly, Maeve responded with her million-watt grin. "I can't say for sure. We'll have to wait until all the auditions are done." She put her hand on the boy's shoulder and pulled him a little closer. Her voice dropped into a barely audible register. "We really like Tater. I shouldn't say this, but I wouldn't be surprised if we offered him a contract."

"Us," Gloria said. "You wouldn't be surprised if they offered *us* a contract."

The girl dipped her head in Gloria's direction. "Exactly."

Gloria glanced, yet again, at the building and decided it didn't look nearly as sinister as it had a little while before.

"We'll be in touch soon," the girl said, and then she was gone.

Gloria gathered her two companions close and ushered them back to the car. Skeeter chose to sit in the back seat with Tater, and despite Gloria's best efforts to pry some details out of the boy, he consistently responded to all her questions about the audition with single syllable answers.

And none of them satisfied her need to know what went on in the squatty little building.

~*~

Ormsby Ivanov had looked forward to a victory celebration, something his enemies had denied him for far too long. But that same long delay had taught him many things about them, not the least of which was their uncanny ability to bypass the roadblocks he strove to put in their way.

Though he had never met the Boss, he knew the man's reputations—one of which painted him as a saint. Another, the one Ormsby had every reason to believe was true, painted a picture of someone who fouled the very essence of the holiday he supposedly embraced.

According to the message Ormsby had just received, the Boss and his minions had completed their recruitment efforts and located enough animals to continue their plans. Once again, the Boss was poised to win. Was there no limit to the resources that sinister figure called upon?

Despite having a spy within his enemy's ranks, Ormsby continued to be outmaneuvered. He had lost count of his failures, and yet he remained dedicated to his objective. His resources were considerable, and he maintained a prominent place in worldwide financial markets, but he lacked the mystical elements his foe employed to achieve his ends. Yes, Ormsby's resources were substantial.

But were they enough?

After a great deal of concentrated prayer, Ormsby concluded that the solution called for a bolder plan and more direct action. That would undoubtedly require more effort from his informant in the Boss's organization.

~*~

A few days after Tater's audition, Gloria got a call from Michael Bell at Leon Farms.

"With your permission," Bell said, "we'd like to sign Tater to a short-term contract."

"You want to use Tater in a commercial?"

"We have several openings right now, and I can't say for sure exactly how we'll use him. All I can promise is that he'll be given extraordinary care while he's with us. Our handlers and trainers are the best in the business."

"Tater is my son's dog," Gloria said. "My husband picked him out at the pound." She didn't mention her husband's disappearance shortly thereafter. Though it had been five years, neither the police nor the private investigator she hired had turned up any trace of him.

"Then," said the man on the phone, "I need to talk to your son."

"He's in school right now," Gloria said. "But if you'll give me the details, I'll pass them along and call you with his answer."

Bell agreed and filled her in on the basics. She promised to call him back by the end of the business day.

"We'll be here around the clock for the next few days," he said. "Call any time."

When the school bus pulled up to the corner, Gloria was waiting for it. She gave Skeeter a hug, and the two walked back to their house. The rental wasn't much to look at, but it served their needs, and didn't take too big a chunk out of Gloria's limited income.

"So," Skeeter said, "they wanna make Tater a star! I told ya they would. I bet it's a movie. They're always looking for special dogs to be in the movies."

"The man didn't say what Tater would be doing. Only that he was needed, and that they'd take good care of him."

The boy wrapped his arms around the dog, who licked his face as if someone had smeared it with peanut butter. Skeeter laughed, and the dog trundled off, his three-legged gait oddly natural.

"How long would he be gone?" he asked.

"About a month and a half. They'd pick him up before Thanksgiving and return him just after Christmas."

Skeeter pursed his lips. "That's a long time." He stretched out the word "long."

Gloria shrugged. "Five, six weeks. Give or take. But the holidays are so busy. You won't have time to miss him." *And we desperately need the money.*

"Could we visit him?"

"Sadly, no. They said he'd be on a very precise training schedule, and they couldn't take the chance that seeing his owner might distract him."

"What're they gonna teach him?" he asked.

"They wouldn't say."

Skeeter always frowned when deep in thought, a trait he shared with his Dad. Seeing that expression brought an on-going ache to Gloria's heart. *What had happened to their perfect little family?*

"I have to talk it over with Tater," Skeeter said.

Gloria shifted mental gears. "Sure. But let me know your decision as soon as you can. I have to call them back and—"

"Oh, you can call 'em now," Skeeter said. "I'm okay with it. Tater really needs to do this, and I think he knows that.

I just need him to know I understand, too."

"I sure wish I did."

"It'll be okay, Mom. Trust me."

He smiled at her and triggered another memory, one of her husband waving goodbye as he left for work that fateful morning. "You're absolutely positive about this?"

"Yes," he said. "No problem."

But as she watched him walk away, she thought he looked anything but positive.

~*~

Maeve finally felt she could relax. While the efforts of the Georgia unit had only located a few potential recruits, two of the others had come through with enough candidates to promise a grand season.

"I told you not to worry," Artemis said.

"I know, but every year it seems to get harder and harder."

"You make it sound like you've been doing this forever."

She laughed. "Of course not. This is my first full season, but it's been eye-opening. I've seen so much, learned so much."

"And there's a lot more," Artemis said with a knowing smile. "You're just getting started." He paused and handed her a note from their supervisor, Michael Bell. "Looks like you've got a pickup."

She brightened. "Which one?"

"Guess!"

"I don't know. Is it Buck? Augie? No, wait." She closed her eyes and made a wish. "Okay, tell me."

"It's Tater."

15

Maeve beamed. "Yes! He's going to be amazing."

"Maybe," Artemis said. "But don't get your hopes up. You only saw him in the audition. Things could change. Nothing's guaranteed."

~*~

The same girl they'd seen at the audition arrived a week to the day before Thanksgiving to pick up Tater. Gloria tried hard to keep her emotions in check as Skeeter accompanied his dog on the short walk to the girl's car. She opened the back door, and Tater jumped in. She put a padded harness on him and secured it to keep him safe in case of an accident, then turned to address Skeeter.

"You've done a wonderful job with him," she said. "We noticed that right away. Love is a lesson that never gets old."

Gloria smiled at that. Skeeter backed away from the car and leaned against her.

"Now, don't you worry about Tater," the girl said. "He's special. You can't begin to *imagine* how special. So, believe me when I say we'll take good care of him. And we'll have him back as soon as we can."

"The day after Christmas, right?" Skeeter said.

She nodded. "Around then, yes." She climbed behind the wheel of her shiny, little, red car and drove away.

Though he tried to maintain a brave front, Skeeter's stoic facade crumbled before they reached the front door.

"I can call them," Gloria said. "I'm sure they'd let us have him back. I could explain that it was all a mistake, that we—"

"No," he said, wiping his nose on his sleeve. "It's okay. This is important."

"If it's just the money you're worried about, I'm sure we

can get by without it. We've managed so far."

Skeeter shook his head. "It doesn't have anything to do with money."

It doesn't? Gloria opted to change the subject. "How 'bout some hot chocolate?"

"No thanks," he said in a dead monotone. "I think I'll just go to my room."

Gloria swallowed hard and wondered if surviving the holidays could get any tougher. Three weeks later, it did.

Chapter Two

"Not all holidays are holy days." – Charlemagne Fyfe

Though Maeve had not been the first to arrive at the Georgia farm, she was definitely the last one to leave. Her promotion after the last season of voyages meant she'd earned the organization's trust. They had given her a position of significant responsibility despite her youth.

She made her final rounds with pride. All but one of the recruits had been shipped out with the remaining staff, one animal per person. Unlike some of the other posts, hers had a few people more than needed. Despite what Artemis said, she still felt guilty, as if she hadn't tried hard enough to find the proper pets for the coming season.

After checking every building, shed, work area, and playground, she returned to the farmhouse with little Tater following close behind. The dog was remarkably agile despite missing a leg. A ten-year-old, the pooch was well into middle age but remained as frisky as a pup, or nearly so.

She recalled how lovingly his owner treated him. The little boy, Skeeter, had shared the secret of his training

18

success. Tater, according to him, would do almost anything for a bite of cheese. Skeeter favored cheddar, but claimed Tater would eat anything that didn't smell too bad. At least, bad *to him*.

Kneeling down, Maev stroked the dog's head. He had dark eyes and thick, furry brows which made them even more expressive. She had no doubt she'd enjoy working with him and felt certain he'd make the most of the new training, to say nothing of the occupational "boost" he'd soon be given.

Maeve looked forward to going home and getting started. She had tired of Georgia anyway, and longed for cooler climes.

~*~

The first symptoms showed up a day later. Gloria suspected Skeeter had picked up a flu bug and treated him accordingly. Two days after that, his symptoms changed completely. When they changed again the following day, Gloria took him to the doctor who promptly put him in the hospital.

Skeeter's symptomatic symphony generated a succession of diagnoses *du jour*, none of which were more than guesses. That in turn led to one series of tests after another. The process seemed hopeless as the results were never conclusive. Skeeter's illness remained a mystery.

Gloria had no qualms about going even deeper into debt if it meant someone, somewhere, could tell her what was wrong with her son and, more importantly, start him on some sort of treatment plan that would make him healthy again. But none of the specialists consulted seemed able to solve the riddle.

Adding to the dilemma was the absence of the boy's usual good humor. That went missing the day Tater climbed into the back of the little red car from Leon Farms.

"Is there such a thing as terminal sadness?" Gloria asked

the latest addition to Skeeter's team of specialists.

"You mean like depression?"

"Well, yes."

"Depression is common in patients diagnosed with a serious illness. You son is certainly ill, but we have no reason to believe the malady is incurable."

"I don't think he's sad because he's ill. I'm wondering if it's just the reverse."

"I'm not following you," the physician said.

"Skeeter misses his dog," Gloria said. "Could all this just be a case of separation anxiety?"

"Maybe." The doctor shrugged. "It's his profound lack of energy we find alarming. We have something like 6,000 named diseases on record, all of them rare. I believe your son has one of them. Our job is to figure out which one it is."

"And treat it."

"Of course."

"Would it help if he were a little happier?" she asked.

"Absolutely."

"Then I'd like to take him home."

The doctor frowned.

"Is that a problem?" Gloria looked him straight in the eyes. "Your team certainly haven't done anything for him here that I can't do at home." *For a fraction of the cost.*

"It would definitely make things more difficult if we decide to do more testing."

"More difficult for you, or Skeeter?"

"For the team. Arriving at a diagnosis in a case like this

is tricky. Here at Health Haven Research Hospital, unlike most conventional treatment facilities, having the patient readily available makes things easier."

"Again, for *you*."

"Well, yes."

"Then we're outta here." She checked her watch. "I'll be back at six to take my son home. You have four hours to do whatever testing you need to do. I may not be able to make him well, but I intend to do everything I can to make him smile."

She left the doctor with his mouth open and his objection hanging in the air, ignored. One of the nurses smiled and gave her a thumbs up sign as she hurried down the hall.

Unlike Skeeter's illness, her destination was no mystery. She needed to get Tater back before she brought her son home, and heaven help anyone who got in her way.

~*~

Maeve closed and sealed the access to the transport chamber before she and Tater, the spunky little three-legged dog, clambered in for the ride to headquarters. Unlike some of the recruits, Tater showed absolutely no fear. Instead, he snuggled next to Maeve as if he'd done it all his life.

She scratched him gently under his chin and behind his ears, something he clearly enjoyed. They listened to some seasonal music—it was *always* seasonal music—as they cruised toward their destination. Tater put his head on her leg, exhaled as if he'd been hard at work all day, and promptly went to sleep.

Maeve leaned back in the cushioned seat and tried to do the same thing. There was little else to do while confined to the chamber. There were no visible controls, no windows, and as far as she knew, no way to contact the outside world. One simply got in, closed the doors, took a seat, and relaxed. The rest was up to someone else, presumably at HQ. She had heard

21

there were similar portals at each of the recruiting sites, but the one in rural Georgia was the only one she'd ever used.

Even though she had been part of the organization for three years, Maeve realized there was a great deal about it that she didn't know. She knew who the Boss was, of course, though she had not yet met him. He remained incredibly busy, even during the woefully misnamed "slack" season. It was anything but slack as she had learned early in her career.

Still, the slack season offered moments of quiet and some time for relaxation. The season of voyages, however, held little time for anything but preparation and execution. Having weathered two such experiences, Maeve felt ready to begin the third. This time, however, her role would be much more demanding. She prayed she was ready.

~*~

The drive to Leon Farms should have been familiar. The last time she made the trip, the autumn leaves had yet to fall, and they provided a colorful tapestry through which she drove. Now, most of them lay on the ground, and the landscape appeared not only unfamiliar but hostile.

She shrugged off all such thoughts and put Skeeter's welfare square in the middle of her mind. The view might have changed, but the directions certainly hadn't, and she hewed to the list she'd pulled from the internet a few weeks earlier.

When she finally reached her destination, little had changed except for the number of cars parked near the old two-story farmhouse. This time, hers was the only one. In fact, the place appeared devoid of human life.

She got out of her car and marched to the farmhouse. When a vigorous pounding on the front door yielded nothing but sore knuckles, she moved on to the squat, ugly building where Skeeter had taken Tater for his audition. The door yielded easily to her touch, but like the house, this second building apparently sheltered no occupants.

Tossing caution to the wind, Gloria marched toward the barn which the Leon Farms insurer had proclaimed off-limits. Once again, the door yielded at her touch. No lock, nor chain nor even cobweb slowed her entry. But like the other buildings, it too appeared both unused and unoccupied, all but abandoned.

Driven by a growing sense of panic and the need to recover Skeeter's three-legged companion, Gloria searched every building on the property until she worked her way back to the farmhouse. That, she had saved for last. Surely there would be some clue, some *hint* of where she might locate the people who ran Leon Farms, Inc.

Unlike all the other buildings on the property, however, the farmhouse was securely locked.

Ormsby Ivanov's dinner didn't sit well, but it had nothing to do with the cuisine. *That,* at least, had proven as tasty as always. What had him perturbed was impatience. He'd sent word to his informant that he wanted more and better information concerning the movements of the Boss. Unfortunately, he hadn't heard anything he didn't already know about.

If tradition held, the Boss—Ormsby refused to call him by any of his traditional names—would present himself as the guest of honor at one of the big holiday parades that usually occurred around Thanksgiving. The man simply thrived on the adoration of the masses. The very thought sickened Ormsby.

But, he belatedly realized, that very same self-indulgent behavior, that uncontrolled addiction to acclaim could play right into Ormsby's hands. If he could simply find out which parade the Boss would bless with his presence, Ormsby could position his people in advance and be ready for him.

He had no doubt it was the right thing to do. No doubt whatsoever.

When it came to matters of faith, Ormsby had no peers. There were plenty of so-called believers who took the winter holidays seriously, and who professed a deep conviction about the need to keep everything about the season reverent. But few felt as deeply as Ormsby Ivanov. When considering Christmas, there should be no room for crass commercialization, shameless celebration, or a focus on the exchange of tawdry gifts and trinkets, few of which ever had anything to do with the arrival on Earth of the Holy One.

The worst of it all, and the target on which he'd chosen to focus, was the one man who seemed to enjoy greater favor than any other, including Ivanov's God. That had to end, and it couldn't end soon enough.

If only his minion would come through!

For lack of a peer, and weary of dining alone, Ormsby Ivanov bowed his head in prayer. Perhaps when done, the information he needed would arrive while he consumed desert.

"Mordecai!" he yelled. "Bring me some pie."

~*~

Gloria stared in frustration at the front door of the farmhouse. No matter how hard she worked at it, the door would not open. An exterior door, it had no visible hinges, and the knob and locking mechanism proved unbreachable.

She moved to the nearest window and attempted to pry it open, but while the casement woodwork appeared boringly normal, it seemed to have a great deal more in common with steel than wood. She ran a fingernail against what looked like worn paint but failed to scrape off so much as a molecule of it.

Both her anger and her frustration grew, her temper

disintegrated, and she yielded common sense to rationalized mayhem. After foraging briefly until she found a fist-sized rock, she threw the stone at the window.

It bounced off.

She picked the rock off the grass and marched forward until she could reach the glass with ease, then proceeded to bash the stone against it as hard as she could. Each time, the rock left a small deposit of itself on the window, but the glass didn't break.

Gloria pounded away, screaming and carrying on until she staggered away, weary, defeated, and embarrassed. *I can't even break a lousy window. My son could be dying, and I'm out here in the boondocks looking for a dog I'm pretty sure isn't even here. What's the matter with me?*

She stared up at the sky as dark clouds appeared to swallow the setting sun.

Please, dear Lord, tell me what on Earth is wrong with me?

No stranger to despair, having lost her husband and, more recently, her job, Gloria trudged back to her car and forced herself to shift focus. She needed to talk to someone she knew would listen, someone who cared about her and Skeeter. The man she had in mind certainly used to care. She prayed that he still did.

~*~

The vehicle Maeve and Tater had been riding in came to a smooth and silent stop. A modest chime signaled their arrival at the terminal. The door slid open as the music faded, replaced by the sounds of a legion of busy workers hustling throughout the building.

Maeve stepped into the crowded corridor as the door to her transport unit whispered shut. She held Tater in her arms,

25

though he didn't seem concerned with their new surroundings. When Artemis Maker approached her walking a pair of ivory-hued labradoodles, Tater barked a happy greeting, his abbreviated tail wagging like a metronome cranked up to the insanity level. It made her laugh, and the dog sealed the deal by licking her cheek.

"Looks like you've made a friend," Artemis said, straining to hold the two wooly canines in check. "I'll trade you!"

"Not a chance," she replied. "I need to report in. But maybe we can grab a bite later?"

"I'd love it," he yelped as the two dogs in his care dragged him away.

She gave him a smile and went on her way.

Though she'd been in the terminal many times, she still got disoriented. The senior staff members probably knew the routes by heart having negotiated them a thousand times or more. To Maeve, however, everything looked the same. She wondered if anyone had ever considered color coding the place. It would be easy enough to put colored lines on the floor to indicate directionality. Instead, everything was done up in red, white and green with abundant flourishes of gold and silver. She thought the whole thing a bit much but lacked the seniority—and the courage—to mention it to anyone, even Artemis, who *claimed* to have heard everything. She huffed. He hadn't been there that much longer than she had.

Tater barked again, as if to get her attention. While she'd been musing on the terminal's decorating scheme, she'd almost missed her turn.

How on Earth could this little dog know where I need to go?

And then she remembered how he'd scored on the

aptitude test administered the day she picked him up. That brought a smile. Little Tater had shattered the previous record for geographic acuity. The aging pup seemed to know precisely where he was.

But, she thought, that wouldn't account for him knowing where she *needed* to be.

Holding the dog in both hands she held him up and looked at him, nose-to-nose. His dark little eyes sparkled with something she'd only seen after training and modification. Tater appeared ready to go to work right then.

He sneezed on her and broke the spell.

Maeve wiped her face on her sleeve. "Okay, smarty. I think I know which way to go now."

Tater barked in response. She suspected it was his way of saying, "Uh huh. Sure."

Working with him might prove to be a challenge, but it was a challenge she couldn't wait to face.

Artemis let his mind wander as he took the two doodles—one golden, one lab–named Buck and Finley, to their first training session. He felt confident they would work out extremely well in their new assignments. He felt a great deal less confident about himself, especially when it came to Maeve Blessing.

The effervescent redhead had caught his eye the first time they met, and he'd been dreaming about her ever since. Though they'd worked together beginning at the end of the last season of voyages, they'd never been alone together. The upcoming season would put them in constant, and almost certainly dramatic, proximity. They would have to depend on each other as much as they would the team of animals in their care.

Once underway, he knew there would be no time for playfulness, much less romance, though he would eagerly embrace either should it ever occur. He, however, was far too reserved to ever initiate anything. No one who knew him would ever consider him "fun" or "entertaining." He hated that, but lacked the confidence to do anything about it.

That very day, for instance, he could have insisted that he and Maeve take time for lunch right then, not on some distant "maybe" day in the future. He should have made it happen. He should have given it a try, at least. He could have. He *should* have. But he didn't.

What's the worst that could have happened?

He knew the answer. She might have told him to get lost, to go decorate a tree, or just wander off and play in traffic. His hopes would be dashed forever. Dreaming about her without making an advance might seem cowardly, but at least it didn't offer a chance for rejection. That was something, wasn't it? Despite the Boss's edict that relationships among the staff should remain platonic at all times, there were many couples who started out simply as coworkers. So much for edicts.

He found a bench and sat down, flanked by the dogs. They both eyed him with something akin to adoration, just what he longed to see in Maeve's eyes. He allowed himself a deep sigh. Maybe he could take her somewhere, he thought. Some place warm.

Getting to the outside world, other than during the season of voyages, was fairly uncommon. Everyone earned vacation time, of course, but it was easier to stay near home than it was to venture out among the masses.

Outsiders had to contend with so many things he and his coworkers lived without, like civil unrest, war, epidemics, and professional sports. Wasn't that, he wondered, an oxymoron? Sports were meant for personal entertainment, weren't they? Why should someone be paid to play something simply because they were good at it? Rather than watching someone engaged in a sport, wouldn't it be better to self-engage? The Boss made that not just possible, but easy. At least, during the slack season. He was captain of his bowling team and enjoyed arm wrestling, too.

Despite his ongoing failure to generate a warmer relationship with Maeve, Artemis considered himself supremely lucky to live and work where he did. He just needed to be patient. An opportunity would eventually present itself. It had to.

He prayed he would have the wherewithal to take advantage of it.

Buck stood on his hind legs and put his paws on Artemis' shoulders. Meanwhile, Finley cocked her head at him and said, "Art!"

Artemis frowned. *Could he be mistaken?* Maybe it was just a bark. But then, it certainly sounded more like "Art" than "Arf."

Was the dog trying to tell him something? Should he change his name? Shorten it to just… Art?

He patted the dog's big head. "Why not?" he said and let the gentle labradoodles haul him toward their destination.

Raymond Mays smiled as he looked at himself in the full-length mirror on the closet door of his tiny apartment in Decatur, Georgia. His long hair and beard, both thick and changing ever closer to white from blond, gave him the appearance of Kris Kringle in the flesh. One look was enough, but his traditional red and white costume left no doubt. He looked like the real deal—a genuine, bona fide, Santa Claus.

And, as if looking the part wasn't enough, he cherished playing the role. For the fourth year in a row, he would work through the holidays as the jolliest of jolly old souls on the planet.

Ray doubted it would have been different even if he hadn't wrecked his relationship with his daughter, Gloria. She had a son nicknamed Skeeter, but he'd never met the child. That failing left a hole in his heart nearly as deep as the one left by the death of his wife a few months before Skeeter's birth.

He had managed to acquire pictures of both Gloria and the boy, though he'd had to resort to subterfuge to do it. The two, small, framed photos sat on his dresser, the only personal touches in his shabby quarters. Sadly, both images were several years old, and getting updates seemed highly unlikely.

Though he would have loved to restore some sort of face-to-face relationship with his daughter, and create one with his grandson, he doubted she would ever be willing to forgive him for his failings as a father.

It therefore came as a tremendous shock when Gloria called him on the phone.

"Dad?"

"*Gloria?* Is that really you?"

"Yes. It's uhm… me. I—"

"What? Is something wrong? Are you okay?" He made no effort to hide his anxiety.

"I'm fine, Dad. Really. It's… Well, it's Skeeter. He's sick."

Ray didn't want to appear overly eager to get involved, but he couldn't help himself. "What do you need me to do? I'm ready, no matter what. Just tell me."

There was a silence on the other end of the line which

left him twisting in doubt. *Please don't hang up, Gloria! Tell me what I can do. Anything!*

"I need some help. And—"

"I'll do it!"

"You don't even know what I need."

"I don't care," Ray said. "I just… For once, I want to be there for you. I'm so sorry about—"

"I really don't want to talk about any of that, Dad. So, please, just listen. I'm in a real bind, and you're the only one I could think of to call."

"You said Skeeter was ill. How can I help? I don't have a lot of money, but—"

"It's not about money. It's about… It's about Skeeter's dog."

"You want me to take care of it? Sure. No problem. I'll—"

"Please, Dad. Let me finish, okay? Geez."

"Right. Sorry."

"I need to stay with Skeeter. He's going to be in and out of the hospital until the doctors can figure out what's wrong with him and come up with a treatment plan."

"Okay. But what does that have to do with the dog?"

"Tater. The dog's name is Tater. It's short for Tater Tot, 'cause that's what Skeeter guessed he looked like when he was a puppy."

"That's cute. I like it."

Gloria sighed, then followed it with a deep breath before she continued. "Here's the thing. We agreed to let a company use Tater in a movie or a TV commercial, something like that,

31

but they have to keep him for several weeks for training and uhm… I dunno, production."

"Someone hired your *dog?*"

"Right. And they'll pay us union scale wages, whatever that amounts to, but it really doesn't matter. Skeeter misses Tater something awful. He's having a hard time getting by without him."

"And you want me to go get him?"

"Could you?"

"I can certainly try! Who do I contact? What do I need to do?"

"Well," Gloria said, "that's the problem. The contract we signed is with an outfit called Leon Farms. It only lists their address as the place where Tater auditioned, a farm way north of here in a town called Ball Ground."

Ray knew the area. He had friends, former drinking buddies, who lived nearby. "Right. North of Canton. I know where Ball Ground is."

"Well, I drove up there earlier today, and the place is deserted. There's nobody there."

Ray glanced at his watch. He had to report for training in a half hour, not that he felt he needed it. After four years of playing Santa, he knew everything he needed to know. His first real shift wouldn't begin until noon on the day after Thanksgiving. That gave him two days to solve Gloria's problem. "Listen, I've got to head out of here in little bit."

"Please tell me you're not still drinking." Gloria's voice didn't offer much hope.

"I quit drinking four years ago," he said. "And I've got a job. It's seasonal, but it pays pretty well, and the benefits are wonderful."

32

"Like health insurance and retirement?"

"Well, no. Nothing like that. I get to make kids smile."

There was another silence from Gloria's end of the line.

"You still there, Gloria?" he asked.

"Yeah. It's just… Well what you said sounded kinda creepy."

"Aw no," he laughed. "I'm working for the mall as Santa Claus. You should see me in costume. Maybe you could bring Skeeter—"

"He's a very sick boy, Dad. Let's not get ahead of ourselves. Can you just check on the dog?"

"Sure. Text me whatever information you've got about whoever has him, and I'll look into it."

"I can email it to you," Gloria said.

"You could if I had a computer or an email address."

"Oh."

"I had to start over from scratch. I lost everything when—"

"I know, Dad. I know. I'm still not ready to talk about that, any of it. Maybe if you can find Tater and get him back… I dunno. Just find the dog. After that, we'll see about where it goes."

"Okay then," he said. "I'll do my very best. I promise."

"Thanks, Dad."

Chapter Three

"Easter egg hunts and parades are nothing new to any household or city, however nobody does it better than the Big Apple." –Hilary Farr

A neatly printed message lay atop Ormsby Ivanov's expansive desk and represented, in his mind anyway, a god-sent revelation. He read it for what must have been the tenth time, grinning wider with each repetition. The Boss would be joining the turkey day mob scene in New York City.

Ormsby wondered if the man ever deigned to show up at a lesser venue, so great was his need for adoration. But such thoughts quickly dissipated as he hurriedly put together a team to do his bidding. The jolly fat man would soon be in his power, and if that didn't put a sincere dent in the secular portion of the upcoming holiday, nothing would.

As it plainly said in John 14:3 of his well-worn Bible, "…I go and prepare a place for you. I will come…." Yes, he'd taken it completely out of context, but that hardly mattered.

Ormsby chuckled. At last, he'd have the upper hand.

~*~
34

True to her word, Gloria sent Ray a text message with the name and address of the company which had taken possession of Skeeter's dog.

After copying the information on a piece of scratch paper, he checked his watch again, as if that would somehow slow time down, a trick of physics he hadn't mastered. He'd never make it in time for the training session. On top of that, he had no idea how long it would take to drive all the way to Ball Ground, chat with the people there, collect the dog, deliver it, and return home. Just thinking about all that was enough to exhaust him. It would have definitely exhausted the old Ray. More than likely, the old Ray would've just said the heck with it and gone to find a bar somewhere.

Thank the sweet Lord, he thought, the old Ray is long gone.

Picking up the phone again, he dialed the mall and spoke with the woman managing the Santa Workshop and the people who worked there. Ray was one of three Santas, and each worked a pair or two-hour shifts per day. As long as the mall was open, there would be a Santa on-hand every day between Thanksgiving and Christmas.

The lady wasn't happy about Ray skipping the training session, but he assured her his family emergency was genuine; his grandson had some sort of rare illness, and he was desperately needed by the child's single parent. Besides, he told her, he'd had the training four times before and doubted much, if anything, had changed.

She relented and wished him a happy Thanksgiving. In an afterthought, she told him if he missed even five minutes of on-duty time, he'd be fired, then rang off.

"Happy Thanksgiving to you, too," he muttered.

Turning back to the mirror hanging on his closet door, he adjusted his red and white-trimmed coat. Satisfied, he grabbed his red hat, white gloves, and his car keys. "Might as well get started," he told himself. "No time to change into civvies."

It wasn't quite dusk, but by the time he reached the little rural town of Ball Ground, it would be pitch-black outside. He hoped there would at least be some moonlight.

"Don't screw this up, Ray," he told himself. "This might be the only chance you'll ever have to get your kid and your life back."

After sticking his phone in his pocket, he headed out the door to his battered, twenty-year-old Toyota Corolla. Once locked in, and still looking like St. Nicolas freshly arrived from a production of Clement Moore's beloved holiday poem, Ray ventured out to change his life and maybe save that of his grandson.

~*~

Gloria wasn't entirely sure what to make of her father's response to her request. He certainly sounded sincere, but that meant little. He'd also sounded sincere when he walked out of her life shortly after her mother died. He needed companionship; he'd said. He needed to be around people who understood him and understood his grief. As if she wasn't grieving, too. As if losing her mother wasn't equally devastating.

He'd chosen alcohol over family. It was easier for him to drown himself in a bottle than concern himself with those he left behind. A bartender's shoulder to cry on would serve him as well as any other and didn't require much in return.

Had he actually changed as he claimed? How would she know? She had neither the time nor the inclination to look into his life. The life of her son took priority. If he could help, find the dog, and restore a bit of the joy which formerly characterized Skeeter's life, then maybe she could bend a bit and give him another chance. It was entirely up to him.

As she walked back into the hospital, she spied the same nurse who'd given her a happy thumbs up earlier in the day. The woman looked anything but happy now. Gloria instantly shoved all other thoughts out of her head and raced toward her son's room.

~*~

Maeve picked at her salad. The greens looked wilty, and the dressing may have been on the shelf a tad longer than usual. It always seemed that way as fall morphed into winter. A new season called for new food, but not until they'd used up the old. Still, it wasn't simply the condition of the rabbit fare in her bowl; Maeve had another concern.

Artemis noticed her sad vibe and attempted to cheer her up. "You won't believe this, but one of the dogs talked to me the other day. Even before training!"

Maeve eased her eyes up from the salad and looked across the table at him. "Which one?"

"One of the big doodles. Finley, I think. Or maybe it was Buck. Nope. It was Fin. It's hard to say. They look so much alike."

"So, what'd she say?" Maeve's query lacked interest, as if she was merely being polite.

37

"She suggested I shorten my name to Art."

At that, Maeve examined him more closely, perhaps expecting something weird to pop out of his head. "Did she offer any reasoning?"

"Nope. She just said—"

"Arf?"

"No. I'm absolutely certain she said, 'Art.'"

Maeve blinked. "You astonish me," she said. "You really do."

"*Really?*" He sat up straighter. "That's maybe the nicest thing you've ever said to me."

She shook her head and gazed once again down into her salad.

"Okay, so what's got you so bummed?" he asked.

"Just the stupid rumor."

"Which one? Seems like there's a new one every twenty minutes."

"Oh, you know. The one about the Boss. They say he's gone off to be in a parade. The big one, in New York City." She humped her shoulders up around her ears. "Why does he do that? We're all working overtime to get ready, and he—"

"He takes off to have a good time, right?"

Maeve gave him a look that reeked of disappointment. "Yeah. I don't get it. It just doesn't seem fair."

"It's not. But then, neither is public opinion. If he

doesn't appear in public once in a while, there's a chance people will forget about him or lose interest."

"That's crazy!" Maeve said. "At this time of year, there's some sort of Santa Claus on every corner. People aren't going to lose interest in him. It's not like he's some kind of Hollywood newbie. He'll never go out of style."

"Unlike his wardrobe."

She nodded. "Well, there's that, I suppose. One could argue he's just keeping up with the times."

Feeling he might have made a dent in her mood, Art went on. "And then there's the whole industrial approach to gift-giving he had to adopt. I sometimes wonder if Jeff Bezos got his ideas from us."

"Who's Jeff Bezos?" Maeve asked. "Does he work in distribution?"

"Sort of. He invented Amazon.com."

"Oh," she said. "Him. He's bald y'know."

Art felt perplexed. "I didn't— I uh… I have no idea how to respond to that."

Maeve chuckled. "Never mind. He probably shaves his head so he'll look like a genie. Promise me you won't do that."

"Me? No. Never." He pushed strands of hair behind both ears. "Although I probably oughta get it cut before we take off."

Maeve reached across the table and touched his brown locks. "Don't let 'em take too much. I think your hair looks cute, unlike this unruly red mess of mine."

Artemis sat speechless, a look of surprise on his face.

"What is it?" she asked.

"I— It's… Uhm… Nothing."

"You sure?"

"Yeah." He smiled. "I'm very sure."

"Sometimes," Maeve said, "I worry about you."

Art sighed. He still didn't know how to tell her how he felt about her. *Maybe now's the time. I'll just—*

"Oops," Maeve said, standing and whisking the remains of her lunch from the table. "Gotta go."

~*~

Ray stopped for gas on the way to Ball Ground. The gauge didn't work when he got the car, and he'd never had the money to fix it. Consequently, he spent a good deal of time wondering where he'd be when the cranky old import coughed and died for lack of fuel. He certainly couldn't let that happen on this mission.

So, rather than buy himself something to eat for dinner, he filled the tank and made a mental note of the mileage. With any luck, he'd remember it for the next time. All in all, it wasn't a difficult decision.

He had the address of Leon Farms but no directions for finding the place. That also required a stop along the way. Fortunately, folks in Cherokee county were generally friendly, and no one seemed to mind helping him.

As anticipated, the sun had long departed the sky when he arrived at the driveway leading to the location Gloria had told him about. And, just as she said, the place looked deserted.

This is nuts. I need my head examined. There's no telling what I'll find way the heck out here. Bears, probably. Hungry ones.

The need to be useful outweighed his fears, and he aimed his arthritic vehicle down the gravel drive and kept going.

Though no expert on farms or farming, he thought the location had more in common with a ranch than a farm. There weren't any fields or signs of something to harvest that he could see. The land bore mostly grass, all of which looked overdue for a trimming.

Leaving his car next to one of the larger outbuildings, Ray walked the short distance to what looked like a farmhouse. A porch the size of a shipping pallet lay before the front door. He could not see a single light in any direction, inside or out, but when he stepped on the porch, a tiny red one winked on just above the door. Had he not been looking up at the time, he wouldn't have seen it.

Assuming it was some sort of security arrangement, Ray went ahead and knocked on the door, then waited in silence for something to happen. For a long moment nothing broke the silence or suggested anyone or anything would respond. But just as he turned to walk away and look for another entrance to the building, something quite unexpected *did* happen.

~*~

"I don't get it," Mordecai said. "If we grab the guy before the parade, the cops'll be all over us."

"And if you don't," Ormsby said, "no one will know he's missing. Not only that, but he'll still get to wave at thousands of adoring fans, many of whom came just to see him." Ivanov ground his teeth. "Tell, how is that going to help us diminish his image? How will that put some tarnish on his saintly shine?"

"Okay, okay. We'll do it any way you want," the big man said. "I just don't want to spend any time in jail. Once was enough, and while I'm grateful that you got me out, I ain't ever goin' back. You've gotta know that."

"I've taken care of everything," Ormsby said. "Just follow my instructions, and it'll all work out okay. Even better than okay. If you pull this off, I'll double the bonus I promised you. And—" he paused dramatically, "—you'll get to spend a few nights in a luxurious Big Apple hotel. How 'bout that?"

"But—"

"Relax. I paid the parade managers to let some of my people man the costuming and make-up tent for the float. You and the rest of your men will be in it when the target arrives. He'll have a white beard and a red—"

"Everybody on Earth knows what he looks like. What do we do with him?"

"Once he's inside the tent, tie him up and drag him out the through the back. There will be a van waiting. The driver knows where to go. After that, all you'll need to do is keep an eye on him, and don't let him out of the hotel room."

"What about food?"

"Order room service. Whatever you want. And for him…" Ormsby chuckled at the thought that popped into his head. "For him, just order milk and cookies. Preferably with sprinkles. He'll love those."

"That's it?"

"Yeah."

"How long will we be stuck there?"

"Until the day after Christmas."

Mordecai groaned.

"What's the problem?"

"Well, see, I got invited to this... Uhm... This Christmas party, and I kinda—"

"Silence," hissed Ormsby. "How dare you even think of such a thing?"

"I— It's just—"

"One more word about going to a party of that kind, and I'll send you for retraining. And I'll conduct the hard parts!"

"Right. Sorry, sir."

"Any more questions?"

"Where's this tent we're supposed to operate?"

"I'll text you the address," Ormsby said. "If you or any of the others screw this up, don't bother coming back. Ever. Is that clear?"

"I'm worried," Mordecai said.

"About what?"

"All of it. I've never been in charge of something before. And all this... I dunno."

Ormsby let out a prolonged sigh. "Never mind. Just

meet me at the airport. I'll fly up tonight and take care of everything personally."

"Thank you." Mordecai's voice sounded almost childlike in its relief.

"No problem, son," Ormsby said, knowing he'd have to find someone else to handle his more important concerns. Mordecai lacked the backbone.

~*~

When Gloria reached Skeeter's room, she was relieved to see the boy sitting up in bed watching TV. He appeared weak, however, and barely managed a smile in her direction. "Can we go home now?" he asked.

She stepped quickly to the bed and gave him a gentle hug. "I sure hope so. Have they put you through a bunch of tests?"

"A couple. They don't tell me much, so I don't know what they're tryin' to find out. I really just wanted to watch one of my favorite shows, but they keep doin' stuff, standing in front of me so I can't see the screen. And every time they say, 'This won't hurt,' it always hurts. Why do they lie to me? Why can't I just go home?"

Gloria felt her stress growing more pronounced with every word he said. She understood the need to correctly diagnose his illness but found it increasingly difficult to keep her frustration over their failures in check. When a nurse entered the room, Gloria was tempted to take it out on her.

"How's our patient?" the woman in pale blue scrubs asked.

"He's not happy," Gloria said. "Neither is his mother."

44

The nurse responded with a slight smile and a nod. "That's understandable." She glanced down at the boy's chart. "Lawrence's test results—"

"He prefers to be called Skeeter. It's a nickname his Dad gave him."

"Of course. I'm sorry. And... Oh, yes, there's a notation right here." She tapped the clipboard as if to underscore the discovery. "Uh... Skeeter's doctor has ordered one more test procedure for the day." She smiled at him as she closed the cover on his chart. "I promise it won't hurt much."

Skeeter's hand on Gloria's arm tightened. "You know what? I think we're already done for today."

"But the doctor—"

"Can wait. We're going home."

The nurse shook her head. "Do you really think that's wise? I mean, considering the boy's condition."

"It might be different if you actually knew what my boy's condition is," Gloria said, trying not to spit the words out as venomously as she felt.

"If you absolutely insist. But you'll have to sign an acknowledgement that you're doing this against doctor's orders."

"Fine. Got a pen?"

"I don't even have the form."

"Well, then. Get it, or we'll leave without it. As far as I can tell, all you've done so far is torment my child. I promise you that won't be the case once he's safe at home."

At that point a doctor dressed in a white lab coat entered the room. "Is there a problem here?"

"Not really," Gloria said. "We're leaving."

"Both of you?" the doctor asked.

Gloria had already advanced to the closet where her son's clothing had been stored. She pulled shirt, pants, socks and shoes from their respective shelves and tossed them on the bed.

"I'm sure you think you're doing the right thing," the doctor said, "but have you stopped to consider that the problem might be environmental?"

"Like what? Allergies? I'm the only one who sneezes, and that's usually in the spring, not this time of year."

"I'm thinking more along the lines of something in your home that's making him sick."

"Nonsense," Gloria said. "We've lived there for a good long while. If it was something in the house, it would've made him sick before now, wouldn't it?"

The doctor shrugged. "It might be something new in the home. Paint, maybe, or a new wall covering. How old is the building?"

Gloria helped Skeeter get dressed. "I have no idea. We just rent the place. And it hasn't been redecorated since we moved in. I doubt much was done to it *before* we moved in."

The doctor reached for Skeeter's medical chart. "I'd like to have someone who specializes in allergies to look at him. If I can set up an appointment, will you take him? If so, I'll approve his release."

The nurse appeared slightly stricken. "But, Doctor—"

"The boy's condition has not changed in any material way in the past 48 hours. This isn't a children's hospital. We're not set up to provide the sort of comfort and distractions that young patients need. I've no doubt he'll rest easier at home than he will here."

Gloria felt a modest wave of relief. "Thank you. Just let me know where to take him and when he needs to be there."

The doctor made a notation on the chart, initialed it, and handed it to the nurse. "Will you please see to Skeeter's immediate discharge?"

"Of course," the nurse said.

The physician then focused on Gloria. "If anything changes, I trust you'll bring him back here immediately."

"Count on it," she said and prayed she wouldn't have to.

Maeve walked into the training room she had reserved for her new charges and smiled at them as they inspected the room and each other. It was a motley crew, as she knew it would be, and as it always was. A majority of the recruits came from shelters, and while they'd only be gone from their previous quarters for a short time, their chances for being adopted were vastly enhanced by the time they spent with Maeve and the other team leaders.

She reviewed the roster and worked on connecting the various dogs to the names and descriptions she'd been given.

Tater came first, of course. She'd made sure he was part

47

of her team. His missing leg had nothing to do with the fact that he'd endeared himself to her on their travel from Georgia to the transport center, and from there to Temp Housing and the training facility. When she called his name, he stopped sniffing about and responded with a short, sharp bark that sounded a great deal like, "Here!"

She recalled that Artemis mentioned one of his charges barked in something that approached English and wondered if the dietary team had dispensed some of the special supplements earlier than usual.

"Foster?" she called.

A medium-sized dog whose white coat was marked by two large black spots—one at each end of his body—and a variety of much smaller ones, perked up his ears, tilted his head, and looked straight at her. The other dogs continued doing whatever they'd been up to. "Good to meet you," Maeve said. Foster wagged his tail in affirmation.

"Spike? Where are you?"

A small, dark-gray schnauzer perked up and barked, twice, as if wanting to make sure he was recognized. Maeve chuckled. She'd been expecting another almost-human voice, one marked by a German accent. Spike seemed quite sure of himself, and after being acknowledged by her, went back to work looking for a vantage point from which he could keep all the other dogs under observation. Drill sergeant material, she thought, and checked his name on her chart.

"Augie? Are you here? Augie?"

A stout, brindle boxer lumbered about on his axis until he faced her. His greeting was more grumble or growl than bark, but his shiny eyes and general demeanor signaled his desire to be friends. A bit of drool dangled from one side of his mouth. When he shook his great head, the saliva landed on at least three of his canine companions. He gave them a quick glance and then appeared to smile.

Oh, you're a sneaky one, aren't you? But you'll do fine if anyone or anything gives us trouble. "Welcome to the team, Augie."

The big dog wagged what little bit of tail he had, then turned and continued his inspection of the training area.

"Who's next," Maeve asked herself, then ran her finger down the list and stopped at the next unchecked name.

"Cody? Are you—"

She was halted instantly by a barrage of barking from a small dog that the record indicated was a cross between a beagle and a Jack Russel terrier.

"Right," she said. "Gotcha." But Cody continued barking.

"Okay, okay! I've checked off your name. You can calm down now."

Cody either didn't hear her, didn't understand what she'd said, or just didn't care. He kept on barking until all the other dogs in the room stopped what they were doing and looked at him. They stretched out in front of him in a broad semi-circle.

Finally, he dialed back his frantic messaging when a similar looking mixed breed dog mix peeked out from behind him. The second dog appeared less than half his size and no more than a few months old.

49

What in the world?

Cody barked once more. The sound, like that of Tater, sounded vaguely like English, and the one-word message he conveyed sounded very much like "Zoe."

She couldn't imagine how a dog could form such a word without having first undergone the training and modifications all of them would soon undergo. Shaking off the thought, she ran her finger down the list again until she came to the name, Zoe. An asterisk took her to a comment in the Notes section. Zoe and Cody came as a pair. Whoever agreed to recruit Cody agreed to let Zoe tag along like a little brother, though the two were not truly related.

Maeve couldn't imagine what she would do with the pup while the adult dogs were working. She reached down and petted the little dog's soft, puppy coat. She turned her big, brown eyes toward Maeve and licked her hand, all the while wagging her tiny tail.

"I'm sure I'll figure something out," she told the pup. "If nothing else, you can keep me company while the others work."

Cody and Zoe seemed satisfied with that arrangement and wandered off to continue their explorations.

Only two more names remained on the list, though the last one also bore an asterisk. A large one. In bold type.

Maeve squinted at the name, which took up more space than the names of the others. "Pinot Noir," she read out loud as she surveyed the pack at her feet. Not a one of them looked back at her or responded in any other way.

Another look at the chart revealed the animal had a

nickname, "Peanut."

Well, that'll be a lot easier to pronounce!

"Hey, Peanut? You in here?"

The room remained quiet.

"Peanut?"

Silence.

"Oh, Peeeeeee-nut! Where aaaaaaaaare you?"

Tater sauntered over to her, nudged her leg with his nose, then turned and struck a pose. With only three legs, he couldn't point like a bird dog, so he used his nose instead and aimed it at the top of a cabinet at the back of the room.

A coal black cat with luminous eyes raised its head and looked back at her. The color of those eyes startled her. They weren't actually green, as she had thought at first. Their color lay somewhere between green and yellow. *Chartreuse? Yes.* That was it.

Spooky. Is this some kind of joke? We're doing Christmas, not Halloween. "Well," she corrected herself out loud, "Christmas Eve."

She couldn't imagine how the cat might fit in with all the dogs, but reasoned that someone who'd done the recruiting must have figured it was a good idea.

"Good to see you, Peanut," she said, mostly for the dogs' benefit. "Welcome aboard." She gave the dogs a stern look, her arm sweeping the room and allowing her to point at each one in turn. "I don't want to hear any nonsense from any of you. Peanut is a valuable member of this team, and I expect you to treat her as such."

The dogs didn't look particularly impressed with her warning, so she added a caveat: "If one of you even looks like you're giving Peanut a hard time, you'll find yourself headed home. In shame. You'll get the full reversal dose for language and understanding, and any modifications done will be returned to their original state. Do I make myself clear?"

The only dog to respond was another small mutt with an un-behaved coat of tri-color fur in shades of brown and black. The dog sat at her feet looking straight up into her face. She barked twice as Foster, the white dog with black spots, crawled next to her and dropped to his belly beside her.

Maeve processed the barks as she looked at the pair which had obviously bonded somehow in the short time they'd been together. A more unlikely couple she couldn't imagine.

The only remaining unchecked name belonged to Maple, a canine whose heritage embraced several noble lines including Yorkie, chihuahua, Lhasa Apso, and quite possibly some form of rodent, most likely a rabbit. Clearly, Foster didn't care. He only had eyes for Maple.

Maeve checked her name off, then clapped her hands to call them all to attention.

"I'm happy to welcome all of you to your very first Christmas class. We've got a lot of material to cover, so I hope you're ready." Though tempted to ask them if anyone had questions, she decided to leave that option open for later.

Chapter Four

"If a dog will not come to you after having looked you in the face, you should go home and examine your conscience." –Woodrow Wilson

When the porch light came on, and the lock on the front door clicked, Ray flinched as if someone had poked him with a pin. He recovered quickly though and pushed the front door open. Lights had come on in a hallway across the front room, inviting him in that direction.

Fearing some sort of trickery, he called out, "Hello? Anyone home? I've come to pick up a dog. My grandson's dog. He's sick. My grandson, I mean. I'm sure the dog's fine. I'm sure y'all have taken good care of him, right?"

No one responded. The house remained frighteningly, silent.

Ray moved cautiously forward. When he had stepped past the door, he stopped and waited to see if it would close on its own. It didn't, which, for some reason, seemed reassuring. He pushed it shut, and the lock once again clicked. His mild sense of reassurance dissipated as the deadbolt turned on its own while he watched.

Ghosts? No! I don't believe in ghosts… ordinarily. Telling himself that, however, didn't entirely remove the nagging worry that something unnatural shared the building with him.

He kept going, headed toward the hallway. He stopped when he reached it and looked in both directions. Two, low-wattage ceiling lights provided illumination. A small, tidy kitchen stood at one end while two open doors punctuated the wall opposite the front room and another, closed door, sat opposite the kitchen at the far end of the hall.

A quick glance in the kitchen and through the two open doors revealed nothing out of the ordinary. Each of the two side rooms held twin beds and dressers but little else. He wondered why the house had no bathroom, then found one opening off the room he traversed when he first entered.

Only one unopened door remained, and he assumed it was either a closet or a hall bath. He turned the knob and found it locked. Within moments, he heard a tiny click, just as he had when he stood outside the front door. He immediately looked up to see if there was a miniature red light above the door as well. There was, and he couldn't believe he hadn't seen it earlier.

The door unlocked itself, just as the front entrance had, and Ray opened it to reveal a stairway leading to a lower level.

A light in the lower level went on as the hall lights behind him went off.

He felt like he'd just stepped into the plot of a drive-in B movie from his teenage years, one featuring a maniac armed with a chainsaw who lived in a basement and lured the unsuspecting to their deaths by turning house lights on and off. *All I need now is a ghost or two, and I'll have to run back and use the bathroom I found.*

"Get a grip," he told himself.

Taking a deep breath and holding on tight to the handrail, Ray started walking down the basement stairs.

~*~

Gloria answered her phone on the second ring.

"Mrs. Malone? This is Anthony Parker, I'm one of the doctors working on your son's diagnosis."

Gloria inhaled sharply. "Have you found something? Is it… is it can—"

"Cancer? No. I seriously doubt that. But I must confess his condition involves something I've never seen before."

"What is it?" Gloria wanted to scream.

"His blood contains an array of odd elements. His genetic make-up is—" He exhaled in a way that made Gloria think he shared her frustration. "—Well, I'm not exactly sure. I've never seen anything like it. We'd love to have blood samples from you and his father. That might help us isolate what's causing his problems."

"You can have as much of my blood as you need," Gloria said. "But my husband…."

"Yes," Parker said. "What about him?"

"Jim's not available," she said, unable to keep a sigh out of her voice. "He hasn't been… *around*… for nearly five years."

"He's deceased?"

"No! I don't think so. I— I certainly hope not, anyway."

"I don't understand."

"My husband kissed me goodbye and headed off to work one morning—"

"Five years ago?"

"Right. And he never came back."

"He made no effort to contact you?"

The doctor's persistence had grown annoying. "No. And I don't know why. Almost anything could have happened to him. I called all the hospitals in the area, and I notified the police. They said they had searched for him, but it's like he just vanished."

"No credit card usage? No changes to your bank accounts?"

"Don't you think I'd have noticed things like that?" Gloria asked, her voice snappish.

"I apologize. I'm sure it sounds as if I'm prying, but I'm really not," Parker said. "I can't imagine how difficult and frustrating such a thing is for you, for anyone. But I have to ask; did your husband have any unusual illnesses or symptoms before he disappeared? I can't help but wonder if the blood issues we think are causing your son's problem may have come from your husband, if not from you."

"Other than growing a little more forgetful than normal, Jim was perfectly fine. I don't ever remember him getting sick."

"And your son? Does he get sick very often? Cold? Flu? Allergies?"

"Nothing out of the ordinary. And I've made sure he's had all his vaccinations."

"Interesting," Parker said. "When do you think you might drop by and give us a blood sample?"

"Any time," Gloria replied. "Night or day. Just say the word."

Ormsby Ivanov arrived at his hotel despite the best efforts of his hirelings to get lost in the Big Apple. Ormsby blamed them; they blamed him, for not allowing the use of certain "high tech" gizmos like GPS. Instead, they were reduced to map reading, a skill no longer taught anywhere, it seemed. Ormsby liked maps. They offered a solid understanding of what and where, and he insisted on their use. The command was one of several which didn't sit well with his troops.

When they finally arrived at his hotel, Ormsby had Mordecai arrange all the men, in ranks, so he could address them.

"I do not care if you don't share my preferences," he told them. "As long as you are in my employ, you will carry out my wishes exactly as I direct you to carry them out. I will not brook any deviation. Is that clear?"

Mordecai and several of the others exchanged looks, but none were willing to say anything which might draw attention to themselves.

"You got that?" growled a man standing close beside their employer. "Do what he tells you, and do it the way he tells you to do it."

Ormsby glanced at the man who had a thick head of jet-black hair and gave him a quick nod of thanks then marched into the hotel to inspect their accommodations. He intended to enjoy a good night's sleep before he oversaw the abduction of the Boss. He felt sure he would have pleasant dreams both before and after his capture.

~*~

Cursing himself as half fool and half idiot, Ray slowly traversed the stairs to the lighted area below. Once there, he inspected the walls and floor for clues about ways in which the space might have been used. To his surprise, there wasn't a great deal of space to examine, certainly less than that occupied by the rooms above.

The only feature of interest in the entire room was a wall which appeared tubular. It curved into the room from ceiling to floor like the side of a huge sausage. He felt it with both hands but noted no unusual texture. It felt like any normal wall aside from the inescapably obvious—it protruded into the room to a depth of three or four feet.

He looked above and below it and saw nothing else of interest. The wall had no molding at the ceiling, which appeared smooth and flat, or at the floor which appeared to be made of cement.

A pair of plain, wooden armchairs sat opposite the peculiar wall, and Ray took advantage of one of them, hoping some clue would soon present itself.

His stomach rumbled, and he remembered spending his dinner money on gasoline for the wild goose chase he'd embarked on. He was about to chastise himself for all the foolish things he'd done that day: miss a training session, drive around half the state dressed like Santa, and search what appeared to be an all but abandoned farm house for a dog he'd never seen and about which he knew precious little.

It's only got three legs. I know that much. There can't be that many dogs like that, and all the others are probably called "Tripod." On the other hand, I don't know what kind of dog he is, whether he's big or small, whether he's trained or crazy, or... or....

His ruminations stalled when a door in the curved wall popped out and slid up into the ceiling. He had been utterly unprepared for that and made a mad dash toward the stairs to the upper floor, all the while expecting something—he had no clue what—would almost certainly come tearing out from behind the raised door and do something profoundly grim.

By the time he'd gone halfway back up the stairs, it became clear there was no pursuit. There were no other changes at all. No menacing men, no armed guards, not even an annoyed homemaker. Only silence.

He crept back down the stairs, as slowly and cautiously as he'd raced up them before. Not surprisingly, the overhead lights in the room began to dim as lights in the newly exposed area beyond the door grew brighter.

Walking to the door, he paused and looked inside at a neatly appointed chamber that sported two well-padded lounge chairs. Though not lavishly furnished, it appeared pleasant and comfortable. Christmas music played in the background providing the first break in the silence he'd experienced inside the building.

The chamber hardly looked threatening, and if visual clues meant anything, the chairs promised a degree of comfort he'd not enjoyed in ages.

"What the heck," he grumbled as he sauntered over to one of the seats and lowered himself into it. He'd earned a break. A little rest wouldn't hurt, and he felt as though he needed one. As his tension eased, and he grew relaxed, he was tempted to close his eyes and take a nap. It would have been so easy. So natural.

His eyes snapped wide open, however, when the door to the chamber slid closed.

Ray was out of the chair and pounding on the surface of it with both fists.

"Open up! You can't keep me in here! Open. The. Stinking. *Door!*"

The words had barely left his mouth when he felt movement and detected a slight vibration, as if the chamber had somehow left the farmhouse basement and was at that very moment hurtling through a large tube of some kind to an unknown destination. He picked up no additional sensory clues—sensations, aromas, nothing.

Ray staggered back to the chair and once again sat down. He made a slow, 360-degree scan of the chamber in hopes of finding something that would give him a clue about what was happening. There was nothing. There were no windows. The door was little more than an outline, a seam. The few decorations on the walls were pleasant but revealed nothing about where he was, why he'd been trapped, or what might come next.

A fleeting thought raced through his head. Had something like this happened to his son-in-law, James? Had he been whisked away in the dark by nameless, faceless ghouls to some dreadful fate, never to be heard from again?

No, that wasn't right. Jim had simply gone to his office, just as he had a thousand times before. This was different. This was no office, and despite the soft, seasonal music playing in the background, this was *not* a happy place.

This was nothing like anything he'd ever imagined in his entire life. And while Ray had experienced dramatic highs and lows, not to mention the absolute worst kinds of depression, he'd never encountered anything like this. This was new. This was beyond weird.

This was downright scary.

"Artemis!" Maeve called as she knocked on the door of his bungalow. She'd never been inside and hoped that he was. She'd looked for him in the Training Wing, and when he didn't show up there, she searched Temp Housing as well. But she came up empty once more, so unless he'd gone off to an early dinner, he just had to be in his house.

Knocking again, with only slightly less intensity, Maeve waited for a response of some kind. If he wasn't home, the only other explanation was that he'd gone out somewhere after work. There was only one tavern close by, but she couldn't imagine him going in it unless some of his rowdy friends dragged him in. A nagging thought at the back of her mind kept insinuating itself in her consciousness: *maybe he'd gone with a female.* He'd talked about dining with her somewhere, and somewhen, but he'd never actually asked her for a date. She couldn't imagine why not, unless… She sighed. Unless he'd found someone else.

"What is it?" Artemis asked when he finally yanked open his door. His gruff tone disappeared the moment he spied Maeve. "Oh! Hi!" he said, clearly taken by surprise. "I— Uh— I wasn't expecting you. I was… Well… If you must know, I—"

"I'm sorry to disturb you like this, out of the blue, but I had to come. I had to talk to you. There's something very strange going on."

Artemis smiled. "Around here, there's *always* something strange going on. It's kinda what we do here."

"Yes, yes, I know that. But this is something different."

"Are you going to tell me or make me guess?"

"I'm sorry, I didn't mean to sound so… I dunno, mixed up."

He reached out and patted her shoulder. "It's fine. Take a deep breath. Let it out. Do it again. And when you're ready, begin at the beginning."

Maeve did as he suggested and immediately felt herself calm down. "All right. I'm… I'm fine."

Artemis nodded and gave her a reassuring smile.

"I got a call from my friend Maximillian in Transport."

"*Max the Monster?*" Artemis asked.

Maeve felt her eyebrows draw down instinctively. "He's no monster. He's a friend."

"Right. Sorry. Bad habit. I listen to too many stupid—"

"Let me finish, okay? Max is a great guy. A little hard-headed maybe, and kinda jumpy when it comes to security, but I like him."

"You do? A lot? I mean—"

"Please just listen, okay? I'm trying to tell you about something important. Well, maybe important. I just don't know. I'm not—"

"Spill it. I'll shut up," Artemis said.

"Fine. According to Max, the Boss just showed up at the transport terminal in Georgia."

"The one we just left a few days ago?"

"Yes!"

"I thought he was in New York City."

"Well, that was the rumor," Maeve said. "Maybe he was up to something else."

"And miss a parade? That's unlikely."

"But, there aren't any Thanksgiving Day parades anywhere in the southeast United States like the big one in New York."

"Are you sure?" Artemis asked, then waved her to silence and answered his own question. "Never mind. We both know the answer to that."

"What should we do?"

Her friend frowned. "I don't think there's much of anything we can do. Security will handle it. That's what they're there for. Your big buddy Max will see to that, I'm sure."

~*~

Ormsby's contact in the company running the parade guaranteed that Ormsby's men would not be bothered while they worked with the man playing the role of Santa Claus. Ormsby had assured him the man was perfect for the role and told him he couldn't think of a soul who might do it better. It was all he could do not to laugh.

As they stood in the tent designated for wardrobe and make-up, Mordecai shuffled his feet, clearly uncomfortable in the setting. The costume rack was empty except for a glitter-covered bikini, and the "elves" and other assorted characters who would join Santa on the float had already finished their preparations. A pair of make-up tables, complete with lighted mirrors stood empty, no longer needed.

He was still scratching his head about the bikini when he asked, "Wouldn't it have been easier to grab your man when he left his hotel?"

"Perhaps. But that would mean we knew where he was staying, wouldn't it?"

Mordecai nodded.

"But we don't even know *if* he's staying in town. He could fly in almost any time. He's got his own aircraft, y'know. It may be weird, but it works." Ormsby resisted the temptation to cuff the big man's head as his own father had when he was a child. If he'd been as big as Mordecai, things might have gone much differently. He shrugged it off and said, "So, we wait. Right here. He'll show."

A voice from outside the tent called, "Roll out in ten minutes! Where the heck is Santa? Anybody seen him?"

"He's coming," Ormsby yelled back. "He's running a little behind, but I'm sure he'll be here any minute."

"Pray that he does. We've got a tight schedule," the voice yelled back. "If he isn't here on time, it's your problem, not mine. Don't forget, this whole thing is on network TV."

Ormsby prided himself on his ability to remain calm, but that hallmark patience had worn thin. He checked his watch again, as he had repeatedly since they arrived at the tent an hour earlier. Mordecai and the others appeared agitated.

"What's wrong with you?" Ormsby asked them.

"He's late."

"Yeah. So what?"

"What'll we do if he doesn't show? The parade guy will be furious."

Ormsby glared at the man. "Do I look like I give a da—"

At that moment, an older, bearded gentleman dressed in the familiar red and white garb of Santa Claus entered the tent. "I'm ready," he said with a hearty laugh, smiling at all the men standing around waiting for him. "I must say, however, I've never had to use make-up or anything else in the past, but the man outside insisted that I come in here and see all of you before I climb up on the float."

"Looks like our patience has been rewarded," Ormsby said, turning to Mordecai. "Grab him!"

65

Santa looked utterly shocked, and except for swiveling his head from side to side, stood stock still while Mordecai and the others raced toward him.

"Whatever you do," Ormsby yelled, "don't let him put his hands near his face!"

Mordecai gave him a questioning look. "Huh? Why?"

"Because of the poem."

"What poem?" Mordecai appeared mystified.

"The one about the night before Christmas, you idiot!"

"Uh… Okay."

Mordecai wasn't the only member of the team who had no clue what Ormsby meant, so he explained further. "There's a line in it where Santa puts his finger alongside of his nose and—"

"And up the chimney he goes!" shouted the same, dark haired man who earlier told the crew to obey Ormsby's commands.

"Right!" said Ormsby, once again nodding his thanks to the speaker. "Now let's get out of here."

Santa did not put up any resistance. If anything, he looked amused, and that alone was enough to completely spoil Ormsby's mood.

~*~

Ray's fear stayed with him and kept him awake for quite a while, but eventually he found himself getting bored. Aside from the background music, absolutely nothing else happened in the comfy chamber where he sat. His thoughts grew fuzzy, and he eventually fell asleep.

He had no idea how much time might have passed before he heard the door open once again. The sound wasn't startling and seemed more like a whisper than a crunch or a grind. Sitting upright, he turned toward the sound, trying to make himself appear composed. Whatever might be coming through that door didn't know him from Adam. He hoped there might be some advantage in that. And besides, what else did he have going for him?

Two young men and a woman hurried into the chamber, their faces reflecting concern rather than annoyance. Ray found that most puzzling.

"We didn't know you'd be coming back this way," said the first of the three.

"We thought you were in New York City, not out in the Georgia hinterlands," said the second.

"Are you feeling all right? Do you need anything?" asked the third.

None of their comments did anything to alleviate Ray's confusion. "I'm fine," he said. "But I'm… Uh… I'm a little confused, that's all. I'm looking for a dog."

The three who'd greeted him looked at each other, then back at him. They all appeared just as puzzled as he was.

"You're looking for a *dog*, sir?"

"Yes," said Ray as he got to his feet. "It's a mixed breed, and he only has three legs. At least, I think it's a he. Anyway, he answers to the name 'Tater.' Have you seen him?"

Once again, the three looked at each other before

returning their attention to him.

"I assume you're talking about a recruit."

Ray frowned. "Well, maybe. There was some sort of talent thing, a tryout or something, and—"

"Oh! If that's the case, he's in Temp Housing," said the second member of the trio. "But why do you need to find any dog at all? There are, as you well know, hundreds of them, plus an assortment of other animals. They're all in training."

Ray squinted at them, then shook his head as if that might clear it. "No. You see, it's my grandson's dog I need to find." He took a deep breath. "The boy's sick, and his mother thinks having the dog at his side might help. The doctors don't know what's wrong with him, and this is the only thing we can think of. It's probably silly and stands little chance of doing anything at all. But... but who knows? It might actually work. That's enough for me. I'll do all I can to find him."

For the third time, the trio looked at each other, their faces reflecting consternation. The first male spoke up, "But, sir, it's a well-known fact; you don't *have* any children, much less grandchildren."

Ray went speechless, but the condition didn't last long. "Don't be ridiculous. Of course, I have a child! Her name's Gloria. She's named after my wife's mother. Her son's name is Lawrence, but he's called Skeeter."

The three greeters huddled briefly then approached him, all smiles. As they accompanied him out of the chamber, the female commented, "We think it would be a good idea for you to talk to Doc."

"I feel fine," Ray said. "I don't need a doctor."

"We don't have doctors here," said the female, a comment which nearly made Ray's head spin even more.

Once outside the tubular chamber, he glanced at a setting rapidly growing surreal. "Really," he said, "I just need to find that dog, that one single dog. And if you'd help me find him, I'd be the most grateful person on the whole planet. After that, you can show me how to get back home, and I'll get out of your hair. You won't even know I was here." He looked over his shoulder at the door he'd just walked through as it slid shut.

"Right this way," the second male said. He and his male counterpart each had a firm grip on one of his upper arms. "Doc will know what to do. We'll have you over there in a flash. You'll like her. She's really smart."

Ray looked around at a scene reminiscent of his last visit to a major airport. But the plentiful signage gave him no clues about where he might actually be.

At least, he thought, they didn't shoot me.

Chapter Five

"Go not to the elves for counsel, for they will say both no and yes." –J.R.R. Tolkien

Gloria arrived at the hospital early on the day after they'd drawn her blood for testing. She had no intention of letting anyone there blame her for delays in figuring out what was wrong with her little boy. Rather than drag Skeeter along, she'd arranged for him to spend some time with a neighbor and her kids. Making those arrangements had been a little testy, but Gloria assured the neighboring mom that whatever it was that knocked the energy out of Skeeter was definitely not contagious. The doctors had been quite adamant about that.

The doctor's office occupied a corner suite and was guarded by a nurse/receptionist who was only slightly smaller than the Statue of Liberty. Thoroughly intimidating even when she smiled, the woman directed Gloria to a chair in the waiting area where she parked without a word.

At the appointed hour, she was summoned to the doctor's office where she took a seat next to his wide, cluttered desk, and continued waiting for another quarter hour.

Eventually, Dr. Parker walked into his office, deposited an armload of paperwork on top of an existing pile and settled himself into a large, leather-padded armchair behind the desk.

"I'm running a little behind, I'm afraid," he said. "I hope you don't mind."

"Of course not," she lied.

"I find your son's case extremely interesting."

Oh, Lord. "Does that mean you need to do more tests?"

"Not necessarily. I have the results from your blood work, but they don't reveal anything terribly helpful."

Gloria had no idea how to respond. "I'm... Uh... Sorry."

"What? No." He smiled at her. "I didn't mean to be dismissive. The results were definitely informative." He looked directly into her eyes. "The unusual elements we found in your son's blood absolutely did not come from you. They could have only come from his father."

"So, Jim had—" she cleared her throat, "—some sort of blood disease?"

"Not necessarily." He interlaced his fingers and lowered his hands to the paperwork accumulated atop his desk. "I've contacted an old colleague of mine, Dr. Mingus. He's retired now, but he used to teach at Oxford. I met him at a seminar shortly after I graduated from Medical school. Anyway, he's an expert in rare blood disorders. I sent him all the data we have on your son."

"And?" she asked.

"He asked for permission to examine the boy. He also wants to speak with you and the boy's father."

Gloria shook her head. "I already told you, his father's not—"

"I know," Parker said, his voice low but not patronizing. "I wish there were something we could do to help locate Skeeter's Dad, but that's not the sort of thing we're set up to do. Your best bet would be to hire a private investigator."

"Yeah. Like I could afford that," she said. "Don't let any of this slow down anything you might do for Skeeter."

"Of course," he said. "Of course."

~*~

Art stared at the clipboard containing his team's roster. Though he'd done at least as many tours as Maeve, he knew she had better rapport with her recruits. While his crew milled around in the assembly area, he thought having her input would make this first, formal gathering proceed more smoothly. By the time he'd picked up a phone to ask for her assistance, he'd convinced himself he hadn't just found an excuse to see her.

"Do you really think you need *my* help with your new associates?" she asked when he explained what he had in mind. "You've been at this longer than I have."

"True," he said, "but you have a certain special way with them that I lack."

"If that were so, you wouldn't have adopted the nickname one of them gave you."

Art imagined he could see her impish smile, parked between dimpled cheeks, and framed by flame-red hair. His heart beat a little faster. "So, is that a yes or a no?"

She chuckled. "As it turns out, my gang's getting their first dose of enhancement today, so I've got a little time on my hands. I might be willing to observe you and your crew. However…" Her voice trailed off.

"However, what?" he asked, hoping he didn't sound too needy.

"Well," she began, "if I do this for you, you'll owe me something in return, won't you?"

"I suppose. Did you have something in mind?" His overactive imagination churned through several possibilities: *would she tell him to quit calling? Would she want something valuable? Wait--what valuables did he even have? Was she simply tormenting him?*

He pictured her with a whip making him jump through the same hoops the animals used in some of their training and held his breath waiting for an answer.

"I was thinking…."

"Yes?" *C'mon, Art, you big doofus; don't sound so pathetic.*

"I'd like you to take me to dinner.

"You *would?*"

"Yes. Someplace nice."

"Sure!" he said, unable to hide either the relief or the excitement in his voice. "Anywhere you want to go. Tonight? Tomorrow night? I can—"

"Relax," she said, giggling. "Let's talk it over and

decide together."

"Yeah. That'd be great. I hear they have some new items on the menu at the pub, and—"

"Actually," she said, her voice adopting a mysterious sort of undertone. "I thought we might rumble over to the South-Central Terminal. They have a brand-new place nearby that I'd love to try. I hope you like deep, *deep sea*-food."

Art's heartrate increased another level. He'd dreamed of traveling with her at some point but assumed it would likely never happen. "I'd love that! Other than working in Georgia, I haven't been away from here in ages."

"Then it's a deal," Maeve said. "We'll flesh out the details when we finish the orientation for your team."

Art searched for words but couldn't find any.

"Art? Are you still there?"

"What? Oh, Yes! Right here." *Glued to the floor in complete shock, actually.*

"Super. I'll be over at the start of the session."

"Thank you so much," he murmured.

There was a brief pause before Maeve continued. "By the way, I heard something disturbing from Max."

Max? The Monster? Again? "What's that?"

"The Boss didn't show up in the big New York City parade. They had a showgirl dressed up in a skimpy Santa's helper costume waving at the crowd. From what I hear, a lot of kids were disappointed."

"A showgirl?"

"Yeah, like one of the Rockettes or something."

"No kidding? What did her costume look like?"

"From what I hear, there wasn't much to it, beachwear maybe. It definitely didn't look like anything our folks wear. At least, not when we're working."

"Imagine that," Art said, his mind once again careening down fantasy pathways. Oh, what *I'd give to see Maeve in an outfit like that!*

"You don't sound very concerned," Maeve said.

"I'm not worried. The Boss has been at this a long, long time. He can take care of himself."

"If you say so. But we both know he's getting old, and from what I hear about his wife—"

"That's just rumor, Maeve. There might not be any truth to it at all."

"I hope you're right," she said.

~*~

At Ormsby's direction, his henchmen hustled their charge into the Montague Hotel through a service entrance and deposited him in a suite on the top floor without being seen by anyone who hadn't already been paid off. The expansive living space would house the captive along with a half dozen guards who would ensure the man couldn't leave until after Christmas.

"You still want us to only give him milk and cookies?" Mordecai asked.

"For a day or two," Ormsby said, unable to keep a straight face. "He looks like he could lose a pound or two."

The man in question had removed his red overcoat, his white gloves, and his broad, black boots. He lounged in an overstuffed chair with his stocking feet propped on a coffee table. He watched them all with a bemused look on his face.

Seeing the man so relaxed struck a nerve. "What's so funny?" Ormsby asked.

"Nothing. Nothing at all. It's not every day one gets kidnapped. I'm curious about what comes next."

Ormsby glared at him. "Just be glad we're not going to torture you for information."

"I'm delighted to hear that." The man's expression didn't change. "But I'm happy to tell you anything you'd like to hear. Where should I begin?"

Ormsby ignored the question. "You understand you'll be locked up here for the duration."

Santa cocked an eyebrow at him. "For the duration of what?"

"Christmas," said one of Ormsby's subordinates.

Ormsby recognized him as the man he considered as a replacement for Mordecai. "What's your name again?"

"It's Bud," he said, "it's short for—"

"Budforth," interjected the prisoner.

Everyone in the room stared at him.

"It was in your letter," said the man reclining in the

easy chair.

"What letter?" asked Ormsby, suddenly very suspicious about the man he was about to put in charge of the operation.

"The one he sent me when he was... Oh, I don't know. About eight or nine. It's been quite a while. But a great many of those letters stick in my mind for some reason. His is just one of them."

"And just what, *exactly*, was in this letter?" demanded Ormsby.

"I don't recall precisely what he asked for; that's not terribly important. What caught my eye was the fact he'd been given a name he didn't fancy. Said the other kids in school made fun of him and gave him trouble about it. He'd been bullied. Can you imagine? It's not as if he got to choose the name on his birth certificate. I imagine the name Budforth is some sort of family heirloom, passed from one generation to the next like a cherished teaspoon. What I find odd, is that anyone who got the name would even want to pass it on, and make the next poor link in the chain suffer the same way."

"I'd never give that name to anyone," Bud said, his voice menacing. When he realized everyone had turned to look at him, he added, "but I don't remember writing you any letters. That's just stupid. And if it's one thing I ain't, it's stupid."

"*Budforth?*" Mortdecai chuckled. "Sounds like a sweet little flower about to bloom." He stepped close to Bud and looked down at him. "Now I think on it, you do look a little like a flower. Them pink ears are just... I dunno. Oh, I got it. They're *adorable*."

Bud landed a punch roughly three knuckles higher than the center of Mordecai's navel. The big man folded over his fist with a rush of exhaled air.

Ormsby watched with detached amusement. For a brief moment, he could not have cared less if the two men killed each other, but given the option, he would prefer that only one would survive. And that one, more than likely, would be given charge of the prisoner's care.

Bud didn't allow Mordecai any time to recover before he followed up his assault with a number of other stiff and well-directed punches. When Mordecai hit the floor, he followed those up with a few kicks to various parts of his opponent's anatomy. Mordecai passed out before he could surrender.

Ormsby touched Bud's shoulder to get his attention and nearly earned himself a roundhouse punch of his very own. Bud managed to restrain himself and backed away from the body at his feet.

"That's a wise move," Ormsby said, noting the bloodstains on the carpeting. The cleaning bill would be enormous, he felt sure, but if it meant they could put an end to all the Santa Claus nonsense, it would be worth every penny.

"I guess maybe I overreacted a little," Bud said. The adrenaline in his system continued to do a job on him. He appeared as tense as a leopard about to strike.

"Well, you can calm down now," Ormsby said. "I think you've made your point." He smiled at the man. "Besides, I like the name 'Bud.' It fits you." He then looked down at Mordecai, still sprawled on the carpet. "When he wakes up, tell him I'm putting you in charge. If you need anything, you can reach me back in Atlanta."

The fat man in the easy chair simply closed his eyes and shook his head.

~*~

Ray found it incredibly odd that he was being treated more like a celebrity than a common trespasser. He couldn't understand the deference paid him by everyone they met or saw. When he and his little entourage left what they called the Transport Terminal, they boarded a pleasant, horse-drawn carriage that rightfully belonged in a Currier and Ives print.

He noted a thick layer of snow on the ground, but for reasons he couldn't fathom, he didn't feel cold. Nor, apparently, did his three companions. The short trip did, however, give him an opportunity to study them along with the countryside through which they passed.

The three who'd met him when he arrived were dressed in a casual sort of uniform. None bore any insignia which might represent some sort of rank, and they treated each other as equals. Based on his two painful years in the Army, he doubted any of them was an officer.

"So, how far is it to the hospital?" he asked.

"Doc's house isn't far. We'll be there shortly."

That's a new one, but suppose it makes sense. Maybe the doctors here actually live on-site. Ray smiled and reminded himself that thus far, everyone had been nice to him, something he hadn't expected at all.

The carriage pulled to a stop, and his companions were already out and on the ground while he was still in the process of standing up. They offered him steadying hands as he stepped down a narrow set of folding stairs to the neatly swept surface below.

They guided him to the front door of a house with a thatched roof, something he'd only seen in photos of rural England. He figured such roofs had fallen out of use sometime around the time of the American Revolution.

An attractive woman he guessed to be in her late thirties opened the door and welcomed him in. His travel companions waited outside.

"I'm Docquinella Bright," she said. "But everyone calls me Doc. Why don't you have a seat over there?" She pointed to a padded bench in an adjoining room. "I'll be right in. Would you like a cup of tea?"

Ray felt his brows furrow. "I'd love some coffee if you have any." *What the heck is she up to?*

She left the room only to return moments later bearing a tray supporting two cups of steaming beverages, an assortment of bakery treats, plus cream and sugar. These she settled on the bench beside him.

"Now," she began, after testing her brew, "what brings you to see a healer today?"

"What or who?" he asked. "I feel fine, but the three who brought me here have a different opinion. I think they've mistaken me for someone else."

"Like whom?" She framed the question simply and gently, as if she were deeply interested in his opinion.

"Well," he chuckled, "I suppose it's only natural, seeing

the way I'm dressed, which, I promise you, I can explain." He leaned toward her and lowered his voice. "I think they believe I'm actually... him."

"Him who?"

"You know... Santa Claus."

She crossed her arms on her chest and gave him a warm smile. "I see."

"But what you don't understand is, I'm just passing through." He gestured toward his Santa costume with both hands. "This is all just pretend. I'm only wearing it for my job at the mall."

"The mall?"

"Yes, a shopping mall. They're all over the place. I work at one on the perimeter." When her expression remained blank, he continued. "You know, on I-285, the multi-lane Interstate highway that goes all the way around Atlanta."

"I've never been there," she said.

"Oh. Well, anyway, I got a call from my daughter." He went on to explain the reason for his trip to the Leon Farm where he hoped to retrieve Tater.

"I see," she said without giving him a hint as to whether or not she believed him. "Would you mind if I gave you a quick examination?"

"Sure, feel free. But I've gotta warn you, I don't have any insurance. I may look like it, but I'm not old enough yet for Medicare or any of that stuff."

She nodded understandingly. "That won't be a

problem. Would you please remove your coat? I imagine you're feeling a bit warmish. Just give me a moment, and we'll get started."

Ray was only too happy to comply. The cool air in the room relaxed him.

He took advantage of the silence to give the woman a visual examination of his own. His first impression hadn't changed. In addition to being attractive, she was pleasant and gently conversational. Her skin appeared flawless, and he doubted she wore any make-up. She returned, checked his pulse, then probed his chest, arms, and neck. Meanwhile, he looked at her dark hair, green eyes, and the tops of her ears.

The latter caught his attention as they seemed to be slightly pointed.

He squinted for what he hoped would be a better look. As best he could recall, the ears of his three companions for the ride to Doc's house kept the tops of their ears covered.

"You have the most delightfully shaped ears," he said.

"Oh. Well, thank you," she replied, "but I assure you, they're simply elfin. Quite common." She bent close to him and held a reading glass in front of his eyes, one at a time.

Elfin? I thought that was a descriptive term. What had they called 'em in school? Adjectives. Yeah, that's it.

"I'd have to agree," he said. "They *are* elfin."

She gave him a puzzled look, much like those he'd gotten from his three previous companions. "And you find that odd?"

He laughed. "I'm thinking more like 'charming.'"

"How else would you expect an elf's ears to look?"

"Pardon me?"

Doc's lips twisted slightly. "I doubt there's anything wrong with your hearing."

"I— Uh. Well, to be honest, I've never given it much thought. Ears are just… ears."

She shook her head. "We'll get back to that in a bit. First, I'd like to give you a little test."

"Like blood work or something?"

"No," she said, her face reflecting some revulsion. "It's a memory test."

"Sure. Go right ahead." He wondered briefly if he would ever reach a point where he wasn't totally confused.

"I'm going to say five words, and I'd like you to commit them to memory. Okay?"

Ray nodded. "I'm ready."

"The words are 'blue,' 'radio,' 'sink,' 'melody,' and 'hat.' Can you remember those?"

He ran through the words in his mind, then nodded. "Okay, got 'em." He tapped his forehead with his index finger. "I remember stuff way better than I used to, back when I was still drinkin'. Back then, there were days I could hardly remember my own name."

"Really," she said. "How long did that last?"

He put his hands in his lap and stared down at them. "Way too long, I'm afraid. But that's all behind me now. I know my limits. I haven't had a drink in a long time, and I don't intend to ever have another." He looked up as a tear crept out from the corner of his eye. He quickly knuckled it away. "I promised myself. More importantly, I promised my daughter."

Doc smiled at him. "Tell me about this daughter of yours. Do you mind?"

"Not at all," he said. "Her name's Gloria." He went on to describe their rocky relationship, his wife's tragic death, and his desire to not only make amends but to restore the family ties he'd abandoned five years earlier.

"You have all these details memorized so perfectly," Doc said. "And you sound so convincing. I'm almost ready to believe you."

Ray couldn't believe what he'd heard. "You think I've made all this up?"

"If you are who I think you are, the answer is yes."

Ray put his head in his hands and moaned. "Oh, please. Not you, too."

She patted his shoulder. "There now, take it easy. We'll get to the bottom of this in no time."

"Wait!" Ray said, suddenly remembering he still had his wallet in his possession. "I can prove who I am." He dug the billfold out, removed his driver's license, and handed it to her. "There! See? It says Raymond Mays. It's got my address and everything. It says I'm an organ donor on the back, although I don't know they'd want anything from me nowadays on account of the booze."

Doc examined the plasticized card as if it were an

ancient artifact. She used her looking glass on it, held it up to the light, and stared at the photo for a long time. Eventually, she handed it back. "The resemblance is absolutely uncanny."

"What resemblance?"

"You and the Boss could be siblings. Do you have an older brother?"

"What? No. What are you talking about?"

"You and the Boss are nearly identical."

"Whose boss? Yours?"

"I'm talking about *The* Boss. The man who created and runs this whole gigantic enterprise: Santa Claus."

Ray pinched himself. Surely the dream would come to an end soon, and he'd wake up. The look on Doc's face, however, suggested otherwise.

~*~

Maeve walked into Art's training room and smiled at the assortment of dogs that greeted her. Art stood in the middle of them trying to get their attention. He wasn't having much luck.

When Maeve clapped her hands, the sound reverberated in the room and brought an immediate silence to the space. "That's much better," she said. "Now, Art, if you'll hand me your roster, I'll call out the names, and you can introduce yourself."

Art complied and took up a position beside her.

"Rosie?" Maeve called. "Sing out, girl."

The dog, a little Maltese, stepped forward confidently and responded with a low bark. She looked from side to side at the others, her head held high, then sat down as if she were royalty.

"A natural born leader, that one," Maeve said to Art as he knelt to pet her.

He agreed then asked, "Who's next?"

"If your name is Rascal, step forward please, and let us have a look at you."

On cue, a Pomeranian that easily weighed twice as much as Rosie worked his way forward and took a seat beside her. They made quite a pair. He gave a short bark to make sure everyone recognized him.

"Welcome to the team," Art said.

Rascal nodded and edged even closer to Rosie, who then pushed him away.

"We'd better keep an eye on those two," Maeve said. "Okay then, next up is MacKenzie." She looked straight at a Westie that matched Rascal pound for pound. The dog pushed her way *between* Rascal and Rosie, gave them each a look normally reserved for assertive schoolteachers, then refocused her attention on Maeve and Art.

"Art's the boss of this team," Maeve said. "But based on the notes and what I'm seeing here, MacKenzie might make a pretty good lieutenant for you."

"I'm thinking along the same lines," Art said, as he stroked the fluffy dog's thick coat. He gazed into the stalwart canine's eyes. "I look forward to working with you."

MacKenzie nodded.

"According to the notes," Maeve said, "you've got two more little ones and two big ones. Let's get a look at JJ first."

The Shih Tzu mix pranced forward as if she were entering center stage, and Maeve couldn't help but wonder if she normally wore a frilly bow and a sparkly collar. At that moment, she had neither.

Art leaned toward Maeve and whispered, "Oh, my. What a diva!"

"She's a charmer all right," agreed Maeve who reached down to pet the little dog. I believe you're going to fit right in."

JJ yipped a greeting then turned in a pair of full circles–canine *pirouettes*–before sitting down beside the others.

"The last of our tiny team members is Maggie. Let's have a look at you."

Maggie burst through the wall of seated dogs, walking on her front legs. The back pair pedaled air. The other dogs looked at her with surprise, and several gave her appreciative barks. Maggie responded with all the aplomb of a Hollywood starlet, wiggling her little tail, and touching noses with all those she could reach.

The two remaining dogs, Buck and Finley, looked on as if it was the sort of display they observed every day.

"I've worked with these two a little bit," Art said.

"Right. The nickname thing."

"Yep." He gestured for the two much bigger dogs to

come forward.

They looked so much alike; Maeve wondered how Art would tell them apart. Then she noticed how Buck seemed to trail a half step behind Finley. She didn't seem to notice, but it was obvious Buck was seriously interested in her.

"Hm," Maeve muttered. "Looks like you've got another pair to keep your eyes on."

At that point, MacKenzie strutted forward and insinuated herself between the two much larger dogs. With a barely audible rumble, she seemed to be advising them, especially Buck, to be on their best behavior.

"Security types, you think?" posed Maeve.

"Definitely," Art said. "If I can keep them focused."

Maeve responded with a grin. "I wish you the best of luck!"

Chapter Six

"I never believed in Santa Claus because I knew no white dude would ever come into my neighborhood after dark." –Dick Gregory

Ray was still processing Docquinella's pronouncement that he and Santa Claus were virtual twins. In his mind, the "real" Santa looked like the cheery old soul pictured in vintage advertisements for Coca Cola. That fellow carried quite a few more pounds than Ray. His cheeks were permanently red, and the images of him had become iconic. But, as he recalled, they were painted images, not photographs, in which case the guy in them was likely to have been imagined if he wasn't simply an ad agency model.

"I really don't know what to say. I never actually believed— Okay that's not completely true. When I was a little kid, I'm pretty sure I believed in Santa. But when I got a little older somebody, probably my parents, told me the 'truth.'"

"Did you believe it?" Doc asked.

"As a kid? No. Christmas was special in my family.

We did it all—the tree, the stockings, the milk and cookies. I can remember leaving some carrots and lettuce out for the reindeer, though I really had no idea what they ate."

Doc smiled at him. "That's not unusual. Most kids who've heard about him had a similar experience."

"But you're saying that's all wrong? That there really *is* a Santa Claus."

"Yes."

"So, my parents *lied* to me?" He felt suddenly indignant.

Doc continued to smile. "Let me put this in perspective for you. The population of this planet is closing in on 8 billion people. Now, let's say just one fourth of them believed in Santa and expected him to deliver a gift of some kind on Christmas Eve. How many gifts would that be?"

"Almost two billion, I guess."

"Right. And do you have any idea how big a number that is?"

Ray shrugged. "I've never really thought about it."

"Hardly anyone does. So, let me clarify it. An American dollar bill is just a bit over a half a foot long. The circumference of the Earth is a little under 25,000 miles. How many of those dollar bills do you suppose it would take to circle the planet if they were laid end-to-end?"

Ray assumed the average middle schooler would be better prepared than he was to answer such an odd question. "I have no idea at all."

"Let me help." She grinned. "I've had this

conversation several times before."

"Thanks, I think."

"All right. Consider this: if you placed one *billion* American dollar bills end to end, they would stretch for five hundred, million feet—that's a five followed by nine zeroes."

"Uh... Okay." Ray still had no idea how to process anything she'd told him.

"That means if you somehow managed to line them all up, you wouldn't run out of one-dollar bills until you'd circled the Earth nearly four times. Now, *double* that number. And *that's* how many Christmas presents Santa would have to deliver, in one night!"

"That'd be impossible."

"Correct, even given the advantage of magic. The numbers are just too big to manage."

"Where are you going with all this?" he asked.

"Simply this: Santa had to find a way to reduce the numbers, so he didn't make any effort to keep his existence 'alive,' so to speak, in the minds of humans about to leave childhood."

Ray nodded. "That seems reasonable."

"Of course, it is. Santa's no fool. But even with that, the numbers were still too high. He couldn't stand the thought of disappointing millions of little ones. It would have destroyed him."

"So, how did he fix things?"

"Out of necessity, he chose to focus only on those who

sent him letters. They're most likely the true believers. That decision alone reduced the numbers dramatically, but even so, there were still far too many for him to deal with individually. Santa's good. Believe me; I know. But he's not *that* good. No one is."

Ray had grown weary of the protracted explanation. "What does this have to do with my grandson's little dog? That's what he really wants for Christmas."

"Once Santa figured out how to generate the quantity of gifts he needed to give away, he had to come up with a way to actually deliver them. One sleigh and eight reindeer would never get the job done. So, he set up special delivery teams, composed of all sorts of animals. Since terrain and weather conditions vary so much all across the world, he needed animals of every stripe to negotiate neighborhoods of unimaginable variety."

"But, how… I mean, wouldn't the houses be locked at night? And surely not all homes have chimneys. The place where I'm staying doesn't have a fireplace." He looked around the room. "Do you even have one here?"

"No. I don't. And that's where the elves come in."

"Elves? Seriously?"

"I couldn't be more serious. The world's elf population had been on the decline for centuries. Santa, almost single-handedly, reversed that. He gave us jobs and responsibilities which ended ages of struggle and competition. He gave us safe places to live. He put an end to the class warfare which had plagued our kind for millennia."

Ray waved his hands as if surrendering. "Please. Stop.

All this sounds really noble and fine, but I just wanna find my grandkid's dog and go home. I've got a job waiting for me. Kids who'll be heartbroken if—"

"If you don't show up?"

"Yeah," he said.

Doc sat with her hands in her lap, much as Ray's were. "You say your grandson is sick, and your son-in-law disappeared, right?"

"Right."

"I think I might know why."

Ray eased forward in his seat. "Really?"

"Possibly. It's a reasonabe hypothesis anyway."

"Let's hear it."

Doc took a deep breath before she continued. "Please bear with me. You're going to hear some things you've never heard before, and it's important that you understand."

He nodded. He couldn't remember a time when he'd been more focused.

"I suspect your son-in-law is a half." She pronounced the letter "L."

"A what?"

"A half—half human, half elf."

Ray couldn't keep himself from squinting at the woman. *Half elf?*

"If your daughter is human, that means your grandson

93

is a qualf."

"A *what?*"

"He's one quarter elf, three-quarters human."

"You're beginning to scare me." He paused. "Actually, you were starting to scare me a while ago when you were talking about numbers. Now you've pushed me pretty close to my freak out point."

She chuckled. "Please, relax. I don't know this to be fact; I'm just speculating, though I have a strong feeling I'm right."

"So, what does all that mean?"

"It's not uncommon for halves to develop sudden amnesia. It's based on their living a human lifestyle and missing out on the traditional foodstuff and nutrition elves thrive on. Fortunately, the condition is reversable, though it can take time."

"You're saying Jim, that's my son-in-law, simply forgot to go home?"

"If he suffered from the kind of amnesia I'm talking about, he would have had no idea who he was or where he came from. It wouldn't be hard for someone with evil intentions to take advantage of him." Doc reached out and patted his hand. "The reason I think this might be the case is because, unfortunately, it's happened before. Too many times. Halfs aren't all that rare."

Ray felt profoundly tired. Doc's words seemed to have pulled all the energy from his body. "And what about Skeeter? What's wrong with him?"

"I fear his situation is even more dire," she said. "Qualfs tend to sicken and die if they have no access to typical elf nutrition. We have no idea why they're more susceptible than halfs, but they are. The physical deterioration usually begins around age ten or eleven. How old is your grandson?"

"Ten," Ray said.

"That would be about right."

"You're saying Skeeter's going to... *die?*"

"Not necessarily. It's simply a question of diet. Just like his father, he needs the nutrients on which elves thrive."

"That's it? We just need to change his diet? That's crazy. He's really sick. He needs special medicines or surgery or God only knows what."

"I doubt that," Doc said. "Given the right things to eat, I imagine he'd be just fine."

Ray stared at her, still not ready to believe her.

"Look at what's happened to humans in the last century, at least, those in the more 'advanced' societies. They don't eat like their ancestors. Everything's processed. Their fruits and vegetables have been chemically or genetically altered, not for nutritional values, but for quantity. Humans never used to be so fat! Not all of them are, of course, but way more of them are than ever before."

His head began to ache right along with his heart. "I feel... defeated. I don't know what to do. I haven't got the slightest idea where to find elf food. It sure isn't on any of the aisles in any grocery store I've ever known."

She smiled at him. "We can take care of that. In the

meantime, however, it's quite possible we may need *your* help. A lot of it, in fact."

Ray shook his head. "I have to focus on my number one priority, Skeeter. If I can round up Tater and a bag of elf food, I'm outta here."

"You don't understand. I'm talking about a lifestyle change for that little boy, and his father, if we can find him."

"You'd help me do that? Find Jim?"

"Of course, provided you're willing to help us."

"This all feels so… bizarre. I'm losing my mind."

"I doubt it. Oh, by the way, do you remember the five words I asked you to memorize?"

Ray looked hard at her, straining to recall that part of the conversation, let alone the five words she'd tossed out for him like treats for pigeons in a park. "I— Uh… Geez, I dunno. I can't really think about that nonsense right now. My mind—"

"It's all right. You've merely forgotten them." She gestured at the treats on the tray at his side. "You haven't touched them. Try one of those," she said, pointing to a green confection.

Ray took a bite, expecting something on the order of fresh dish towel. Instead, he found the treat to be excellent, a tasty blend of salty and sweet. "This is pretty good."

"Take your time," she said. "Chew. Enjoy. Swallow. Relax."

"Those aren't any of the words you wanted me to memorize, are they?"

"Nope."

But as he consumed another of the salty/sweet treats, all five words came back to him. In order: *blue, radio, sink, melody,* and *hat.* He felt a timid but growing sense of confidence and smiled at Doc. "I've got 'em," he said.

She smiled back at him. "I knew you would."

~*~

Gloria didn't own a computer. When she had to do anything dealing with the Internet, she relied on her phone, though it was far from being the latest and greatest. At least it worked. Most of the time. But she doubted it could handle an online video chat with Dr. Mingus, the man Skeeter's doctor wanted her to talk to.

Though she couldn't imagine what he wanted to know, or what he might be able to tell her, she didn't want the discussion's success to hinge on her sad, little phone. Instead, she went to the local library and used a computer there. Fortunately, none of the others were in use when she arrived, so there was a good chance she'd have some privacy.

The connection went through smoothly, and before she knew it she was facing the neatly bearded professor. He removed his pince-nez spectacles, quickly introduced himself, then went immediately to the subject at hand.

"I just needed to ask you a few questions about your husband," he said.

Gloria hesitated, then spoke. "I thought this discussion would be about my son."

"It will be, eventually. I'm merely attempting to place him geo-genetically. Your son's DNA contains some rarities.

97

Without going into great detail, which you likely wouldn't understand anyway—"

"I beg your pardon," interjected Gloria. "I'm not exactly stupid."

"I meant no offense," said Mingus. "So, you're familiar with genotypes and alleles?"

Gloria swallowed. "I've... *heard* of them."

"Good! So, you'll understand what I'm talking about." He returned his glasses to the bridge of his nose, picked up a sheet of paper, gave it a quick glance. "Your son's DNA contains characteristics of a genotype I'm greatly interested in. Based on the DNA sample I have from you, I can conclude that those characteristics would be even more evident in your husband's DNA which, I understand, we won't be able to obtain."

Suddenly, Gloria's chair ceased to be comfortable. "What kind of characteristics do you mean?"

"I'm sure you're familiar with our species, *Homo Sapiens,* supposedly the only human species which still exists."

"*Supposedly?*"

"There are a number of extinct human species. There are also the Neanderthals and Denisovans; they're also extinct. But even so, some of their DNA remains in our genetic makeup. It's greatly responsible for things like hair and eye color. If you have a DNA test done today, you will often be told what percentage of such material you've inherited."

"You're saying my son has *caveman DNA?*"

Mingus laughed. "No. Certainly not. At most he has

inherited perhaps one percent of such DNA. That's not what caught my eye, however."

Gloria shook her head. "This is all quite fascinating, but my concern is my son. Is there anything you can tell me which might help cure him?"

"Ah." He frowned. "That's not really my area of expertise. I'm not a medical doctor."

Making a conscious effort to avoid grinding her teeth, Gloria asked, "Then what good will it do me to even talk to you? You're the only one getting anything out of this! My son may have a very limited amount of time left, and you're wasting it!"

"Maybe not!" Mingus exclaimed. "The more we learn, the more we can do. Please, I just need to know a little bit more... about your husband. Do you know where he was born?"

"In the Midwest, somewhere. He was adopted."

"Oh." Mingus appeared as crestfallen as Gloria felt.

"Do you know what agency handled it?"

"No. Why does that matter?"

"They might have additional records. I have reason to believe there is a race of near-humans with whom we've co-existed for many thousands of years. I suspect one of your husband's biological parents was a member of that group."

"I've never heard of such a thing," Gloria said, feeling certain Dr. Mingus was a certifiable lunatic.

Mingus hurriedly asked one final question. "Do you happen to recall if your husband had pointed ears?"

Gloria cut the connection without giving him an answer.

What a complete idiot! Pointed ears. What in the world was he thinking? For that matter, what in the world was I thinking?

"I've got way better things to do than worry about the shape of Jim's ears!" she announced to the empty computer stations around her.

She hadn't heard a peep out of her father since she'd asked him to retrieve Tater, not that she held out much hope of his success. If he operated true to form, he probably went to a bar somewhere and used Skeeter's condition as a means to connive someone into buying him a drink.

As she walked out to her car, she wondered if maybe she wasn't being too hard on him. After all, he had certainly *seemed* sincere and eager to do whatever he could to help. Maybe what she needed to do was to see if Skeeter was feeling strong enough to make a quick trip to the mall. Maybe having a visit with Santa Grandad would lift his flagging spirits. At the very least, it was worth a try.

The drive from the library to her home was mercifully short, and she dropped her keys and purse on the kitchen counter the minute she walked in the door. After checking on Skeeter, who was sound asleep, she ventured back into the kitchen and thanked the neighbor who had stayed with her son while she was gone. It was time to see when her father might be on duty so they could visit.

It required a number of calls before she finally reached someone in charge, a woman who, after learning the point of Gloria's call, seemed eager to get the conversation over with.

"Raymond Mays? Yeah, he worked here. Last year. He skipped the training session yesterday and was supposed to work the first shift today. He didn't bother to show up."

Gloria's hopes faded instantly. "What happened to him?"

"I don't know," the woman said, "and frankly, I don't care. If you see him, tell him I want our Santa Claus costume back. Oh, and he can forget about ever working here again!"

<Click>

Gloria stared at the phone in her hand. "Well done, Dad, and congratulations. You've proven yourself to be everything I thought you might be."

She put the phone back in her purse, sat down at her small kitchen table, and wept.

~*~

Art went through the motions of seating Maeve at a table in a posh little dining establishment located a short distance from the South-Central Terminal. The trip had been uneventful, other than giving him a chance to be alone with her for a good half hour.

Maeve filled most of that time talking about their teams and how excited she was to get the Season of Voyages underway.

"That little Tater is something else," she said. "I don't know how he does it, but he acts as if he can sometimes read my mind."

Art seriously doubted that. "Give me an example."

"Okay. This morning, for instance, I somehow

misplaced the roster and the outline for their training. I didn't say anything to them; I didn't want to give the impression I could be so fallible. You know how important it is for them to believe fully in their team leader."

"Yeah. So?"

"While I tried to locate the missing paperwork and simultaneously look like nothing was amiss, little Tater sneaked out of the room. I didn't even notice he was missing until he scratched at the door."

She giggled. "I couldn't believe it. Even though the door was partially open, and he could have come in, he waited until I came to the door. There he sat with the paperwork in his mouth. I honestly believe he didn't want the others to know what was going on."

Art whistled. "That's amazing."

"I thought so, too."

When their meals arrived, the conversation shifted. "This is undoubtedly the most tender musk ox I've ever tasted," he said. "How's the arctic salmon?"

"Sublime," she said, gently applying a corner of her napkin to her lower lip. "By the way, I got another note from Max today."

Oh, great. My competition just happens to be Mr. Muscle himself. "How nice. And what did our dear friend have to say?"

"They've lost track of the Boss."

Art stopped chewing. "You're kidding."

"I wish I were."

"There was a rumor he somehow traveled, on his own, from New York to Georgia and returned via the terminal there. But that turned out to be just another rumor. Max called it a misunderstanding." She fixed him with a worried look. "How could something like that be a misunderstanding?"

Art struggled to find a way to turn what she'd said into a joke but failed. "Mistakes happen," he said. "Besides, we don't really need to have the Boss on hand at all times. He's taken time off before."

"I know, but having him around is great for morale."

"My team members couldn't care less," he said.

"You don't know that. There's not a single dog on your team that doesn't like people."

"That doesn't mean they'd know the difference between the Boss and a Beefeater."

She giggled again. "A Beefeater?"

"You know. The guys who guard the Tower of London. They're uniforms were mostly red back in the day, just like the boss's."

"You're a nut, y'know that?" She blew him a kiss. "That's what I love about you."

Art's mind had been mentally cruising the grounds of the Tower when he heard her words, and suddenly just one of them took center stage. *Love? Don't mess this up, old chum. Find something to say. And fast!*

It took a moment, but he liked what he came up with.

"I can't think of *anything* about you that I don't love."

Maeve flashed one of her ultra-high voltage smiles at him. "I think you've had enough wine for one evening."

~*~

Comfortably ensconced back home in his upscale Northside Atlanta estate, Ormsby put in a call to his man in New York City. "Budforth? What've you got to report." He'd intentionally pushed the man's buttons to see if he could handle a little pressure. He felt doing so at a distance of some 800-plus miles would be fairly safe.

Bud, however, didn't take the bait. "We're good here," he said. "Although I wish there were a way to get our special guest to shut up. If he's not jabbering about his sleigh and his eight not-so-tiny reindeer, he's singing or humming Christmas carols."

"That tells me I made the right decision about coming home," Ormsby said.

"I swear, if I hear him launch into another rendition of 'Grandma Got Run Over by a Reindeer,' I'll choke him to death."

Ormsby laughed for the first time in what felt like months. Just having the Boss under his thumb gave him a psychological boost of monumental proportions. "Just keep your eye on him. If it absolutely comes to it, I suppose you could put a gag in his mouth, but only as a last resort."

"Yes sir," Bud said.

"How's Mordecai doing?"

"I can't say we're on the best of terms."

"How are you keeping him occupied?"

Bud exhaled into the phone. "I put him in charge of exterior needs."

Ormsby frowned. "What does that mean?"

"Anything we need from outside the hotel, he has to get. He only takes over inside when I'm not here."

"You leave? I thought we had an understanding." Ormsby had no intention of letting Mordecai mess things up.

"I have to get away from our friend here every once in a while. It's my understanding you don't want him killed."

"*Of course,* I don't," Ormsby said.

"Well then, that means I have to get away from time to time. Otherwise, I promise, I'll do something I'm sure we'll both regret."

"Bud?"

"Yeah?"

"Keep him alive. Understand?"

"Yes, sir."

"At least," Ormsby added, "until after Christmas."

~*~

When Maeve returned to the team's quarters, the entire crew lined up to greet her. They sat hip-to-hip, from tallest to smallest: Augie, Foster, Cody, Spike, Maple, Zoe, and Peanut. Tater marched up and down in front of the line like their commanding officer. If they'd been wearing uniforms, he would have been inspecting them.

"Relax, guys," Maeve said, and suddenly the unmoving line broke into constituent parts, and all of them wanted to get as close to her as possible. The exercise made it difficult to walk.

Maeve worked her way to a sofa and dropped into it. The dogs followed. Peanut, the cat with the strange green eyes, held off until the rest were settled, then climbed over them to reach Maeve's lap where she curled up in a tight ball after giving Maeve's chin a kiss, and then either went to sleep or pretended to.

The modifications had clearly begun to take effect. Whatever animosities the animals might have had before completely vanished. Neither Cody nor Spike barked, something they both loved to do. Maple and Zoe conceded the center of Maeve's lap but took up positions on either side of her. They also followed her lead and either went to sleep or faked it. Maeve didn't care; she was simply happy to be the focus of so much attention. Augie didn't even drool on her.

Life was good. Dinner with Art had been wonderful. She was still blushing over his seemingly heart-felt remark that he loved everything about her. She still had some secrets, but none of them would change anything if and when he discovered them.

She had almost fallen asleep, right where she sat, when thoughts of the Boss crept back into her head. Art's comment, that they'd gotten along without him several times in the past, didn't make her feel any better.

Something about his latest disappearance just didn't feel right.

Chapter Seven

"Christmas is never going away; it's always going to be here. And there's always room for one more Christmas song, I think." –Johnny Mathis

"Are you hungry?" asked Docquinella.

"Yes," Ray said, though he wasn't sure what time it was. He didn't know if what he needed was breakfast, lunch, or dinner. "What'd you have in mind?"

"That sort of depends on your last meal. You've definitely changed time zones."

That explained a lot, but not with any specificity. "Where *am* I, exactly?"

"Exactly?" She chuckled. "That I can't say. Let's just say you're significantly north and west of where you were when you began your journey here."

"Like the Rockies?" he asked.

"More like the Canadian Rockies, the seriously remote part."

Ray's grasp of geography had never been stellar, but he knew where the Rocky Mountains were, and he knew where Canada was, so he had little trouble putting the two together. He just found it hard to believe it could get more remote.

"What I need more than food, is sleep," he said. "I've gotta be sharp for work tomorrow. You wouldn't believe how smart some of the little kids are who come for a visit. I definitely have to be on my toes. Some of the questions they ask demand creative answers."

"About that," Doc said, her lips twisting to one side. "I'm afraid you won't be going back very soon. Certainly not today, and perhaps not even this week."

Ray felt stricken. "But— But that's my job! It's what I do. You don't understand; if it weren't for my Christmas gig, I couldn't make it through the rest of the year. Kids see me in stores and out on the street, and they wave and say, 'Hi.' Some even call out, 'Merry Christmas!' It keeps me going from one season to the next. So, y'see, I can't afford to lose this job. I just can't."

He remembered what his boss at the mall had told him about showing up late. She'd given him a 5-minute buffer. "Please, I'm begging you. Help me get home so I can hang on to at least *something* good in my life. It may not mean much to you; it may not mean anything at all, but it's important to me. More important than you can imagine."

Doc smiled at him. "You don't give us much credit when it comes to caring, but then you haven't been here very long. You don't know what we do."

"That's true, I suppose. And, to be honest," Ray said, "I'm surprised by how well I've been treated. Y'all don't know me from Adam's housecat."

"Has it worked for us?"

"I beg your pardon?"

"Adam's housecat. Did we recruit it at some point?"

"What, like Tater?" Ray snorted. "No. It's just an expression. I— Never mind." He yawned.

"Let me show you to one of my guest rooms. You can lie down and take a nap. That'll give me time to make some inquiries and see about getting you back home."

"With Tater? That would be a huge blessing, especially if I've lost my job."

Doc smiled again. "I'll do what I can. You get some rest."

~*~

As the doctors had suggested, Gloria monitored Skeeter's temperature and his blood pressure, faithfully noting both on a chart provided by the hospital. For a while, he seemed to be doing slightly better and was able to sit up and watch television for an hour or so. He would then close his eyes and nap for about the same length of time.

His appetite, once as robust as any active ten-year-old's, had dropped to a subsistence level, and Gloria had to coax him to eat. Even his favorite foods—mac 'n cheese, ice cream, peanut butter—no longer appealed to him. If not for vitamin supplements, she feared he would starve to death before the doctors figured out what was wrong with him.

When he started taking longer naps between shorter

sessions watching the tube, she knew his problems had become worse. She called Dr. Parker and pleaded with him to do something, *anything*, that might help.

He hemmed and hawed, and even suggested they try herbal remedies and non-traditional healing methods.

"Like what?" she asked. "Acupuncture? Voodoo?"

"There are quite a few different non-traditional options available. Unfortunately, I'm not very familiar with them. My training has been strictly traditional. However, I've had a number of patients who have reported success with therapies such as herbal medicines, Chiropractic, and even Tai Chi."

"Skeeter can barely lift his head. You expect him to hold a pose? Get real."

"There's Reiki and Qigong, too," he said, sounding as if he was grasping at any straw he could reach.

"*Qigong?*"

"Like Reiki, it's an alternative, energy-based healing practice."

Gloria pursed her lips. "It sounds like you're reading it from a list."

"From my computer screen," he said. "I'm so sorry. I just don't know what else to tell you."

Gloria's heart beat faster. "I hope you're not saying what I think you're saying."

"Well—"

"Are you giving up on my son?"

"No!" he replied quickly, "it's just that we seem to be out of options. I've consulted a number of specialists, and not just Dr. Mingus. Hopefully, one of them will—"

"So, you *have* given up," Gloria said. "You're sending me out to visit faith healers and snake oil salesmen, is that it? Do you happen to have a shaman on staff? I can supply the feathers and sweetgrass. I'd be willing to build a sweat lodge if I thought for one second it might help."

"Mrs. Malone, please be reasonable. We're trying—"

"The thing is," she said, "you're not trying hard enough!"

Gloria clicked off and dropped her cell phone on the kitchen counter as she slumped forward, crossed her arms, and lowered her head. All the better to cry her heart out. She tried not to make too much noise so as not to disturb her son.

"Mom?" Skeeter called out, his thin voice plucking her heartstrings. "Are you okay?"

"Yes," she replied, grabbing a tissue to blot away her tears. "We're both gonna be fine. I promise."

~*~

Art lined up his charges in hopes of figuring out which of the dogs was best suited to handle specific tasks required of a delivery team. He knew it wouldn't be easy, and one or more of them might not be good at any of the options available. It had happened before.

According to more than one team leader, it wasn't unheard of for entire teams to be dismissed for an overall lack of competence. The mission was too important to leave to chance. Dogs could be flighty. Everyone knew it, but they could also be intensely loyal. Coupled with native intelligence and the modifications, training, and the special treatment they received, most of them served brilliantly.

He reviewed the various tasks his team would have to perform. They included filling stockings of virtually any size and shape with hard candies and small toys. A special tool had been devised to make the process easier, but it required at least two dogs to operate: one to support the loading tube, and one to position it and start the goodies flowing. He thought Rosie and JJ could handle it, with Maggie as a back-up in case one of them got tired. The smallest members of his team, they would most likely be his Fillers.

Sentry duty would certainly fall to Buck and Finley since they were the largest. They could also pull double duty if a larger gift needed to be hauled in. Though presents were pre-loaded on small, wheeled carts, the little dogs sometimes struggled to pull them. Hopefully, Buck would be able to focus on the job instead of romancing Finley, though she seemed adept at ignoring his advances. He checked off the box for Guards.

Rascal would be an ideal Hauler. He was just the right size to drag packages from the delivery vehicle to their destination. For that matter, MacKenzie was also the right size. Both, however, had already lived long lives—fourteen and fifteen years respectively. The job wasn't terribly demanding, and they could probably take turns. He made a note to look into providing extra vitamin supplements for both of them.

Once he'd decided on their roles, Art began putting them through their paces. It wouldn't be long before the team loaded up and began the most important journey in the Season of Voyages. He prayed they would be ready.

~*~

"Your Santa finally did it," Bud told Ormsby on the phone. "I was out getting a drink, and your brain trust, Mort, was supposed to be keeping an eye on him."

"So, what happened?"

"The old guy was carryin' on as usual, according to Mort—"

"It's Mordecai. He's a little sensitive about his name," Ormsby said.

"Yeah, whatever. Anyway, room service shows up, and who do you s'pose got to the door first?"

"Oh, for cryin' out loud. Not the Boss! No one's even supposed to *see* him."

"I know, right? Chalk up another one for Morty. Mordi. Whatever. Anyway, the guys tell me Santa looks the busboy in the eye and tells him he's been kidnapped and then hands him a slip of paper with a phone number on it. Says if he calls that number, he'll get a big reward."

Ormsby stopped chewing on his lip but not until he'd nearly drawn blood. "And?"

"Finally, your guy pulls Santa away from the door and yanks the note out of the busboy's hand. When the kid objects, your guy tells him the bearded weirdo is crazy, and that he's not being held prisoner, he's being treated for Alzheimer's or some such."

"When did you get there?"

"An hour or so later," Bud said. "I wasn't gone all that long. And I never dreamed any of the guys would mess up so badly."

Ormsby considered what he'd been told. "Do you still have the piece of paper with the phone number on it?"

"I imagine it's kickin' around here somewhere. Why?"

"I want the number," Ormsby said. "It might come in handy."

"Okay then, I'll look for it. My guess is Mordee-cry still has it."

"Text the number to me when you find it."

"Will do," Bud said. "And by the way—"

"Shut up and listen," Ormsby said, "this nightmare is on you. If you ran a tighter ship, this never would've happened. From now on, you don't leave the apartment unless it catches fire. Understand?"

He hung up without waiting for a reply.

~*~

Ray woke up feeling refreshed even though the bed he'd slept in wasn't terribly comfortable, and the general fragrance suffusing the house didn't appeal to him. He wondered if there had been something in the snack Docquinella had given him that made him sleepy.

Did she drug me?

He'd been told repeatedly by his AA sponsor and other recovering alcoholics to avoid anything and everything that might prove addictive. He'd done his best to follow that advice and hoped that, if Doc had actually given him a knock-out pill of some kind, he wouldn't develop cravings for it.

He left the room and returned to the parlor where he'd previously chatted with the attractive female elf. He found her there, seated beside an athletic-looking man with long hair and a dark, five o'clock shadow.

"Oh, good! You're awake. Ray, I'd like you to meet a member of our security team."

I knew it! He's going to arrest me for trespassing. She was just stringing me along. Ray began looking for a way out of the house, a path to freedom, even though he doubted he could outrun the much younger man looking at him.

The man smiled and held out his hand. "My name's Maximillian," he said. "But everyone calls me Max. I'm pleased to meet you." He glanced at Doc. "You're right. He *is* the spitting image of the Boss."

Ray accepted the outstretched hand, fully expecting to be yanked across the room, cuffed, and thrown in a paddy wagon. Instead, the firm handshake ended without incident, and Doc gestured for both men to follow her lead and have a seat.

"Max was one of the first to discover our problem," Doc said.

Ray squinted at her. "*Your* problem?"

"Yes," said Max. "And it's a big one. I was working in transport and had arranged for the Boss's trip to New York City. He wanted to be in a parade there."

"Why?"

"Kids love to see him, and the whole thing's broadcast on network television. It's great coverage for very little effort." He pressed his lips together in a tight line. "At least, that's the way it always worked in the past. This time…" He shook his head. "This time was different."

"How?"

"He never made it to the parade. We watched the whole thing; he was supposed to be in the very last float, the grand finale. We were stunned, as you can imagine, when we saw his float go by without him. Some woman in a bikini had taken his place. She was smiling and waving to the crowd like nothing had gone wrong."

"A *bikini?* In November?" Ray scratched his head.

Doc quickly chimed in, "It was unseasonably warm that day, which is beside the point. Switching places, especially with someone dressed like that, is definitely not the sort of thing the Boss would ever do."

"And then, not much later," Max said, "we saw him—or *thought* we saw him—get into a transport module leaving from our facility in Georgia."

Ray thumbed his chest. "Hey, I'm sorry about that. I didn't mean—"

"There's no need to apologize. It could've happened to anyone."

"Right," said Ray, unable to restrain a note of sarcasm, "as long as they wore a costume and happened to look like Santa Claus."

"Well, yeah," admitted Max.

"We still don't know where the Boss is," Doc said. "We're far enough along this year that our entire operation should be able to function normally, or nearly so, even if he doesn't make it back by Christmas day. But next year? Who knows?"

"Who's going to deliver his gifts *this* year?" Ray asked.

"The usual teams. It's the highlight of the Season of Voyages; it's the reason we exist. Our teams go out all over the world and make those deliveries."

"Wait. I thought Santa did it. You mean I've been lying these past few years? Kids sit on my lap, look me straight in the face, *and I lie to them?*"

"Back in the day, the Boss did make all the deliveries himself, but the job's grown so much, there's no way he can do it all now," Doc said. "We talked about this, remember? Two *billion* presents?"

"Yeah, yeah, sure. I remember." Ray gave it some more thought. "If *delivering* so many gifts is crazy hard, how about making them? He couldn't possibly do all that by himself. That's where the elves come in, right? In the workshops? They must be gigantic."

"They used to be," Doc said. "Not so much anymore."

"Kids today aren't often interested in wooden trains or handmade dolls," she pointed out. "They're keen on mass manufactured toys, games, and books. There's very little call these days for the kinds of things the Boss and the elves used to make."

Questions swirled in Ray's head, but one in particular stood out. "Who pays for all this?"

Max and Doc exchanged looks, then Doc spoke. "We can't say anything more unless you sign a Non-Disclosure Agreement."

Ray had heard of NDAs, but he never thought he'd ever see one, much less need to autograph one. "Okay, I'll sign, but why are you telling me any of this?"

"Because we really need your help," Doc said. "We're in a bind, a big one. We need you to stand in for the Boss, at least until we locate him and bring him back."

Ray shrugged. "I've already lost my job over this, so I don't suppose hanging around an extra day or two will matter. But I really need to find my grandson's dog. If—"

"We can make that happen," Max said. "A friend of mine has been working with him. She can deliver him for you. The problem is, we can't guarantee we'll find the Boss any time soon. We have a security team in New York City right now, and they're investigating, but so far they haven't found anything useful."

"And what do you expect me to do? Drive a sleigh? I've never even seen a real, live reindeer by the way. How—"

Doc interrupted him. "We need you to do some public relations work. We want to schedule a press conference to show the world everything's okay. We'll come up with a cover story to explain why the Boss wasn't in the big parade. Hopefully, that'll take some of the steam out of the rumors."

"What rumors?" Ray asked.

Doc grimaced. "All kinds. Social media thrives on this stuff. We've seen all sorts of stories: Santa's on vacation; Santa's been kidnapped; Santa's working for the CIA. There's even one claiming he's dead."

She looked him in the eye. "We can't let that nonsense go unanswered, and you're the perfect candidate to do it."

"Because I sorta look like him?"

"No," Max said. "It's because you're a dead ringer for him. You fooled both the transport department *and* security. They had no idea you weren't the real deal."

"And you want me to go on national TV?"

"Yes," the two said at once.

Ray looked at them in amazement. "You're crazy. Both of you!"

~*~

Maeve walked into Art's training room, pleased to see his crew practicing their new skills. She felt a jealous pang noting that most of his team had progressed beyond the point hers had reached. And now she had still another task to perform. It didn't seem fair.

"Art?"

He hadn't heard her come in and spun around in surprise. "Hey there! This is a pleasant way to start the day."

She eased the door shut behind her. "Sorry to interrupt."

He waved the apology off. "What's up?"

"I had a chat with Max, and he says Security needs me to take one of my dogs back to its owner. One of my best!"

Art frowned. "Well, if the order came from Max the Monster himself, you can't very well—"

119

"C'mon. He's not a bad guy. He's just big. That's not his fault."

"Max didn't *inherit* those big muscles he's always flaunting," Art said. "He makes me nervous. Sometimes I wonder if he's one of them."

"Them?"

"Humans. A body builder or a wrestler. Elves don't normally get that big. Maybe he's a qualf. Yeah. I'll bet that's it. Sure would explain a lot."

She smiled at him. "You aren't jealous, are you?"

"Of the *Monster?* Hardly. I just—" He shrugged. "Whatever. So, anyway, why do you have to return a teammate? I presume you're talking about Tater."

"Yep. I don't have all the details yet. I'm supposed to leave today, but Max told me to wait for final instructions."

~*~

Ormsby kept an eye on anything he could find in social media that pertained to his nemesis, and there was quite a bit. Some of it, he noted, hadn't come from his own posts. That would normally have made him gleeful, but in light of Bud's failure to keep Santa in complete lock-down mode, there was a chance someone might post something on the not-so-jolly fat man's behalf.

It hadn't taken long, nor a great deal of effort, to start rumors on the internet about why Santa failed to show up for the parade. The fact that a scantily clad female had taken his place all but guaranteed any post which included a photo of her would receive wide circulation. Ormsby congratulated himself for having the foresight to provide the lovely young thing, complete with light-up, two-piece swimwear in Christmas colors. Her perky little Santa hat, sporting a sprig of mistletoe, completed the ensemble. The social media copycats were all too happy to take care of distribution.

In no time at all, someone suggested Santa had fallen ill and may have been poisoned by a religious fanatic. Ormsby found that rumor unsettling and a little too close to home, though he hardly considered himself a fanatic. *Righteous?* Certainly. *A warrior in the cause?* Absolutely. And if there were ever another grand Christian Crusade, like those storied battles of the Middle Ages, he would happily step forward and help fund it.

Another rumor, one he'd have preferred to quash, suggested that Santa had been kidnapped and was being held for a big ransom. Who would actually make the payoff wasn't mentioned. Ormsby consoled himself with the knowledge that while he may have removed from the gameboard a major player in the war on a religious Christmas, he certainly wasn't holding him for ransom. Such a thing was simply beneath him. He'd sooner have the man taken somewhere and shot.

Still another claim speculated that one of the major political parties was somehow behind the disappearance. Naturally, both the Democrats and the Republicans blamed each other. Finger-pointing soon displaced the message, however, and devolved into the usual back-and-forth that most people just found tiresome.

The only other rumor Ormsby could claim for himself was the one about Santa's demise. This one he thought had just the right fanciful quality. According to this explanation, Santa was headed to New York City from the North Pole when he ran afoul of the North American Aerospace Defense Command, known universally as NORAD. Santa and his team of flying ruminants had entered protected airspace and were shot down somewhere amidst the frozen wastes of far northern Canada.

A spokesman for NORAD immediately responded. He reminded anyone interested that for sixty-some years, the organization had provided an "official" Santa Tracker for anyone who cared to find out where he was, and when.

Ormsby knew it was all complete nonsense, though he disliked the idea that a government entity would so readily comment on his post. Of course, as always seemed to happen, new stories quickly appeared about a conspiracy within NORAD, an attempted coup by the NSA or CIA, and other tales depicting Santa's woes amid the icebergs and the dwindling population of polar bears.

Why can't they just let him die in peace?

And that provoked a new option. What if Santa really did die?

~*~

"Yes, of course I'll help," Ray said. "It's not like I've got anything else going on in my life that would take precedence." He paused. "Except my grandson. I'm sorry about how sad so many kids around the world are about Santa, but my family has to come first."

"That's completely understandable," Doc said. "What do you want us to do?"

"Don't just take Skeeter's dog back. Instead, I want you to bring the dog, the boy, and his mother here. And I want you to start treating Skeeter. Do whatever you have to do to make him well."

Deep in thought, Doc tapped her fingertips together. "That might be difficult."

"Why?"

"For openers, how likely would your daughter be to travel to an unknown location, guided by someone she has no reason to trust?"

Ray saw her point. "Why can't I just call her and explain everything?"

"That might work, except your cell phone is useless here."

"Can't I just use yours?"

She shook her head. "We don't use them. They generate too many distractions. We have our own ways of communicating. And there's another issue as well. Both your daughter and your son would have to sign a pledge that they won't say anything about who we are or what we do here."

"More NDAs. Even for a child?"

"Especially for him. You know how children love to talk. We have to impress upon him the importance of keeping all of this—all of our operations—a secret."

"What if I wrote her a note and explained all that?" Ray asked. "Surely that would do the trick."

Doc held out her hands, palms up. "Maybe. I suppose it depends on how much she trusts you."

"It's worth a try," Ray said.

"Why not just record a short video? That way, she'll get a glimpse of what's waiting for them. We can shoot it right here, right now."

Ray agreed, and the two worked together to get it done. They filmed the video with a camera Doc provided, and Ray reviewed and rejected the first couple takes. When he was finally satisfied, Doc contacted Max and put their plan into action.

"I'm still wondering about one thing," Ray said, "at least for now."

"What's that?"

"Who pays for all this? It's gotta be expensive, and I'm not just talking about all the gifts and toys."

Doc smiled. "Mostly it comes from corporate donations. Think for a moment about how many companies depend on a thriving economy and huge populations of Christmas shoppers. If it weren't for the holiday season, many of those companies would quickly go bankrupt. They *need* Santa. Santa is imperative for their survival. And without us, there wouldn't be one."

Chapter Eight

"Mother considered a press conference on a par with a visit to a cage of cobras." –Margaret Truman

Pleased that Art was willing to take care of her team during her brief absence, Maeve headed back to the transfer portal for her return to Georgia. The little car was still in storage there, and she would use it to take Tater home, and with any luck, bring his owner and his owner's mother back with her.

She had reviewed the short video Max had given her and which she would share with Tater's family. The word "family" conjured a number of images in her mind. While Tater settled his head on her lap and went to sleep, Maeve daydreamed about a family of her own, one that didn't consist solely of dogs and a cat.

Still young by elf standards, Maeve knew the time was right for her to find a mate. Art was the obvious choice, though he lacked the nerve to come right out and propose to her. But he wasn't a child anymore, either. He had a good half century under his belt, and he'd worked in any number of positions within the Boss's worldwide operation. It was high time for him to make a move. And since they were roughly the same age, it only made sense that he should make that move *on her*.

She often wondered how humans managed when they had so many fewer years in which to figure things out. She was every bit as old as the man on the video she carried, but he looked twice her age!

As the door slid shut and the music no longer competed with noise from the transport terminal outside, Maeve relaxed and prepared to take a nap. She'd need all her wits, and as much energy as she could muster, to fulfill her assignment. With any luck, she'd be back working with the remainder of her team the following day.

And maybe, just maybe, she'd squeeze in a lunch with Art the following afternoon.

"Hi, Mrs. Malone? You probably won't remember me, but we met at Leon Farms when your son's dog tried out for one of our productions."

"Yes," Gloria said. "I remember. But would you please tell me your name again?"

"I'm Maeve Blessing, and I need to see you right away."

Gloria's tone abruptly shifted from pleasant to pained. "This is about Tater, isn't it? Oh, Lord. Please tell me he's all right. If my son—"

"Tater's fine, Mrs. Malone. He's a wonderful little guy. In fact, he's sitting in my lap right now."

Though she strained to hear him, Gloria couldn't make out any Tater-ish sounds.

Maeve continued, "Your father has been in touch with some influential people around here, and he asked me to do him a favor."

"Really? *My father?*"

"Actually, he's become something of a celebrity where I come from," Maeve said. "You'll be amazed."

"I'm uh… Well, a little surprised. I knew Dad wanted to contact y'all, but I had no idea he'd done it. In fact, since we last spoke, I haven't heard a single word from him."

"Then you'll be happy to know I've got a recorded message, a video, that he made just for you and your son. That's Skeeter, right? With an owner like him, it's no wonder Tater turned out so well. You must be very proud of both of them."

"Oh, I am. I am. Although, right now, I'm afraid we're having—" She stopped and took a breath to steady herself. "We're having a really hard time."

"I know," Maeve said, her voice softening. "Your father filled us in. That's why Tater and I are here. I just wanted to touch base and make sure you were home before we drove over for a visit. I'm sure Skeeter would like to see his pet again."

"You can't imagine how much that would mean to him." She allowed herself the first sigh of relief she'd had in days. "It's nearly dinner time; would you like to join us? It's just meatloaf, but we'd be happy to share."

"That would be wonderful," Maeve said. "So, we'll be leaving in just a bit, and we should arrive in an hour or so."

Gloria thanked her and rang off, then called to Skeeter in their diminutive living room, "Hey, you up for a special guest?"

The boy looked at her from his regular sprawl on the sofa in front of the TV. "I'm kinda tired," he said, then took a closer look at his mother's face and saw something there that triggered a change of heart. "Who's coming?"

"You remember that pretty girl with the bright red hair who met us for the audition and picked up Tater for his training?"

"Yes'm."

"Well, they're both on their way here now." She grinned. "Still tired?"

For the first time in days, Skeeter sat up straight with a huge smile on his face. "No kiddin'?"

"No kiddin'," she assured him. "Now, you'd best skedaddle and get cleaned up."

Skeeter skedaddled.

~*~

Art realized Maeve could be accused of taking advantage of him, but that wasn't the case when someone in the upper echelon of the organization handed out a special assignment. Those jobs always took precedence. But, since Maeve's task came down the pipeline via Max, he could have given her a hard time about it. That, however, would simply have proven he had issues with the big guy.

He pushed all that out of his mind as unproductive and surveyed the oddball crew that had temporarily joined his team. Some of the names sounded familiar, but that may have been due to memories of crews he'd work with in the past.

Tater was missing, but he knew Maeve had him with her. The two largest canines under Maeve's command were Augie and Foster, though the boxer, Augie, massed twice Foster's weight. They sat behind a short row of smaller dogs who watched him with various degrees of curiosity.

A black cat completed the company and lay stretched out on the floor as if unaware of the dog pack which, under other circumstances, might have torn her to shreds.

Art acknowledged her with, "Good morning, Peanut. I see you're comfortable." He found that a little hard to believe since his own gang, lined up at the opposite end of the room, all seemed intensely interested in the lounging feline.

He went through the rest of the list after assigning Guard and Hauler duties to the two big dogs. "Spike? Speak up."

The dark little schnauzer responded instantly with a series of sharp yips, each one propelling him slightly backwards. Spike's size and attitude suggested he'd make a great Hauler, as would the much younger but equally vocal, Cody.

That left Maple as the only candidate for working as a Filler, although young Zoe might help if she responded well enough to training. He marked their assignments accordingly and hoped Maeve would return with Tater. He would make an excellent Filler and would work well with Maple provided Foster didn't get jealous. Art had seen how closely Foster watched Maple, while Augie seemed oblivious of everything except a box of treats on a nearby counter.

He whistled both teams together and gave them some time for the usual sort of nosey greetings dogs required. Peanut took the hint and adopted a position on the counter next to the dog treats.

Art squared his shoulders and tried to prepare himself for the long day ahead.

~*~

Doc handed Ray a cup of tea which he sniffed before tasting. His trembling hands testified to his emotional state. The tea seemed awfully hot and far too spicy, but he managed a whispered, "Mmm. Good."

"I doubt that," Doc said, "But it should help settle your nerves."

Ray hoped so. He still couldn't believe how quickly things had progressed. It seemed as if he'd only just agreed to do a press conference, and suddenly he was about to go on live TV in front of millions of people. Saying he had unsettled nerves ranked as the understatement of the century.

"Are you sure I should wear my uhm... *traditional* outfit for this?"

"That's what people expect you to wear," Doc said as a network makeup artist smeared some sort of cream on his face. The woman appeared intense, and that only added to his discomfort level.

"This is the Big Apple, New York City. It's Times Square and Broadway. It's all new to me. And in here, it seems like everyone who might be on camera is dressed for church. So, it occurred to me I might look better in a shirt and tie. And maybe a suitcoat? I just don't wanna look like a clown."

"You look fine," Doc said as she cast a worried glance at the woman who'd quickly switched to powdering Ray's cheeks, nose, and forehead. "The world needs to recognize who you are from the very start."

"But—"

She waved him to silence and asked the makeup mechanic if she would be done soon. "We need a few minutes to prepare. Do you mind?"

"I'll be finished in just a sec." She quickly fluffed Ray's hair and beard, all the while making faces which suggested she wasn't happy with the results. Eventually, however, she pronounced him ready and stepped away from the dressing table in front of which Ray sat.

"C'mon," Doc said, "we can chat in the Green Room."

"You've been here before?" he asked, surprised.

Her look suggested he was the most naive man in the world, something he thought reasonably possible.

"Theaters and studios usually have rooms where guests can relax before an interview or broadcast. There's even one behind the stage in our little community theater. For some reason, they're always called Green rooms. I don't know why."

Ray groaned. "I'm guessing it's 'cause folks like me who're scared stiff look a little green when we think we're gonna barf."

"Have some more tea," she said, "and just follow the

talking points we prepared."

"You really think there'll be reporters there, asking questions?"

She smiled. "That's the plan."

"Oh, Lord," he said.

"Hey, you said you had to be creative when talking to kids who ask questions. Why would this be any different?"

Ray shrugged. "Kids usually don't have an axe to grind. God only knows what motivates a journalist."

"I'm sure you'll be fine. Just…." Her voice trailed off, and she pursed her lips.

"Just what?"

"Two things: first, see if you can dial back your cornpone accent a bit. Nobody thinks Santa grew up in Dogpatch."

"Okay," he said. "I'll try. And the second thing?"

"Right. Try to remember: Ho, Ho, Hos tend to be hokey."

~*~

As soon as Maeve pulled into the modest, suburban neighborhood where Gloria and Skeeter lived, Tater grew excited, and the closer she drove to their destination, the more he wiggled, squirmed, and whined from his harnessed spot on the back seat.

"We're almost there," Maeve said. "For goodness sake, try not to explode!"

Skeeter and Gloria sat waiting on their front porch when Maeve drove up. Tater's antics had grown more frantic. When Maeve released the buckle on his harness, he launched himself like a cruise missile.

Smiling from ear to ear, Skeeter held out his arms as the little dog bounced on his one back leg, snuggled tight against the boy's chest, and licked his face. All the while, his tail wagged itself into a blur.

Gloria laughed and wiped a happy tear from her eye at the same time.

Maeve couldn't help but smile. "I used to think Tater liked me, but I never got a reception like that!"

When Tater eventually calmed down, Gloria ushered them all indoors. Eventually, they sat down at the family's petite table and prepared to eat.

Maeve checked the time as they dug into Gloria's meatloaf. "There's a program on television tonight that I think you'd enjoy. It starts in a little while."

"There's nothing violent in it, is there?" Gloria asked.

Maeve grinned. "I certainly hope not."

"And didn't you say my father made a video for us?"

"He did, and I'll be happy to play it for you when the TV show is over," Maeve said. The expression on Gloria's face prompted her to explain. "I'm told your Dad wanted it done this way."

Gloria reacted with pursed lips but didn't object.

"There's a video, too?" Skeeter asked.

"Your grandfather made it," Maeve said.

"*My* grandfather?"

Gloria squeezed his hand. "I didn't tell you about him because… Uh… Well, I thought it might be a nice surprise. You know, for later."

"I have a grandfather," he said. "That's kinda cool. But I still don't get why you never told me about him."

Maeve felt suddenly guilty, as if she'd betrayed a confidence, but no one had told her the family wasn't close. Her own family hadn't been close either, but she always believed that was the exception rather than the rule.

"I didn't want…" Gloria began, then changed gears. "The thing is, my dad—your grandfather—has been really ill. He's doing better now. Much better, apparently. He didn't want you to see him when he was sick, but now, hopefully, that's all behind him."

"We'd better finish dinner," Maeve said. "The show will start pretty soon."

They gobbled down the meal, and Maeve insisted on helping with the dishes. Gloria seemed appreciative, and the two of them whispered conspiratorially while watching Skeeter and Tater play tug o' war on the living room floor with one of the dog's toys.

Eventually they all crowded onto the sofa to watch the show.

"I think it's on Fox News," Maeve said.

Gloria brought the TV to life and switched to the appropriate station. When a picture steadied on the screen, she

134

gasped. "Oh, my heavens! It's Dad."

Skeeter's face reflected awe. "My grandfather is *Santa Claus?*"

Raymond Mays, decked out in full Christmas regalia, stood at a podium and looked directly into the camera. "Good evening," he began. "I want to thank all of you for giving me a chance to talk with you tonight, and, hopefully, to be the first one to wish you all a Merry Christmas."

He adjusted the microphone, stared briefly at his notes, and continued. "As you probably know, I was unable to participate in this year's Thanksgiving Day parade in New York City. There's been some speculation about what happened, and I've come here tonight to set the record straight."

Clearly, the studio's bright lights bothered him, and his heavy clothing didn't help. Perspiration broke out on his brow. He removed his hat and dropped it on the podium, then looked up and smiled. "I'm usually outside at this time of year. The reindeer like it better there, too."

He cleared his throat. "So, the parade. I wanted very much to participate, again, this year. The weather forecast said it would be nice outside, and the wonderful folks who organize the event did a splendid job, as always."

Pausing for a quick sip of water from a bottle placed conveniently on a podium shelf, Ray swallowed before going on. "As I said, the weather was beautiful, warmer than usual, so there was no snow. Can you imagine trying to land a team of flying reindeer and a sleigh when there's no snow on the ground? It's murder, I'm tellin' ya."

Skeeter whispered, "Ouch."

"So, we had to land farther north. Way farther north, and I had to switch to ground transportation, which isn't a big deal for most people, but when you look like me, and dress like this—" he gestured to his costume, "—people naturally want to stop and chat. And, if they're wearing a uniform, they often want to ask for a passport."

"Oh, dear," Gloria said.

Maeve swallowed. Based on what she'd heard, he'd already abandoned the script. She had no idea where he had gotten the storyline he continued to lay out.

Ray broke into a huge smile. "You know, back in the day, nobody had a passport. If you had a team of flying reindeer and a sleigh, you could land anywhere. Nobody cared where you came from. Nowadays, everyone has border guards. Everyone wants to see your papers. And that's a real problem when you come from a place like the North Pole where *nobody* has a passport."

He took another swig from the water bottle. "But try explaining that to the average border guard." He shook his head. "Now, I understand those guys, and gals, are just doing their jobs. They're trying to protect their homeland and do what's right. I get it. I really do. And I admire them for the hours they put in and the toll it takes on their families. But it still makes me sad that a hearty 'Ho, ho, ho!' doesn't go anywhere near as far as it used to."

Maeve sighed and glanced at Skeeter who could do nothing but stare at the screen as if somehow attached to it.

With a dramatic sigh, Ray went on. "So, the long and the short of all this is that I got hung up in border crossings, bureaucratic red tape, and hurt feelings, among other things.

136

And by the time I arrived at the staging area for the parade, my float had already traveled several blocks down the street. The tent I reported to was mostly empty; wasn't even anyone there for me to apologize to. I felt really bad about that. It was all my fault, a clear case of poor planning, and I promise I'll do better in the years to come."

Gloria turned to Maeve. "Where is he—"

Maeve silenced her with an upraised hand and a hard look at Skeeter.

Gloria closed her mouth and eased back into the sofa cushions.

Once again, Ray paused to take a drink of water and a deep breath. "And now, I understand it's customary to open the floor for questions." He smiled. "I'm as ready as I'll ever be."

A short, bald-headed man in the front row stood up and waved his arms. Ray pointed at him.

"So, Santa," he began, "how long have you been doing this?"

Ray blinked at him. "How long? Uh… Y'know, I'm not really sure. A long time."

"Could you be a little more specific?"

Ray checked his notes then smiled. "You're familiar with the Clement Moore poem, I'm sure. The proper title is 'A Visit From St. Nicholas.'"

The man appeared significantly less sure of himself than before.

"That," Ray said, "came out in…" He tapped his temple. "The early 1800s if I'm not mistaken, 1822 or 23. Anyway, I'd been involved in Christmas deliveries for quite a long time before that."

"But—" the reporter began.

"Of course, there *were* some errors in the original poem, but I chalk that up to poetic license."

"What kinds of errors?" someone shouted.

"Well, for one thing, Mr. Clement made up some of the names of the reindeer so they'd rhyme. He did a wonderful job. I think it's a lovely poem, even though he claimed I was 'chubby and plump.' Mrs. Claus has been ribbing me about that ever since."

A woman near the back of the room didn't wait to be recognized. She outshouted the others in the room. "Why wasn't Rudolph mentioned in that poem?"

Ray smiled. "He didn't come along until much, much later."

"Are all nine of the original reindeer still working?" asked a rail thin man at the side of the room.

"Sadly, no," Ray said. "You might not be aware of it, but reindeer normally only live about ten years. Most of ours live twice that long, because they get extraordinary care. They deserve it."

"What's the secret of your own longevity?" someone shouted.

"How many houses do you visit each year?" asked another.

"What do you do when there's no chimney?"

"Has anyone ever tried to stop you from making a delivery?"

"Do you visit every continent on the whole planet? In one night?"

"What are the names of the reindeer currently pulling your sleigh?"

"What do you do when there's no snow on the ground?"

"Don't the reindeer get tired? I'll bet the ASPCA would love to know."

There were so many questions from so many people, Ray couldn't possibly answer them all. Fortunately, the moderator rescued him when she stepped to the podium. "As you can all imagine, Mr. Claus has a very busy schedule, and we've already used up the time he said he'd have available. So—"

Ray touched her shoulder to get her attention, and she stepped away from the microphone. He settled his hat back on his head and smiled at the reporters spread out in front of him. "I'm willing to take one more question," he said, then scanned the crowd for someone he hadn't previously called on. He spotted an older gentleman with a pad and pencil who had been taking notes while everyone else relied on microphones and recording equipment. The man had raised his hand only slightly, but it was enough.

"You, sir," Ray said. "What would you like to know?"

The room quieted as the man slowly got to his feet. He gripped the back of the chair in front of him for support. When he spoke, his voice was low and had a gravely tone. "Here's what I'm curious about," he said, looking straight at Ray. "Why do you do it?"

The question stunned Ray. He didn't smile; he didn't laugh. He doubted he looked anything remotely Jolly. It took a moment, but he managed to settle himself and respond, knowing it would hurt.

"A long time ago," he began, "I made a big mistake. I had the opportunity to be a part of someone's life, someone very dear to me. But I let my problems turn my head. I let them force me away from those I loved."

Maeve turned from the screen to Gloria who watched with rapt attention.

"It took a long time, but I got help from some wonderful, caring people, and I eventually put my life back together. I realized that I'd let a very special child down, and there was no excuse for it. I couldn't blame anyone but myself."

He swallowed hard. "If she could see me now, I'd like to think she might forgive me. At the time, however, I thought it was too late for that, and so I turned my attention to making some other children happy. I wanted to reward them for being good and decent people, just like that very special little girl I stupidly walked away from."

Ray looked at the old man who had asked the question. "I'm trying to make up for lost time, missed opportunities, and a failure of character." He wiped his brow. "Does that make sense to you?"

The old man smiled. "It does, and it should make sense to every caring person on the planet. I hope you'll keep it up for a long time to come."

"I plan to," Ray said.

"Thank you all for coming," said the moderator who clicked off the microphone and accompanied Ray out of the room. A used car dealer's commercial blared forth, and Gloria turned off the TV.

Skeeter appeared to be in a mild state of shock. "*That* was my granddad?"

Gloria nodded. "In the flesh."

"And… And he's really Santa Claus?"

"Well," said Maeve, "that's kind of a tricky question."

"And do you intend to answer it?" Gloria asked.

"I think I'll let your father do that," Maeve said. "He has something very important to say in the video I mentioned."

"I'd like to hear it," Skeeter said. "Now, please."

Maeve smiled. "Okay."

Chapter Nine

"Once again, we come to the Holiday Season, a deeply religious time that each of us observes in his own way, by going to the mall of his choice." –Dave Barry

Ormsby Ivanov had enjoyed the day. His dinner couldn't have been better, and he sent a quick text message to the chef at the restaurant which had delivered it to him. He allowed himself an occasional glass of wine, and for reasons he didn't quite understand, that evening seemed like a proper time to indulge. If Jesus could turn water into wine, then a glass of it once in a while couldn't possibly do him any harm.

He lounged on a luxurious sofa with his tablet computer in hand and looked up from time to time at whatever was on the screen. A brief note someone had posted on social media claimed that the one and only Santa Claus would be conducting his first-ever press conference right after the local news ended.

Despite his annoyance at the abundance of commercials urging the public to go out and spend their hard-earned money on toys and trinkets "in honor" of the most holy of holy days, he opted to see what the fuss was about. Obviously, the "real" Santa could not possibly be involved. He'd already checked with Bud to make sure there had been no further slip-ups. Bud assured him all was well. He didn't bother to talk to Mordecai who also remained on his "govno" list.

He smiled at that thought. *Govno* was the Anglicized word for excrement in Russian. His father, a staunch Christian and Russian by birth, had moved to America as a young man and vowed never to learn or use vulgar words in English. Though it defied logic, he had no trouble translating the old-world versions of such words which ably filled the gutter language gap in his English vocabulary. Ormsby found it equally useful though it typically left his subordinates scratching their heads.

As the press conference began, he found himself leaning ever-closer to the wall-sized, flat-screen in his den. The man at the podium dressed in a Santa suit looked exactly like the man he'd had kidnapped in New York.

He dialed Bud immediately.

"Are you watching TV?"

"Yeah. I found a re-run of a great episode of 'Columbo.' You should—"

"Switch to Fox News. There's a press conference going on."

"Okay, but the guys aren't going to like me changing—"

"Do I need to promote Mordecai? Just do it. *Now!*"

Ormsby thought he might have heard someone mumble

143

the word "grouch," but he couldn't be sure it was Bud. He let it go.

"Okay," Bud said. "It's on."

"Who does that look like to you? The guy talking, I mean."

There was a short, sharp intake of breath followed by, "That's impossible. Hang on!"

Ormsby could hear shouting and a good bit of commotion over the phone, even though Bud most likely had his hand over the mouthpiece.

"Well?" Ormsby was finally able to ask.

Bud sounded a little winded but relieved. "He's still here. The guy on the tube is a lookalike. Probably a phony. We're good."

"That's a relief. Keep an eye on our guest."

"Will do," Bud said and rang off before Ormsby could.

While the man in red yammered on about Canada and border guards, Ormsby used his tablet to keep an eye on his favorite social media site. He couldn't wait to see how the faux Santa would be received by the trolls on the internet.

A highlighted message flashed quickly on his tablet screen: "Fraud Alert!" it said. He couldn't wait to open the message which hailed from some woman in Georgia. She claimed to operate a Meet N' Greet for Santa at a mall somewhere near Atlanta.

"That guy's a fraud!" she wrote. "He used to work for me, so I know he's bogus. He's wearing a costume he stole from me! Where's the justice? Where are the cops when you need 'em? It isn't right. This is terrible! We should boycott Fox. They're probably owned by some super-rich, rightwing gang of social misfits. Boycott the Fox News Network!"

Ormsby couldn't resist smiling as he reposted the woman's diatribe. For all he knew, she'd made the whole thing up, but he didn't care. Anything that tarnished the reputation of the man with the bag of presents slung over his shoulder was fine with him.

He did, however, make a note of the woman's contact information. One could never tell when such data would come in handy.

As he eased back on his plush sofa, a disturbing thought crept into his head. What if the one on TV was real, and the one he controlled was an imposter?

~*~

Gloria put her arm around Skeeter's shoulders. She could only imagine how tired the boy was. He hadn't moved much since Tater crawled up in his lap, and the two seemed to bring a sense of peace to the room that had been sorely missing.

Maeve had a device which allowed her to play Ray's video message on the TV in Gloria's living room, and all three occupants paid rapt attention as an image flickered to life on the screen.

A smiling Ray appeared, sans hat and coat. His suspenders dug little furrows in the white pullover he wore. "Hey there," he said, his smile as wide and welcoming as any Gloria had ever seen. The man actually looked healthy, though she found that more than a little hard to believe.

"I would much rather deliver this message in person, but I've got some work to do, and I think it's completely worthwhile. I presume you've watched the press conference, and I hope I didn't do anything to embarrass myself or my hosts."

He drew an attractive woman into the picture. "This is my new friend, Docquinella. She's a brilliant woman and an accomplished doctor."

"Healer," the woman corrected.

"Right," he said. "Anyway, she's familiar with the illness Skeeter has, and she's pretty sure—"

"I'm *absolutely* sure," she interjected.

"—that she can help him." He smiled at the woman, and she stepped out of camera range. "There's just one thing, and it's really, really important. You and Skeeter need to come here in order for her to do what she does. You'll be safe, well fed, and taken care of. And you'll be able to wander around, talk to those who live here, and get a feel for life in a very different environment. Everyone I've met here has been nice to me."

He took a deep breath, and his features relaxed into a pose of comfort and satisfaction. "There's a good chance I might move here permanently. I have a job offer, of sorts, and it would be a complete game changer for me. I'd love to have both of you in my life, and I'm hoping you'll find this place as pleasant and welcoming as I have."

From behind his back he withdrew a sheet of paper and held it in plain view of the camera. "All you need to do is sign this form that says you won't tell anyone about what you see or do here. You'll have to keep it a secret whether you decide to come permanently or only long enough for Skeeter to get well. That's entirely up to you."

He lowered the document. "Coming here, and going back if you chose to leave, won't cost you anything. So, please," he said, "*please* give this serious thought. I promise you won't regret it."

At that point the image faded, and Maeve clicked the video off. "Well," she said, "what do you think?"

Under the watchful eye and overshadowing presence of Max, Ray and Doc headed back to her cottage by way of the New York portal. Much like the one in Georgia, the portal in the Empire State was hidden beneath a Leon Farms house on property located about a two-hour drive from the Big Apple.

"You said you thought I might be needed for other things," Ray said as he settled into a seat by the healer. He liked being close to her and realized his positive thoughts about her made him more willing to go along with her requests.

"That's right." She loosened the top button on her blouse and fanned herself with one hand. "I feel like I can finally relax."

"Me, too," he said. "Now, about those 'other things' you mentioned?"

"You've never met the Boss," she began, "and we keep a really tight rein on information about his health. But there's one thing that's inescapable: he's getting on in years. Don't get me wrong, he's still got a strong mind and a willing heart, but we're all mortal. We all slow down as we get older; we have to."

"Elves, halfs, and qualfs, too?"

"Of course. We aren't robots. I just celebrated a big birthday, and—"

"Your 39th?"

Doc burst out laughing. "You're sweet, but you're off by a good six decades."

Ray stared at her. "I— Uh…."

"What?"

"You're *a hundred years old?*" He shook his head. "That's not possible! You look like a yoga instructor or a lingerie model."

She blushed. "What a sweet thing to say."

"I'm serious!"

She patted his hand. "It's not a big deal, really. Elves tend to live a good bit longer than humans, but once we start to age, most of us go downhill rapidly." She adjusted her seatback and raised a padded footrest.

Ray shook his head, still stunned by her revelation. The woman sitting beside him looked younger than he did, and yet she claimed to be twice his age.

"So," she continued, "we think—"

"*We?*"

"There's a committee; I'm on it. The Boss appointed us to keep an eye on him and the whole operation. He knows his limitations and has no intention of letting all our efforts go for naught if or when something happens to him. His wife, bless her wonderful heart, has some serious issues of her own, and we're sure the Boss would like to be able to spend more time with her."

"I'm sorry to hear that," Ray said. "But what's it got to do with me?"

Before answering, Doc glanced at Max who was charged with making sure no one bothered them during the trip. He appeared to be asleep. Ray followed her lead and stared at him, too, stunned by the amount of space he occupied.

Doc faced forward again and continued. "With the Boss gone, you could take up a great deal of the slack. You could meet with the corporate execs who produce so much for us, and you could be the focal point for our talks with government agencies that want to monitor and control our travel. We constantly have supply chain problems that don't get the attention they need unless our top man gets involved." She leveled her beautiful smile at him. "You could be that man."

Ray chuckled. "You know I'm an alcoholic, right? My whole life went into the dumpster 'cause I lacked the gumption to hold it together when things got tough. And you want *me* to rub elbows with corporate hot shots? Government bigwigs? You're more out of your mind than I am!"

"Maybe not," she said. "You did a great job at the press conference. Now, I admit, I got a little worried when you went off script, but you pulled it together nicely. You didn't seem the least bit worried."

"It was an act, all of it. Believe me."

149

"I do," she said. "But it was a *convincing* act. It's one you could duplicate in all sorts of settings. We don't expect you to be an expert on any of this. You'll have very capable staffers to assist you and keep you on track."

"Won't these commercial giants get a whiff that something's not on the level?"

"But it will be. We'll conduct business as usual. Best of all, they'll have you to look at. If *we* all thought you were the Boss, I'm sure *they* will think the same thing."

Once again she looked at Max, still slouched across two seats.

"Are you expecting something? You keep looking at him," Ray said.

"It's nothing. He just seems to give off an odd vibe." She shrugged. "I can't explain it."

Ray contemplated what she'd said for a while and thought she had fallen asleep. Max didn't represent a threat. If anything, he represented the exact opposite. Who'd want to go up against that big pile of muscle? What worried him most were Doc's remarks about the Boss's age. *What would they do when he passed away? No one lives forever. Who's next in line?* It was a question he desperately wanted answered, but one he didn't want to ask.

Doc lazily turned her head in his direction, opened one eye, and smiled. "You okay?"

"Yeah. I'm just…" He paused, frustrated. "Who *is* the Boss, really? I don't know when Santa came on the scene, *officially*, but it must've been a couple hundred years ago, at least."

150

"It depends on whose version you believe," she said, keeping her voice low. "Stories about him have circulated for a very long time. Some go back to 270 BC." She grinned. "His history has been bandied about forever, it seems. Father Christmas hailed from England; Saint Nicholas dates back to the 400s in what is now a small town in Turkey; Sinterklass, from the Netherlands and Belgium, seems to work *two* days a year, December 6th and 25th. And there are others. Are they all the same? Is there a different Santa for every culture? I don't know. I'm not smart enough to figure that out. Maybe someone will, one day. But until then, we stick with what we know. He was here before we were, and he was in desperate straits when we arrived. The world was changing faster than he could keep up with it."

Ray pursed his lips. "That's all very interesting, but it's not really an answer, is it?"

"You want to know his *real* name?"

"Yeah."

"Why?"

"I think… Well, maybe it'll help me make sense of all this. I feel like I stumbled into another dimension, something out of a science fiction movie. I used to have a handle on it—the whole thing: Christmas morning, mistletoe, stockings hangin' off the mantle, even 'Secret Santas,' —all of it. But now? Now it's all a jumble."

Doc took a deep breath and exhaled before answering. "Not that it matters, but his real name is Charlemagne Fyfe. His wife calls him Charlie. The rest of us call him the Boss."

Ray responded with a raised eyebrow. "And everyone else calls him Santa?"

She nodded. "Yep, pretty much everywhere outside of our operations. There are different names in use in different countries, of course, but due to advertising and mass media, Santa is the one used most often."

"Charlie Fyfe." Ray chuckled. "Any relation to Barney Fife?"

"Who?"

"A TV character from... I dunno, a long time ago. Funny guy."

She hiked her shoulders up around her ears. "Sorry. Never heard of him."

"It's not important. But, this Charlie guy, he's been around for hundreds of years?"

"Oh, gosh, no," Doc said. "He's not an elf, despite what it might say in the poems, movies, songs, and TV shows."

"So, he's human?"

"A qualf, actually. So's his wife. They've been with us for around twenty years or so."

"Twenty?" Ray couldn't contain his surprise. "Criminy! How many Santas have there been?"

"Now, that's a bit of a mystery," she said. "The earliest ones didn't leave any written records. Stories, legends really, have been passed down over the years, but there's nothing official that I know of. Mr. Fyfe is the fifth Santa I've worked with in my lifetime."

Ray whistled. "Man, I've gotta say, I never had any idea—"

"But that's a good thing!" Doc gently bumped his ribs with her elbow. "You don't *need* to know all the background, all the history, all the details. They really don't matter. What we have to focus on is where we are now, and where we're going in the future. And Ray, we want you to be a part of it. I'm thinking, a very big part."

He looked deep into her eyes, trying not to get lost in them. "You're scarin' me, ya know."

She planted an all-too-chaste kiss on his cheek. "I kinda figured that."

~*~

Maeve allowed herself a sigh of relief when Gloria not only agreed to return with her but had no qualms when it came to signing the NDA. Skeeter insisted on reading it but gave up after wading through the first few paragraphs. Gloria assured him she had checked it out and thought the terms were reasonable.

Skeeter still wouldn't sign it until after he'd posed the question to Tater, who barked his approval as well.

"You'll need to pack a bag or two," Maeve said. "Bring anything you think you'll need for a couple weeks. The height of the season is so very close, it's likely we won't be able to bring you back, if that's what you decide to do, until after Christmas."

Gloria indicated she was content with that and told Skeeter to lie down and rest while she packed for both of them.

"He's got schoolbooks," Gloria said, "but he hasn't had the energy to keep up with his classes. It's not that he's a great scholar or anything, but he's been completely off his game. Hasn't managed to complete any homework since he got sick."

Maeve tried to make light of it. "Bring 'em along if you'd like. With any luck, he'll be feeling both better *and* bored. Maybe that'll be enough to help him buckle down."

"We'll see." Gloria piled his school materials on the kitchen table and went into his bedroom.

Maeve trailed behind her. "Is there anything I can do to help?"

"I'm not sure. How long is the trip? Do I need to bring snacks? How 'bout food for when we get wherever it is we're going?"

"Focus on clothing," Maeve said.

"Cosmetics? Lotions? Oh! I almost forgot. Meds. Skeeter's got a ton of those."

Maeve gave her what she hoped was a reassuring smile. "Bring it all. You may not need it, but if you do, you'll have it."

That triggered a flurry of activity, and Maeve helped where she could, but mostly she tried to stay out of the way. The more Gloria set aside for the trip, the more Maeve worried that it wouldn't all fit in her little car. "This isn't a permanent move, you know," she said when Gloria dragged her sewing machine into the kitchen and set it alongside a growing pile of unnecessary stuff.

"I mean," Maeve continued, "you can come back and get any of this later. You don't need to pack... well, everything."

Gloria turned to her, a look bordering on despair colored her face. "I'm terrified by Skeeter's illness. I don't know what we're getting into, and I doubt I'm thinking straight."

"You'll be fine, both of you," Maeve said. "And you can replace almost anything you might leave behind."

"If you say so." Gloria's shoulders slumped.

Maeve gave her a hug. "C'mon. Help me load the car. We need to get going."

A bungee cord took over for the latch on Maeve's car since she couldn't close the trunk all the way. Gloria held a bag in her lap while Maeve settled Skeeter and his dog in the back seat.

The drive was uneventful, and they pulled to a stop in front of the farmhouse. Stars littered the clear, night sky, and a chill in the air encouraged them to unload quickly.

Maeve opted to move Gloria and Skeeter's things into the basement a chunk at a time. Gloria pitched in but told Skeeter to stay out of the way until they were done. He didn't think much of the command but obeyed it anyway.

Tater, however, had ideas of his own. He seemed completely familiar with the old house and toured every room in it, his nose continually quivering.

"What d'you suppose he's looking for?" Gloria asked.

"I can't imagine," said Maeve. She looked at Skeeter. "What's he doing?"

"He had a chew toy in his mouth when we came in, but I don't see it anywhere now. He prob'ly dropped it

155

somewhere, and now he's tryin' to find it."

Gloria parked a suitcase at the top of the stairs leading to the basement, ready for Maeve to take down and store in the transport unit. "See if you can keep Tater out of the way, okay?"

"Awrighty," he said and pulled the dog into his lap.

Maeve hefted the big bag and gave a silent prayer that it was the last one. She couldn't remember the last time she'd worked so hard.

The first two steps she managed without difficulty, although she needed both hands on the handle of the bag, which left her leaning toward the handrail rather than holding onto it.

"I wish you'd let me help you with that," Gloria called out from behind her.

"It's no problem," Maeve said. "I've hauled heavier stuff. It's just… This one feels a wee bit awk—"

Suddenly, something under her foot rolled, and she twisted her ankle. A sharp pain raced up her leg to her brain, cutting off her voice and replacing it with a shriek.

Oh, how stupid! I can't believe I—

When she hit the bottom, with her leg jammed clumsily beneath the suitcase, she screamed again, louder. The pain from her twisted ankle had been but was merely a tiny taste of the agony she felt in her leg.

Gloria raced down the stairs as fast as she could and made a ballet leap to avoid stepping on Maeve. "Oh my God! Are you all right?"

"No," Maeve gasped. "I've never done anything so stupid. I can't believe—"

"Where does it hurt?"

"It's my leg," she cried as tears coursed down her cheeks. "I slipped on something. Oh, it hurts!"

Gloria bent down to move the heavy suitcase from her leg. "This may hurt, but I need to get it out of the way. I'll have Skeeter call 911. We'll get a paramedic down here to check you out and get you back upstairs."

"No!" Maeve whispered. "That won't work. We need to take the transport. I'll be taken care of at the other end."

"But… Your leg! We can't—"

"Go ahead and move the bag, please. Maybe Skeeter can help."

"I've got it," Gloria said as she lifted the dead weight.

Instantly, new pains shot forth from Maeve's leg, searing her with an electric jolt that had her crushing her teeth together.

She looked down at her badly misaligned limb and cringed. It looked as if she had a second knee joint several inches above the old one. The sight caused her to swoon.

Gloria reached her side in time to cushion her head before she banged it against the wall.

"Got to get going," she breathed once the pain in her leg settled down to something slightly less overwhelming. "Help me up. Please."

"You've got to be kidding," Gloria said. "Your leg—"

"I know. I— I looked at it."

The process of standing proved too excruciating, and Gloria wept along with her in sympathy.

"If it didn't hurt so bad," Maeve said, "I'd send you two back and let you tell them what's happened to me here. They'd come back and get me." She shook her head in anger. "How could I have been so stupid?"

She leaned against Gloria, her injured leg twisted awkwardly, and painfully.

Tater sat on the bottom step with a round, bone-like chew toy in his mouth and a guilty look on his whiskery face.

"It was on a step," Skeeter said as he came down the stairs to join them. "I'm pretty sure that's what tripped you up." He frowned at the little dog. "I yelled at him, but he didn't understand. I know he'd never want to hurt you. Never! I'm so, so sorry."

"It's all right," Maeve said between clenched teeth. "I don't blame him. I should've looked before I started down."

Gloria tried to lift the smaller woman again and partially succeeded, but Maeve's groans deterred her from doing more.

"I can't take any more," Maeve said. Wincing, she added in a whisper, "I've never felt so much pain."

"There's still time to call 911 and get you to a hospital," Gloria said. "The EMTs know how to deal with all sorts of difficult situations, and this one certainly qualifies."

Maeve shook her head. "I'm sorry. I can't let you do

that. It's not just that I don't have insurance; I'm not an American citizen. They could have me detained and make me stand trial for extradition, but that's… that's impossible."

"Why?" Gloria asked. "Where do you live anyway?"

Maeve looked from the mother to the son. "Do you both believe in Santa Claus?"

"Yes!" said Skeeter without a moment's hesitation.

"Gloria?" Maeve asked.

"Well… Uhm…" She gave Skeeter a sympathetic look. "Yeah. I guess I do."

"Then you won't be too shocked to learn that I live fairly close to him."

"Whoa!" said Skeeter. "The North Pole?"

Gloria stared at Maeve as if she'd claimed to be the reincarnation of Amelia Earhart. "Seriously?"

"Seriously."

Chapter Ten

"The job of the artist is always to deepen the mystery." –Francis Bacon

By day's end, Art needed a drink. He'd done a reasonably good job of keeping his mind off of Maeve, but once his training session ended, he was impatient to see her. He checked the time and decided she should at least be on the way home.

There was a time difference between their homes and Georgia, and he took that into account even though Maeve hadn't given him all the particulars of her mission. He concluded she could be back in an hour or so.

Rather than sit around moping or getting loaded at the pub, he opted to wander over to the transport terminal, locate her arrival port, and wait for her there. He'd still be moping, of course, but he'd be sober when she finally arrived.

He took his time covering the distance and even stopped at a little shop to pick up a ribbon he thought would look nice in her hair. Such a token might even earn him a peck on the cheek.

Finding the arrival port proved somewhat complicated since her mission had a "Secure" level attached to it. That simply meant that whatever she was doing had approval from upstairs, most likely the Committee, but possibly even from the Boss himself, assuming he had shown up. Whatever it was, however, did not need to be a topic for general discussion.

Art finagled the arrival port information and camped out near the appointed location in anticipation of Maeve's imminent arrival.

It turned out to be anything but imminent. It didn't happen at all. After waiting for two hours, he contacted the only person he knew who might have a line on what was going on.

"Max? This is Art Maker, in Team Training."

"Yeah, I've heard about you. Maeve Blessing thinks you're a dork."

Art bit down on his tongue, unwilling to rise to the Monster's challenge. "Yeah, whatever. Listen, I'm camped out here at the port where she's supposed to return from a secure op. You know anything about that?"

"It's not my op, but of course I know about it."

Of course, you do, you gigantic snot. "Y'see, Maeve asked me to hang around and go with her when she heads for home."

"Yeah? So?"

"So, it'd be nice to know when she'll get here."

"I'm sure it would," said Max.

"So? When would that be?"

"I have no idea," Max said dismissively. "I've got a security detail of my own to worry about, so I don't have time to waste talking to you. But here's bit of advice: that little redhead doesn't care about you at all. She just wants a free ride home. Why don't you go somewhere and get a life?"

The connection abruptly ended.

"Thanks, pal," Art said. "I hope the Boss puts something profoundly nasty in your stocking."

~*~

Ormsby Ivanov fingered the crest on his ring, a copy of a much larger crest hanging on a wall in his luxury home in suburban Atlanta. The gaudy Ivanov coat of arms had been commissioned by his father in order to impress potential business partners. The elder Ormsby concocted a story to go with the counterfeit emblem and claimed to have been born into the Russian peerage. As the only family member to survive the purge of the aristocracy, according to the tale, he'd escaped, penniless, to America when the communists took over the country. His favorite saying, which young Ormsby vividly recalled, was, "Trotsky! I spit on your grave!" While graphic, the epithet was wholly impractical owing to the location of Trotsky's remains.

It all made for a dramatic story, and the old man embellished it over the years. Ormsby's mother went along with it as well, proudly claiming her place in the fictitious Ivanov dynasty. When his parents died, Ormsby kept the fantasy alive and used it to woo a bride of his own. When the truth eventually came out, she left him and took one of their two sons with her.

He remained angry about her betrayal, although it had pushed him toward religion. That resulted in multiple encounters with one intensely religious organization after another, none of which met his needs. He finally created his own branch of the faith, one which honored God, but according to the rules Ormsby decreed.

His business acumen, combined with the sizeable fortune left to him by his father, allowed him to construct a beautiful church and hire an ardent evangelist to build a following. Once in place, Ormsby retired to the background, content to remain out of the limelight.

From the church's shadows, he listened to his evangelical spokesman who happily adopted Ormsby's ideas for sermons. The most common of which bemoaned the commercialization of traditional Christian holidays. The cadre of similarly minded followers grew year after year. If Ormsby ever encountered trouble because of his beliefs, they would protect him. He felt sure of it.

Still, it could prove awkward if he ordered his men to do away with their charge. The police had an annoying habit of investigating deaths, especially those involving so-called "beloved" characters. They might not believe the costumed man being held captive in a Manhattan penthouse was really Santa Claus, but if the man turned up dead, there was a good chance they could connect the murder to Ormsby. Neither Bud nor Mordecai could be counted on to take the fall, and he doubted either of them had the brains needed to make the crime untraceable.

Ormsby shook his head sadly. It would be so much easier to kill the snake by cutting off its head. Instead, he'd have to rely on his inside man. With Christmas only days away, there wasn't much time left.

~*~

"Mom!" called Skeeter from the top of the stairs. "Look what I found in the kitchen!" He waved something in his hand as he and Tater crept down the steep set of steps. Despite not moving much, the boy remained visibly fatigued. It had been a long night thus far.

"What's in it?" Gloria asked.

"I'm guessin' band-aids 'n stuff, or some kinda medical junk. I thought maybe it might help."

Gloria doubted a First Aid Kit would be of much use for someone with a fracture as severe as Maeve's. But she figured it couldn't hurt to see what was in it.

The little redhead who rested on the floor next to her eyed the box in Skeeter's hand. She then surged forward until the movement disturbed her injured leg. "That's— Ow!" She took a breath. "Open it, please. There are herbs inside. I need the blue one!"

Skeeter surrendered the prize to his mom. A latch on the box proved a little difficult at first, but Gloria got it open without resorting to force. Inside the box she found several small plastic bags containing a variety of powders and shredded leaves. None of them looked blue.

She shook her head at Maeve. "Nothing blue in here."

Maeve reached for the box and dumped its contents on her stomach. She pushed several of the packets aside until she found the one she wanted.

"That's not blue," observed Gloria.

Maeve nodded agreement. "You're right; you have to add water first. *Then* it'll turn blue."

"How much water?"

"Just a splash. Enough to dissolve the powder. Skeeter? Can you take this upstairs and do it?" She looked quickly back at the remaining bags and frowned. "That's the only one we have, so you need to be careful. Add a little water, then seal it up again. Okay?"

"Sure thing," Skeeter said, taking the bag from her hand. He remounted the stairs though his pace remained as labored as before. Tater opted not to follow him and settled down next to Maeve and Gloria instead.

"What *is* that stuff?" Gloria asked.

"Lavender and chamomile and a couple other herbs I doubt you know about." She winced. "If I could, I'd hug and kiss your wonderful son for locating that kit. I don't know why I didn't think of it."

"Pain can put you off your game." It was a phrase she'd heard her father use as a child, and he certainly proved its accuracy.

Maeve nodded as a look of consternation clouded her face. "Oh, no," she muttered, her voice so low it barely registered.

Gloria heard it, however. "What's wrong?"

"How can I do my job with a broken leg?" She began to cry.

Skeeter came down the stairs even more slowly than he'd gone up, but Gloria was afraid to urge him to move faster.

165

Eventually, he reached them and delivered the bag which now contained a dark blue liquid.

"This is perfect," Maeve said. She adjusted her position so she wouldn't spill any of the fluid when she drank it. Just that slight motion left her grimacing in pain.

"Easy, there," Gloria said.

Maeve sighed. "Okay, here goes." With that she poured the contents of the little bag into her mouth and swallowed. The look on her face suggested it wasn't tasty. "Bleah! That's nasty."

"So, maybe it'll dull the pain?" Gloria asked, a note of hope in her voice.

"Give it a minute or so," Maeve said, "and it should knock me out. Then you can drag me into the transport unit. I won't feel a thing."

"You sure?"

Maeve smiled. "Sorta sure. I've never used it before."

Gloria waited until she closed her eyes. Her breathing slowed, too, and that worried Gloria at first. When she nudged Maeve's arm there was no response, so she gingerly touched the redhead's injured leg. Again, there was no response, and Gloria stood up.

"Skeet, set yourself down in one of these seats," she said. "And strap yourself in."

The boy followed her instructions but stopped when he couldn't find a seatbelt. "Mom? There aren't any seatbelts. Not a one."

"I guess we'll just have to hang on to the armrests."

"Who's driving this thing?" he asked.

"I have no Earthly idea, sweetheart. But according to our sleeping friend here, this is the only way to get where we need to go."

Dragging Maeve across the room and into the transport unit took more of an emotional than physical toll. She couldn't imagine how much pain Maeve would have suffered if not for the herbal knock-out potion she'd taken.

Once she'd finished piling their bags and gear in the middle of the tube-like vehicle, Gloria took a seat beside Skeeter. Tater curled up next to Maeve.

"How do we start this thing?" Skeeter asked.

"Darned if I know," Gloria said. Then, in a louder voice, she added, "If anyone out there can hear me, we're ready to go."

She heard a pair of gentle, pinging sounds as the entry door slid down from the ceiling and sealed itself into the wall. Soft Christmas music drifted out from hidden speakers, and she felt the slightest bit of movement, then nothing more.

"I guess that's all it took," she said.

Tater wagged his tail and whined.

"Did we bring him any treats?" Skeeter asked.

Gloria looked from him to Maeve's damaged leg and back. "You kiddin' me? Give your dog *a treat?*"

~*~

Ray and Doc arrived at the transport terminal where Max bid them a good night and sauntered away.

Doc shivered.

"You okay?" Ray asked.

"Yes. I'm fine. It's Max. He… Never mind. I'm just being silly. I heard him talking to somebody, and he didn't sound very nice."

"Yeah, I heard it, too." He shrugged. "I could use a bite to eat. You hungry?"

"I am," she said.

"I don't know if Gloria and Skeeter are here, or even if they're coming, but I'd love for you to meet them."

"I'd like that, too," Doc said. "I presume it was your daughter you mentioned during the press conference. Tell me about your grandson."

Ray frowned. "To be honest, I don't know him very well." He sighed. "That's not true; I don't know him at all. I've got a photo of him in my apartment, but until a few days ago, I doubt he knew I existed."

"Give me a moment, and I'll see if someone can give me an update on them. I sent one of our trainers with your video. If she was successful, they should be returning almost any time."

Ray waited while she used a phone-like device near the portal they had just exited. She wasn't gone long, and when she returned, she looked worried.

Her worry quickly infected him. "What's wrong?"

168

"Sorry for the delay. I had to use a secure line. I didn't get a good answer, but apparently there was some sort of accident. Maeve, the trainer I assigned to make the contact, was unable to board the transport unit on her own. An unidentified woman dragged her aboard accompanied by a boy and a small dog."

"That's gotta be Gloria and Skeeter," Ray said, his voice rising with excitement. "Where will they come in?"

"Down this way." Doc pointed to a different corridor, grabbed his hand, and started walking. "They're not due in for a while yet."

When they reached the designated portal, they found someone else already waiting. He looked at them with a worried expression that matched Doc's.

She went straight toward him and offered her hand. "I'm Docquinella Bright. Are you waiting for Maeve Blessing, too?"

"Yes," he said, quickly getting to his feet. "I'm Artemis Maker, a friend of hers. I heard she'd be coming in here, but I couldn't get any de—"

He stopped talking when two males in surgical attire arrived with a stretcher. They took up a position next to the spot where the door would eventually open.

"What's going on?" Art asked, concern written across his face.

"We'll know soon enough," Doc said. She introduced Ray and brought Artemis up to date on Maeve's mission.

"How could she have been injured?" he asked. He

turned to Ray, his voice suddenly accusatory. "Do you know anything about this? Did your daughter have anything to do with it?"

"Relax," Doc said. "I'm sure we'll get the full story as soon as they arrive. Let's all just sit down."

She led them to seats arranged along a wall. No one spoke for a long moment, and the silence bothered Ray more than he wanted to admit. "Maybe we could grab a bite to eat or something. Is there a place nearby?"

"In the main terminal," Art said, stabbing his thumb in that direction as if he were hitchhiking. "You go ahead. I'm staying right here."

"I think I'll do the same," Doc said.

Ray closed his mouth, crossed his arms, and waited right alongside them.

Eventually, they heard a slight rumble and felt a mild vibration through the floor. Art was the first one up, though the two who brought the stretcher waved him back.

When the door to the transport unit slid upwards, Gloria was the first one out. She quickly spotted Ray.

"Dad!" she shouted. "We need help."

He and Doc raced toward her with Art right beside them.

The stretcher bearers jumped into the vehicle and went directly toward Maeve.

"She broke her leg," Gloria sobbed as she hugged Ray. "She slipped on a dog toy and fell down the stairs. It looks…"

She took a breath. "It just looks awful."

Doc had already pushed by her and joined the stretcher crew. Art trailed along behind. After assuring the emergency workers she was a healer, they allowed her to give Maeve a quick examination.

"Get her on the stretcher now, before she wakes up," Doc said after a hurried check of Maeve's vital signs. "Then get her to Healer House as quick as you can. We'll follow you."

"Is she going to be all right?" Gloria asked.

"I'm sure she will," Doc said confidently. "It's a good thing you got her into the transporter. She must have been in terrible pain."

"She was, poor thing."

Ray had wandered closer to the action and spotted a boy who looked up when Ray entered. The child gave him a huge smile. "*Grampa?*"

A sudden burst of something coursed through Ray with a warmth he hadn't felt in years. He dropped to one knee and held his arms out. "Yessir, that's exactly who I am. Can ya give me a hug? 'Cause right now, I desperately need one."

Skeeter and Tater raced toward him. The dog reached him first, but Ray kept his arms wide and enfolded the boy when he arrived a moment later.

"I saw you on TV," Skeeter said. "You were awesome! It was the awesomest news program I ever saw. I can't believe you're Santa Claus. I just can't believe it!"

Skeeter delivered a fierce hug, and Ray reveled in it,

ignoring the tears dripping down both his cheeks. He blinked the worst of them away and gazed at Gloria who smiled back at him.

He waved a hand at her, unwilling to let go of his grandson. Gloria knelt down beside them and joined in the first multi-generational group hug Ray could remember.

"I hate to break up the party," Doc said, "but we need to get Maeve back to my house so I can take care of her."

Ray gathered up his family and followed Doc, Art, and the emergency team. He prayed there was a carriage big enough for everyone.

Maeve came awake slowly and did not recognize her surroundings. She did, however, recognize Art who sat beside her bed holding her hand.

"Artemis?" Her voice came out as a whisper, but he heard her and squeezed her hand.

"Take it easy," he whispered back as he moved closer and sat on the edge of her bed. "You're going to be okay."

She glanced quickly around the room, her head still reeling. "Where—"

"Healer's House. Doc put a cast on your leg."

His smile should have made her feel better, but all she could think about was her team and their mission. It was only days away. How could she manage with a huge, heavy cast on her leg? How could she even get in and out of her vessel?

She wept as the reality of her predicament became

clear. When the ships departed on the upcoming Season of Voyages, she would be left behind.

"I said you'd be fine, Maeve. There's no need to cry." Art continued to smile, but his pinched brow conveyed concern. "What's the matter?"

She rubbed at her eyes and grabbed a tissue from a box beside the bed. "I'll be stuck here when everyone else goes on the delivery runs." She barely recognized her own voice and blew her nose into the tear-damp tissue.

"Who says?" Artemis asked her. "Who *says* you can't go?"

Maeve slapped the hard, plaster covering on her leg. "This does!" The statement unleashed another cycle of tears and tissues. She didn't even notice when Docquinella entered the room.

Doc took up a position opposite Art. Both sat sideways on an edge of the bed. "How are you feeling?" Doc asked.

"Foolish," Maeve said.

Doc laughed. "There's no need for that. We've all taken missteps."

"Just days before the Season?"

"Of course! Don't you recall three years ago when the Boss had to have his appendix removed two weeks before Christmas?"

"Well," Maeve said, her voice still blubbery, "but he's Santa. And… there's magic."

Doc grinned. "Of course, there is. Right along with

medicine, herbal treatments, and physical therapy."

Art frowned. "PT for an appendectomy?"

"Certainly not, but it's required for patients with broken limbs." She gazed down at Maeve. "Like that of your sweetheart here."

Two sets of eyes—Art's and Maeve's—instantly spread wide, and Doc laughed. "What? You thought no one could tell you two were in love? Don't be silly."

Maeve strove to get back on topic. "But— But the Season! How will I manage with a cast on my leg?"

Doc pursed her lips. "There is that. I honestly don't see how you'll be able to handle everything that's needed with your mobility compromised."

Once again, Maeve sobbed, and neither Doc nor Art could cheer her up.

A small voice sounded from the doorway. "*Miz Maeve?*" Skeeter said, his voice uncharacteristically shy. "Uhm, why couldn't I go with you?"

The three adults turned toward him, speechless.

"I mean," Skeeter went on, "I'm pretty good with dogs, Tater 'specially. And I could do anything you'd need me to do. I'm already feelin' better. Honest!"

Doc's eyes shifted back to Maeve. "He's been devouring my food supply and a heavy dose of herbs ever since you got here. I swear, the boy is all stomach." She stood and walked toward him. "You may feel a little stronger now, but you're a long way from being cured."

At that point, Tater raced into the room and launched himself toward the bed. He hit the mattress with his chest and began sliding backwards toward the floor. Art reached across the bed and hauled him up. The dog gently worked his way up Maeve's torso and settled down next to her with his head on her shoulder.

"We're a team," said the boy. "Tater n' me, I mean."

"What're y'all talking about?" asked Gloria as she and Ray walked into the now crowded room.

"She's worried about not being able to make her delivery runs," Art said.

Doc nodded. "The cast is going to be a problem. It has to stay on for weeks."

"I'm gonna help her," Skeeter said from his position at the foot the bed. He had his fists firmly planted on his hips.

Gloria cast a worried glance at her son. "You don't say." She shifted her gaze around the room and stopped when she got to Doc. "Just for the record, he's still sick." She then looked at Ray. "And he doesn't know diddly about sleighs and reindeer. He sees snow maybe once a year where we live, and it melts so quick there's no time to get a photo of it."

She ended her discourse looking at Maeve and Art. "If you think you're taking my son off on some crazy—"

"We're not," Maeve said. "I don't even know if _I_ can go."

"You can," Art said. "You've got to." He turned toward Gloria and Ray. "It's not that hard a job, and we don't use sleighs and reindeer. That's old school, and besides, nobody knows how the early Santas pulled it off."

Skeeter appeared shocked. "No *reindeer?* No—"

"We still call the delivery vehicles sleighs, but they're more like ships or barges," Maeve said. "Really well-packed ones."

"So, how does it work?" asked Ray. "I'm totally confused."

"Me, too," said Skeeter.

"That makes three of us," added Gloria. "Someone needs to fill us in."

Doc held up her arms to get everyone's attention. "Let's do this over breakfast. Fair enough? Some of you—" she winked at Skeeter "—may not be hungry, but I am. I just hope I've got some food left."

~*~

Sleep had not come easily to Ormsby Ivanov, but not because he felt remorse or any other emotion, when it came to his kidnap victim. What bothered him was the uncanny resemblance of his captive with that of the man at the press conference. At one point, he did manage to drift off and blissfully enjoy an unencumbered slumber. Unfortunately, that was undone by a dream.

Ormsby suddenly sat up in bed, his mind all but sparking with the energy of the revelation he'd had while asleep. He finally knew the secret to Santa's success.

He couldn't imagine why it hadn't occurred to him previously, and it was so completely obvious. Slapping his forehead with an open palm, Ormsby reached for his cell phone from a bedside table and rang the number for the penthouse at the Montague Hotel.

"Yeah?" grumbled a sleepy voice.

"Bud?"

"Uh-hunh. Wha d'ya want?"

"Let me talk to Mordecai. *Now!*"

"Yeah, sure. Hang on," Bud muttered.

He heard muffled conversation and sounds of movement then more grumbling. Eventually, Mordecai picked up the phone. "Listen," Ormsby barked into it. "I've got it all figured out."

"You've got what figured out?" Mordecai said.

"The secret to Santa's success, you numbskull. I've never understood until now."

"Uh, okay. That's great, I guess."

Ormsby couldn't imagine how the man could be so disinterested. Unfortunately, he couldn't think of anyone else with whom he could share his discovery. "It is great," Ormsby said. "It's— Monumental."

"Well then, congratulations," Mordecai said. "Wanna fill me in?"

Ormsby Ivanov allowed himself a self-congratulatory chuckle. "He's cloning himself."

He got silence from the other end. It lasted a long moment before Mordecai said, "I'm not sure I heard you right."

"Santa Claus is a *clone!* A copy! That's how he's

177

pulling it off; it's how he can be in two places—or more—at once. I'll bet he's cloned himself a hundred times, maybe a thousand. And *that's* how he manages to do so many deliveries all over the world. It's so obvious, I can't believe I didn't work it out years ago."

"That's great, man. Thanks for letting me know. And now my shift's almost over, and I need to get ready for bed. So, bye."

<Click>

Ormsby stared at the phone in his hand. *How could I have ever spawned such an imbecile?*

More than ever, it became necessary that he contact his man on the inside. Hopefully, he had a better head on *his* shoulders.

Chapter Eleven

What lies north of the North Pole?" –Stephen Hawking

Art thought it would be hard to seat anyone else at Doc's dining room table; the six in attendance filled every chair. Doc had arranged for someone to both cook and serve their breakfast so she could stay with her guests and not miss anything.

"Okay now," Ray began, addressing Art, "what exactly does a driver of one of these Christmas delivery gizmos do, besides steer?"

Maeve spoke first, but she deferred to Art. "After all," she said, "you've made three times as many trips as I have."

He patted her good leg under the table. "Like the captain of any ship, our drivers are responsible for everything that goes on. Navigation is largely automatic, but certain decisions have to be made when it's time to choose an actual landing spot. It depends on local weather and other conditions. Once on the ground, a lot happens all at once."

"They don't land on the roofs?" Skeeter asked.

Art chuckled. "We rarely do. It's too hard to get inside from the roof."

Skeeter gestured with both hands. "Just use the chimney, like… you know. Santa!"

"Have you ever looked inside a chimney?" Maeve asked him. She made a face. "They're usually pretty nasty."

"Then, what *do* you do?" Gloria asked.

"First, there's the dream tool," Art explained. "We know there's a letter-writer in the house somewhere, and the dream beam—"

"You're kidding, right?" Ray said. "A *dream beam?*"

Art gave him his bewildered look. "Yes! The beam targets whatever DNA the letter writer left on their letter. That way, we can be sure we're focusing on the right person. The beam won't affect anyone else."

"And what does this beam thingy do?" Gloria's face reflected serious concern.

"It makes them sleepwalk," Maeve said. "We have a technical term for it: directed somnambulism. It just means we use the person's dreams to instill a strong desire to unlock a door so we can get in."

"That's outrageous!" Gloria said. "What if they hurt themselves wandering around in the dark?"

"Sleepwalking is actually pretty common in human kids," Doc said. "I've seen the studies. And those children aren't likely to hurt themselves since they're just going to a door and unlocking it. Then they go right back to bed. They don't remember a thing."

Gloria harrumphed. "It doesn't sound very ethical to me."

Art shrugged. "The alternative is to leave the present outside, where someone might steal it, or just not deliver it at all. We really don't like either of those options. We're graded on the number of completed deliveries we make without incident. We get graded further on how we handle the incidents we do encounter."

"What constitutes an incident?" Ray asked.

"For instance, the beam doesn't always work," Art said. "And if there aren't any other letter writers in the house to try it on, we have a couple tools to help us gain access. Those usually do the trick, especially with deadbolts and chains, but now and then we have to pick the lock."

"Breakfast is here," Doc announced as her hired help deposited bowls of steaming food on the table.

Ray smiled at the scrambled eggs loaded with sausage and cheese, a mound of waffles, enough bacon for a commando unit, a big tray of baked goods, and fresh fruit.

Gloria frowned theatrically. "What, no grits?"

"They're a little hard to find this far north," Doc said. "Sorry. Maybe next time."

"Just kiddin'," Gloria said as she helped herself to some eggs.

Skeeter ignored the platters and bowls being passed around and continued to quiz Art. "What if someone sees you tryin' to break into a house?"

"Thankfully, that's quite rare," he said. "It's always dark, and we can temporarily cut power to any outside lights. We wear dark clothing, too. So, even if someone looks directly at us, we're very hard to see. Besides, we're tested on how quickly we can bypass a lock. We won't let just anyone do it."

"Then what?" Ray asked. "And what'll Tater be doing while you're trying to get in?"

"That depends," Maeve interjected. "Tater is really smart, and he can do almost anything, although I probably wouldn't use him as a hauler 'cause of his missing leg. But he can direct traffic, especially if we need to bring in gifts for more than one child."

She went on to explain about the stocking fillers and the need for two dogs working together to get it done quickly and efficiently. "There's always the possibility of interference, either from inside or out. It's usually another dog, so we always have guards on hand just in case. They're trained to look incredibly fierce, and while on duty, they give off a pretty heavy pheromone that scares off all but a tiny percentage of canines."

"What's a 'fairy-gnome?'" Skeeter asked.

Art chuckled. "It's a fancy word for something dogs can smell coming from other dogs. They can be extremely powerful."

Gloria asked a question while she slathered cream cheese on a cinnamon-raisin bagel. "Don't the pheromones bother the other dogs on the team?"

"Nope," said Art. "They're trained to ignore those

scents. But when the Season of Voyages is over, we make sure they can smell *everything* they need to smell. That includes danger."

"Drivers also monitor the haulers to be sure they get the right packages," Maeve said.

"The trickiest part is handling the unexpected. As you can imagine, that's very hard to train for, although we've had some pretty creative instructors." Art waved at Maeve. "I'm told she earned the highest score at the academy when she was a rookie."

Skeeter had begun to look drowsy, but he wasn't alone.

Doc suggested they all take naps if they felt so inclined. They could decide later what they needed to do next.

Art shook his head. I've got to make sure the four-legged members of our teams are being looked after. He thanked Doc for breakfast and then offered to help Maeve either go back to bed or find a more comfortable place to sit and relax. They waited until all the others had left the room.

Once alone, he steeled himself to ask her about what she had said to Max. "Did you really tell him you weren't interested in me?"

"*What?* No. I'd never say that. Just what did he tell you?"

Art repeated the parts of their conversation that bothered him the most.

Maeve looked very surprised. "I can't believe he said that."

"I'm not making it up."

"Then I have a few choice words for him, too," Maeve declared. "Maybe you're right to call him the 'Monster.'"

~*~

"That was some breakfast," Ray said. He stepped away from Doc and looked her up and down. "I'm pretty sure you don't eat like that every day."

She giggled. "Nope. Just on special occasions."

They had left Doc's house and walked outside. Though the snow looked knee-deep to him, the walkway was clear, and despite wearing the same things they wore indoors, the temperature didn't bother him. He thought that profoundly strange and commented on it.

"We've learned a great deal about temperature control," Doc said. "And we've developed some technologies that help. And then, of course, we have a little something extra we can bring to bear."

"Like what?" he asked.

"I suppose you'd call it magic."

He stopped and looked at her more closely to see if she was trying to hide a smile or some other clue that she was pulling his leg. He came up empty. "Magic?"

"Sure. There's an old quote I'm sure you've heard. It goes something like, 'Any sufficiently advanced technology is indistinguishable from magic.'"

Ray smiled; he'd heard it before. "It's called Clark's Law. Arthur C. Clark was a science fiction writer and a favorite of mine. But you're suggesting something that *isn't* technology. Or am I just confused?"

They started walking again.

"You're not confused; you just don't have all the facts. You see, here in our world," she gestured to the surrounding area, "small though it may be, elves reign. We have our own way of looking at nature, and dealing with it, too. We have beliefs, and we have those who occupy a special, call it spiritual place, in our society."

"You mean like... *wizards?*"

She tilted her head slightly to one side and nodded. "That's not far off. Anyway, they have certain abilities which allow them to manage our weather a bit, among other things. If not for them, we'd all have frozen to death long ago."

"In other words, every day is a beautiful day in the neighborhood."

She clearly missed the Mr. Rogers reference and kept on. "We do have seasons. We have rain and snow sometimes, too. It rarely ever gets very warm though, which is why we like to travel when we can."

"So, no swimsuits for sale around here?"

"Not many," she said, "and those are meant for sunlamps or the pools. We have quite a few of those."

Ray couldn't help but think how amazing Docquinella Bright would look in a swimsuit. "Maybe we could visit one sometime?"

She eyed him suspiciously, then laughed. "Sure. Why not?"

They continued walking for a while, then Ray asked what she thought about Maeve's ability to do her job wearing such a huge cast.

"It will be very difficult, if not impossible. The main issue is her reduced mobility. She won't be able to do some of the tasks required in the short amount of time she'll have to do them."

"Like picking locks?"

"That's a good example. And if a team member runs afoul of something, or someone, she'll have a harder time planning and executing a rescue on the spot." She paused and gave him a serious look. "We never, *ever,* leave a team member behind."

"Sounds like a great policy," he said, musing about his grandson's interest in joining Maeve. "There's not really any chance that Skeeter could help her, is there?"

Doc twisted her lips. "It's unlikely. It'll be a while before he's fully recovered. On the other hand…" Her voice drifted off.

It became Ray's turn to eye *her* suspiciously. "Are you thinking what I'm thinking?"

She bobbed her head from side to side, and when she stopped, she was sporting a smile. "Maybe."

"Gloria?"

"Why not?"

Ray chuckled. "I'd be amazed if she agreed."

"You don't think she'd like a job? There are some really astounding benefits, y'know."

He looked at her appreciatively. "I can only imagine."

Doc answered his grin with one of her own. "Actually, no. I don't think you can."

~*~

Gloria lay stretched out on one of two twin beds in what she thought had to be a row of guest bedrooms, if not rooms for patients. The size of Doc's house puzzled her. It seemed a great deal larger on the inside than it did when viewed from the outside. And that was but one of the mysteries she'd encountered in the short time she and Skeeter had been there.

She had imagined Skeeter would be taken to a hospital of some sort and was surprised when they arrived at what appeared to be a modest rural cottage. Ray, however, insisted that things would be just dandy if she'd only open her mind to the possibility of a different way of doing things.

Thus far, that had proven to be true. Despite the old-style plaster cast which encased Maeve's leg from hoof to hip, the little redhead looked pretty good. She had already announced she fully intended to report for work as usual and didn't seem overly concerned about the obvious problems she was sure to encounter with a plaster anchor on her leg.

To Gloria, Maeve's attitude spoke volumes. No one could doubt her spirit; she was tough. Gloria admired that and wished she had the wherewithal to do the same thing. When her own job was on the line, she hadn't fought for it. Truth be told, she never really liked it anyway. She envied Maeve for having a position that meant so much to her.

Going back over the things Maeve and the fellow who was clearly in love with her had said, her job didn't seem terribly complicated. It did, Gloria realized, require someone who could think and act quickly. She'd been in a few such situations herself and thought she had handled them well. Moreover, she felt quite confident she could do it again.

It occurred to her that she was, technically, already on Santa's payroll since Tater's earnings would be delivered to her. That would only change if Skeeter had a bank account, in which case the little dog's union scale wages would go there. She knew she wouldn't be visiting any banks here in Wonderland, or whatever it was called, and mused about what she might earn as a delivery team member.

And, assuming she took such a job, how would she break the news to Skeeter, since he seemed to want it more than anyone else.

She rolled over and glanced at her son lying in the bed next to hers. He looked so peaceful, and his energy level had definitely improved in the short time they'd been there. Tater lay beside him, his dark brown eyes focused squarely on her.

"What d'ya think I should do?" she asked him.

Tater lowered his head but continued looking straight at her.

"Well?"

The dog responded with a sharp snort after which he closed his eyes and went to sleep.

~*~

"I wish you'd contact me more often," Ormsby said into his phone. "There are times when I have questions, and there are times when… when I need some action taken."

"Phone calls are a problem," came the reply. "A big problem. They don't use 'em around here. They've got their own cockamamie communications system, and it isn't tied into anyone else's."

Ormsby struggled to keep his impatience in check. "So, how are you able to talk to me now?"

"I had to leave the compound and go someplace that offers normal phone service. Do you have any idea how hard it is to locate a pay phone these days?"

"Nonsense," Ormsby said. "You don't need a pay phone. Just go buy one of those... what do they call 'em? Uh... burner phones. That's it. You could buy one of them and call me."

"Assuming it worked way out here where there aren't any cell towers, what would I do with it when done, throw it away?"

"I suppose. They aren't that expensive, are they?"

"Regular cell phones aren't, but I'd need a satellite phone. And one of those good enough to connect at the North Pole? They're very expensive. A pay phone is way cheaper."

"Considering what's at stake," Ormsby growled, "I'm not above paying for a bit of convenience, even if it's not my own. Just keep track of your expenditures. I'll make good on them."

"Okay, I'll get one before I go back north. But what's wrong with contacting you by email?"

"For one thing, it's not secure," Ormsby said. "Or do you know something I don't?"

"Let's just say we're experts in different fields. You don't know anything about what goes on up there."

Ormsby grunted. "Really? Then let me ask you this: did you know they've been cloning Santa Claus?"

The voice on the other end of the line burst out laughing.

"I'm serious," Ormsby said, his voice rising sharply.

"They do nothing of the kind," said his informant. "Their technology is... different. Weird. It's hard to explain. They use some stuff that's common all over the world, like computers, but then they have other stuff that works in ways I can't explain, much less understand."

"Give me an example."

"I'm pretty sure they use a computer to maintain the information they get from letters written to the Boss. You know, things like who they are, where they live, and what they want. But then they've got some other contraption they feed the letter into after they've copied down the information they need."

"And what does it do?" Ormsby asked. "Is it a shredder or something?"

"Partly," said the voice. "And partly something else. I mean, it grinds up the letters to tiny shreds, but then there's some kinda data that comes out of it and goes back to the main computer. I've no idea what it could be."

"I'd have thought you'd make some inquiries, or eavesdrop on some conversations. Surely someone there in that great wasteland has some idea."

"I'm sure they do, but they're not talking to me. I've worked in transport and security, but the folks I know here are all tight-lipped. They don't wanna give up anything. I know.

I've tried."

"Well maybe you just need to try harder," Ormsby said, though he pitched his voice low enough that only he could hear it.

"What's that?"

"Nothing. I'm just curious. What do you know about the computer where the Boss stores all his data?"

"Not much. It's hidden in a secure area somewhere. But there are a ton of workers entering data. It's really something to see."

"Thanks, but no thanks," Ormsby said. "I can't help but wonder how good the security is. Could you, for instance, get access to a terminal connected to the main computer?"

"Maybe. But please don't ask me to develop a computer virus or program the thing to do anything else. I'm no geek!"

But, oh, how I wish you were! "That's not terribly important. If I knew what kind of operating system is used, I could have someone else write a program to erase everything. All you'd have to do is run it."

"And if I got caught? Then what?"

"If you're as smart as I think you are, you'd leave before they caught you. Didn't you just tell me you worked in transport? And didn't you manage to leave the compound to make this call? Surely you could do that again."

"Maybe," the voice said. "But I don't even want to think what they'd do to me if I got caught. They could just haul me off far into the hills. It's a permanent deep freeze. I'd be dead in minutes. Frozen like a popsicle."

"Then, don't get caught!"

"You're crazy."

"Like a fox," Ormsby said, feeling proud of himself. "See what you can find out about the computer and let me know."

"Don't hold your breath."

That felt like the sort of pinch Ormsby's late father used to administer. He didn't like it. "Do as you're told," he said, allowing a tone of menace into his voice.

"Yessir," came the immediate response.

~*~

"When can I go home?" Maeve asked.

"Tomorrow, I imagine," Doc said. "Unless you develop a problem of some kind. How do you feel?"

"Fine, except I've got an itch I can't reach, and it's driven me to start looking for a way to chop my leg off. Got any suggestions?"

Doc snickered. "I've got an anti-itch powder I can pour into the top of the cast. It'll eventually filter down, but it's not magic. Getting it to the precise spot is iffy."

"Then why not use magic? You're a healer, aren't you?"

Doc shook her head. "You've been reading too much Harry Potter. Magic has its limits. You know that."

Maeve looked up at the three humans seated in Doc's living room. All of them were staring at her.

"You guys do magic?" Skeeter asked. "That is so cool! Can you make me taller? And give me some muscles? There's a guy at school who always picks on me. I'd love to—"

"Love to what?" Gloria asked, her eyes narrowed at the boy.

"Give him a taste of his own medicine, I suspect," said Ray. He smiled at the two of them, then spoke directly toward his grandson. "Bullies rarely pick on people their own size. If you were as big as the clown who's giving you trouble, he wouldn't mess with you."

"I'd still like to—"

"*Skeeee_turrrr?*" Gloria said.

"—smack him."

"And you think that'd make you feel better?"

"I don't know about that," he said, "but it sure wouldn't make *him* feel better. That's kinda the whole point."

Ray winked at him in solidarity; Skeeter responded with a thumbs up.

"So," the lad continued, changing the topic. "Can I ride with you, Miz Maeve, when you do your deliveries? I feel a lot better. Actually, I feel great!" He flexed both biceps. "Wanna feel my muscles?"

"It's not up to me," she replied. "That's something you and your Mom need to work out. And that's only if Doc thinks you're up to it."

Skeeter instantly turned to the healer. "You said I'm doin' better, didn't ya?"

193

"I did. But you've still got a way to go. Those gigantic muscles of yours got a little less gigantic while you were sick. We need to work on them, too."

Skeeter appeared crestfallen. Tater seemed to read his mood and barked at Doc.

Gloria turned to Maeve. "How 'bout if I went with you?"

"Aw, Mom," Skeeter said, the second word coming out as two distinct syllables.

"It's okay with me as long as you can pass the proficiency tests," Maeve said. "I can make suggestions to the committee, but they make the final choices."

Gloria looked at Doc. "Is that the committee you told us you were on?"

She nodded. "Maeve's right. But if she asked for you, and you passed the tests, I'm sure you'd get the job."

"So," Skeeter said, "if she goes and I stay here, what do I do if I need her for something? You know, if I get lonely, or decide to take a walk and get lost. She'll have Tater, too. I'd be abandoned."

Doc lightly slapped her forehead. "I can't believe I forgot to give you your compods."

Ray gave her a puzzled look. "I'm not sure I even want to know what a compod is. It sounds kinda… I dunno… kinky."

Maeve giggled but didn't offer any insight. She left that for Doc.

"It's like a radio," the healer said. "Most of us wear

194

them on a cord around our necks. That makes it easy to grab with one hand and get in touch with anyone else who has one. Hold on, I'll fetch yours."

"I want one, too!" Skeeter called out after her.

"Righto!" she said.

Maeve pulled hers out from beneath her blouse and held it out for the others to see. "It's small and light," she said. "I hardly even know I'm wearing it."

"How's it work?" Ray asked.

"Doc'll show you," she said. "There may be some restrictions on yours." She glanced at the boy. "And yours might have something extra since you're in Healer House."

"Like what?" Skeeter asked. "A video game or something?"

She chuckled. "More like a locator. So, if you did wander off and get lost, someone could find you right away."

Doc returned with three of the devices and handed them out. She also held a different appliance which she used to register each of them as valid compod users.

Skeeter looked at his with undisguised suspicion. "There's no screen. How'm I gonna play video games without a danged screen?"

"Language," Gloria cautioned.

Skeeter responded with a breathy, "Yes ma'am," and stared down into his lap.

"It's not a toy," Doc said. "And you don't need a screen. Just hold down the button on the side and tell it what you want."

"Kinda like Siri?" Gloria asked.

Doc's eyebrows scrunched together. "Who's Siri?"

"Never mind," Ray said. "She doesn't live around here." He slipped the cord of his compod around his neck, lifted the little instrument, and asked, "Who'd like to get something to eat?"

There was no response.

"You'll need to be a little more specific, Ray," Doc said. "Otherwise, you'd get responses from all over the place."

"Okay then." He rubbed his jaw and tried again. "Who in this room is hungry?"

The question came out loud and clear from every other device in the room.

"That's pretty neat," Skeeter said. He held the button on his and said, "I am."

Ray's device repeated his words only a split second later.

"Miz Maeve said mine might have something extra in it," Skeeter said. "What is it?"

Doc nodded. "It's something we all have, a locater function. No matter where you are, anywhere in the world, the system knows your location. The only difference between your compods and mine, or Maeve's, is our ability to turn the locater function off."

"So," Gloria said, "you could hide if you needed to."

Doc gave her an odd look. "I suppose that's one way of looking at it. But very few of them are set up that way."

"I suppose there's a reason for that," Ray said.

Doc nodded. "There is, indeed."

Chapter Twelve

"I stopped believing in Santa Claus when I was six. Mother took me to see him in a department store, and he asked for my autograph." –Shirley Temple

I can't believe I'm doing this.

Gloria stared at her alleged "instructor" as he made a note in her file. She had no doubt that it recorded in glaring detail how she'd failed to pick the lock he'd given her to open. It wasn't the first such notation. She'd failed to open any of them, and with each new test she discovered her hands shaking more and more.

"Can we do something else for a while?" she begged. "If I see another locked door today, I may be tempted to throw it at you." Despite the obvious and logical need to find a way into certain homes and apartments, she couldn't imagine Santa Claus picking a lock.

Her mentor during the rushed training session was a stout, bespectacled elf wearing an outfit she thought reserved for bike-riding circus performers. His costume appeared a good three sizes too small, and the image destroyed any illusions she may have had about the hunkier variety of elves. She wondered if they had an organization of some sort to which she could report him for failure to represent his species.

The chubby, latex-wrapped, pseudo-sprite merely frowned and pointed at the first door she'd failed to unlock. "Okay, relax," he said, his voice sounding as though it emanated from one of Tater's squeaky toys. "Let's go over it again. Slowly, step-by-step, and you can give it another try."

"Fine," muttered Gloria.

"In case you weren't listening," squeaked her teacher, "this isn't rocket science. Most of the locks you'll see on doors today, all over the world, are the pin and tumbler variety."

Just like on my own front door. Big deal.

"Did you know they were invented during your country's Civil War?"

"Seriously?" *Were you there at the time?*

"They haven't' changed much since then," he went on. "And when you see how easily they can be opened, without a key, you'll realize they only offer the illusion of security."

"How comforting," she said.

"Thefts and break-ins are almost unheard of here, of course—"

Of course.

"—but in your world, it's a different matter. If you wish to rely on technology that's as old as I am, go right ahead. I'd prefer what we have."

"Which is?"

"An incantation. Most of us get little training in the ancient arts, but we all know a few handy tricks."

"Like how to lock your doors at night?" She tried not to sound snide.

"Among other things," he said. "Now, back to work."

Growling obscenities *sotto voce*, Gloria once again attacked the unyielding lock on a door which looked like a souvenir from a Kansas tornado, possibly from Auntie Em's farm.

"Get out your tension wrench and your rake."

Gloria pulled the two little tools from a set small enough to fit inside a wallet. The tension wrench looked like a miniature golf club—a tiny, flat putter. The rake had three rounded tines. Neither looked clandestine.

"Since you seem to be having issues with your nerves, I won't use the timer for this attempt."

It's not just the timer I have issues with you smarmy little—

"Insert the short end of the tension wrench into the lock first and press the long end gently to one side."

Gloria did so.

"You're applying too much pressure. If the wrench bends, you're pushing too hard."

Yeah, yeah. She backed off.

"Now insert the rake above it and gently rock it in and out while you alternately apply a little pressure to the wrench and then let up."

Gloria tried her best to follow the instructions.

"Don't overwork it, just keep it up until the cylinder in the lock turns."

This is never going to work. I'm just too—

Without warning, the cylinder turned.

"It turned!" she exclaimed.

The instructor gave her the least enthusiastic "Yippee!" she'd ever heard. "And," he added, "you did it within the allotted time."

She looked at him in surprise. "You said you weren't going to time it."

"Yeah. I lied. It's a teacher's prerogative."

"I'm tired," she said. "I want to go back to my room and have a drink."

"Let's run through it once more. If you can beat the clock a second time, I'll sign off on your lock picking skills."

"And then?"

"And then you can go drink yourself silly for all I care." He shook his head. "Humans." His voice carried a note of disgust.

"Elves," she muttered in response. "If only they weren't so hard to kill."

"What's your problem?" he asked, his eyes boring into hers. "You're the one who wanted the training, only you wanted it short and sweet, condensed but easy to learn."

"My problem is you," she said. "I don't understand

201

your attitude. I'm doing this to help one of your own, Maeve, a sweet kid if there ever was one. But you? You're a jerk. So, what've you got against humans?"

He pressed his lips together and appeared to be counting to himself, one nod of his head per number, but eventually he relaxed. "The thing is… I'm worried about the Boss. We all are. Those of us who know the situation, anyway."

"What about him?"

"We don't know where he is or if he'll make it back in time. If he doesn't, we can have someone else complete his run, but it won't be the same. He takes the really special cases and…" He paused. "I don't know how to say this other than… what Santa does calls for a human touch."

Gloria found the admission surprising. "All this time I thought you disdained humans."

"Most of them, yes," he said. "But there are a special few who rise above the rest."

"Like Santa."

"Correct."

"Okay then," Gloria said brandishing her two tiny tools. "Reset your darn clock. I've got this."

~*~

Ray and Doc sat opposite each other in a secluded niche at the back of an old-world style pub. They'd been enjoying each other's company and a small selection of beverages. Doc had wine; Ray found an unusual cider with no alcohol but plenty of taste and body, a drink he'd never heard of before.

202

"I thought I'd never go inside a place like this again," he said.

She smiled and took his hand. "You're stronger than you think, and you know what's good for you." She batted long lashes at him. "Me, for instance. You don't need—"

To his dismay, she went abruptly silent when her compod not only glowed, but vibrated.

"It's an alert, an emergency," she said, retrieving the device from its nesting spot in the center of her chest. Ray envied the gizmo.

She held the device close to her ear and spoke in a tone so low Ray couldn't make out what she was saying.

The conversation was brief, and she let the device drop back to its normal position as she worked her way out of the booth. "We've got a problem."

"What is it? Can't it wait? We just ordered some—"

"No, it can't wait. Somehow or other, all of the animals in Team Housing were released. They're roaming all over the place. I'm afraid some of them may get hurt. C'mon. We'll need your help."

"I'm right behind you," Ray said as he joined her in a headlong exodus from the bar, something he couldn't recall ever doing before. What he knew he'd miss definitely wasn't booze. The realization gave his spirits a lift he didn't know he needed.

Doc hailed a ride in a far less romantic vehicle than the one in which he'd previously traveled. Instead of a horse and buggy, a small but chunky two-seat conveyance rolled to a stop outside the pub, and they clambered in.

"Where's the steering wheel?" he asked.

Doc ignored him and barked the word "trams" into her compod. The vehicle got under way immediately and drove itself.

"*Trams?*" Ray asked. "There's a place called Trams?"

She nodded. "That's where non-motorized vehicles are housed and maintained, along with draft animals of all kinds. Some of them are huge, and of those, a few don't get along well with dogs and cats. A couple think of them as food."

Ray's thoughts shifted to Tater. When he'd last seen him, the dog was curled up next to Skeeter. Ray fumbled with his compod, pressed the button, and called out to the boy. "Are you and Tater okay?"

"I'm fine," Skeeter said. "But Tater wants to go outside somethin' fierce. Think I should let him?"

"No!" exclaimed Doc. "Keep him with you. We'll explain later."

~*~

Having ignored her instructor's suggestion that she summon a ride, Gloria opted to walk back to Healer's House since the distance wasn't all that great. She hadn't covered much ground when she heard a commotion behind her. The sounds grew rapidly louder. She turned and inhaled sharply as a mob of dogs raced through the powdery snow headed straight toward her.

She looked for shelter, but none of the nearby buildings appeared open to strange humans wandering in off the road. A decent-sized tree would've been nice, especially if it had some low hanging branches she could use in an ascent. Trees abounded, but none appeared scalable without the appropriate gear, which she clearly lacked.

Two canines of nondescript breed appeared to be leading the pack. In the lead raced a lean, white, medium-sized dog with a black spot covering one eye. Not far behind charged a larger, reddish-brown dog, its tongue wagging to one side.

Gloria had nowhere to go. She stood fully exposed in the road while the dogs hurtled in toward her overland, leaving in their wake a drift of light, fluffy snow swirling through the cool, early evening air.

Summoning courage from somewhere deep inside, Gloria turned to face the oncoming stampede, raised one hand like a Peachtree Street traffic cop, and yelled, "Stop!"

The larger of the two lead animals slammed on its breaks and came to a stop at Gloria's feet. The white dog fishtailed around her in a tight turn which ended beside the first dog. The rest of the pack, an assortment of breeds in a variety of sizes, assembled themselves behind the leaders.

"You, too," Gloria commanded, her voice surprisingly firm. "All of you. Sit!"

Without another sound, every member of the pack settled on their haunches behind the leaders. All of them focused their eyes on hers.

Gloria felt empowered and crowed, "I'm the Mother of... of... *Dogs!*"

She did a quick tally and discovered the pack consisted of 17 animals in assorted fur lengths, shapes, and description.

Now what do I do with you? I don't mind playing the role of Pied Piper, but only if you follow me and don't attack anyone on the way. On the way? To… where?

She punched the button on her compod, called out to Doc, and explained her situation. "What do I do now?"

"The animals should all have collars and IDs," Doc said.

"Hold on. I'll check." Gloria gave her crew a quick review though it rapidly became apparent they were losing patience. "All have 'em but one," she said.

"Then," said Doc, "be extremely wary of that one."

Gloria looked closer at the dog in question, the second of the pack's two leaders. It had a short, reddish-brown coat, and the most dark-brown, loving eyes she'd ever seen. "You're the color of brandy," she said as she stroked the dog's coat.

In response, the dog snuggled closer to her and wagged its tail.

"Oh. My. God," she whispered into her compod. "I think she's in love with me."

Gloria's father's voice chimed in from the background, "The real question is how do you feel about her?"

"Oh, she's a doll," Gloria gushed as the dog licked her hand. "She may be a mutt, but she's… I don't know how else to say it, special. If I had to name her, I'd call her Brandy."

"See if you can keep them together," Doc said. "I'll send someone to pick them up."

"Who let them loose?" Gloria asked.

Doc exhaled in disgust. "No one seems to know. But there has to be a way to find out, and then whoever did it is going to have some explaining to do."

Gloria leaned toward the second of the two lead dogs, the white one. The name on his collar read "Foster." She scratched his head and received a tail wag in response.

As soon as she straightened up, Foster scampered in a big circle around the canine gathering, dodging in and out as if taunting one or all of them to go after him. Before long, several of his comrades responded, and a massive game of "chase me, catch me" ensued.

While the mass of whirling, racing, barking dogs grew more frantic, Gloria again sought a place of refuge, and again came up empty.

She clicked the button on her compod once more. "Please tell whoever's coming to step on it!"

~*~

"You did what?" Ormsby asked, not sure he'd understood what he'd just heard.

"I let the dogs out," said the voice on his phone. "You know, just like that stupid song." He snickered and sang a few bars from "Who Let the Dogs Out."

"Oh, knock it off. And tell me why I should care."

"Because it'll upset their plans, slow them down. They're trying to get ready for their big delivery night. They call it the Season of Voyages, which doesn't make sense to me at all."

"It would help if I knew what you were talking about. I don't care about dogs. I don't like dogs. I wouldn't have a dog if you paid me." Though tempted to cut the connection, Ormsby gave his caller a chance to explain.

"Most of Santa's deliveries aren't actually made by Santa."

"Obviously," Ormsby snorted.

"Well who do you think makes them? And how do they do it?"

Ormsby sneered. "I don't know. They recruit a great number of animals for some reason. Maybe to pull the sleighs? What difference does it make?"

"If there are no animals to assist, there won't be many deliveries. And if you're holding the main man himself, there may not be any."

"What's to keep them from getting new ones or rounding all the escaped animals up? They can't go far." Ormsby said.

"They're looking for them now. Training new ones would take too long. The point is, they've been distracted from their usual preparations. Almost everyone up here is on edge because the Boss is missing. Anything else that goes wrong increases their anxiety level and wrecks their productivity."

"That's all well and good," Ormsby said, striving to be patient. "But I'd be a lot happier if I knew their computer system malfunctioned or they lost all their data. Or both. Big organizations thrive on organization and information. Eliminate one or the other, and the system collapses."

"But—"

"I think it's nice that you found a way to upset them, but what I'd *really* like you to do is get the information I *asked* you to get." His voice rose as he spoke and hit a crescendo on "asked."

"You want the type of computer they're using and the operating system, right?"

"Correct. And figure out where and how they back up their data. I'd dearly love to wipe all of it out."

"Yes, sir."

He thought he may have heard a note of disappointment in the caller's voice. "You're still with me on this, right? You're still committed?"

"Of course. But I'm worried I'll never get the information you need. It's well guarded. And I don't have the faintest clue where the main computer is even located. The workers are all tight-lipped. It's as if they have a personal stake in what goes on. They don't understand they're just being used. They have no idea what the real meaning of all this is. They don't have the background you gave us."

Ormsby smiled. "You'll be fine. If nothing else, we can always resort to something less sophisticated."

"Like what?" the caller asked.

"Like explosives," Ormsby said. "You'd be amazed how destructive a few pounds of C4 can be."

"And just where am I supposed to get my hands on that stuff?"

"Give me a mailing address you can get to in a hurry. I'll have it delivered. Pronto."

Art waited near the team housing units to which he and Maeve had been assigned. She stood beside him, gamely trying to get around with a cast and crutches. Her efforts seemed awkward, and he couldn't fathom how she would be able to make her rounds.

"Gloria could only read the name of one dog," Maeve said. "It's Foster, and he's on my team."

"Yeah, I remember him. White with a black eye patch. Kinda goofy?"

She gave him a squinty-eyed look. "All right, maybe a little. But he can run like crazy. I'm surprised the others could keep up."

Art glanced up and down the road for the thousandth time. "Gloria also said there was one in the pack without a collar. She named her Brandy."

"*She* named her? That's a bit presumptuous, don't you think?"

He shrugged. "If the dog's a stray, and the owner didn't care enough to provide some identification, then I don't see any harm in it. Maybe she'll adopt him."

"Are you sure they're coming *here?*" Maeve asked. "Seems like we've waiting for—"

"I see 'em!" Art said as he stepped into the road and waved both arms above his head. "Over here!"

When the wagon arrived, the driver jumped down from his seat above and behind the horses, hurried to the back, and lowered the gate. The dogs poured out, excited to see their

210

team leaders.

Art immediately began a headcount and spared a glance at Maeve who was doing the same thing. "I've got four," he said and quickly rattled off their names, "Finley, Buck, JJ, and Maggie. Two big ones, and two small ones. I'm missing my three oldest. How 'bout you?"

"I've got Cody, little Zoe, and Maple. That's it." She thought about it for a few seconds. "Foster's still pretty young, but the other two, Spike and Augie, are both senior dogs. They're missing, too. And Tater, of course, but he's with Skeeter."

"So, we're missing six altogether," Art said.

"Seven, if we count Gloria's stray. And if she's anything like Foster, the two of them are probably having a high old time chasing each other around the whole settlement. We might never find them before lift-off."

"About that," Art said. "I'm really worried about the older dogs. If they don't show up… Look, neither of us can operate with half a team. We may need to merge."

"You don't think I'll be able to go, do you? You must think—"

"I think you're amazing. I think you've got more heart than all the other team leaders put together. And you can toss in Doc and the Grand Committee, too. All of 'em."

"But…."

"If we merge our teams, you and I can work together. What d'ya say?"

She blinked several times in surprise, then favored him

with a relieved smile. "I'd like that. I'd like that a lot."

"Good! Now then, do we hope the other dogs remain lost, or do we pitch in and help find them?" He chuckled.

"We find 'em, of course! We need to make sure they're okay. We'll sort everything else out later."

When he gave her a hug, they both fell over into the snow, and their dogs piled on.

~*~

Ormsby answered his phone for the second time that evening, noting the call was from Bud in New York. "What now?" he groused.

"I'm afraid you aren't gonna like this."

"I'll be the judge of that. Spill it."

"He's gone," Bud said.

"Who's gone."

"You know. Him. Is this line secure?"

Ormsby felt his blood pressure rising. Could no one on the planet follow simple instructions? "No, it's not a secure line, you idiot! But that doesn't matter. No one's listening in. No one knows anything about what we've done. Or, in your case, haven't done."

"Listen, it wasn't my fault I—"

"Just tell me what happened," Ormsby growled. "I'll decide whether or not it's your fault."

"I… We don't know what happened, exactly. We were all in the main room watching TV. Another of those sappy

212

Christmas shows he loved. We'd usually humor him 'cause we got tired of having to say no, as if—"

"Will you get on it with it? *Please?*" Ormsby found it galling that he had to use the word "please."

"Right, right. Sorry. Anyway, the guys said he got up during a commercial and said something like, 'It's nearly Christmas Eve, and it looks like I won't get to fill any stockings this year. But would it be all right if I slipped into my hat and coat? Just once, for old time's sake?'"

"And you said, 'No,' right?"

Bud cleared his throat. "Well, not actually, no. I wasn't there just then. I would have objected, but the other guys—"

"Mordecai, too?"

"No. He was in the other room making himself a sandwich."

"Go on."

"The other guys decided to give him a break seein' as how we were depriving him of the one thing he liked to do the most."

Ormsby couldn't believe what he was hearing. "And then?"

"Well, one of the guys brought in all his stuff, and he got dressed. They said he was humming that goofy tune about grandma gettin' run over by a reindeer, and they all just kinda went back to watching TV."

"So? What happened?"

"See, that's the weird thing," Bud said. "None of them

really know what happened. He just sort of went away."

Ormsby was too angry to be shocked. "So, he just disappeared? Faded into thin air?"

"I don't know! None of us does. He was there, and then he wasn't. Someone said they might've heard the door open and shut."

"So, he just got dressed and walked out? Is that what you're struggling to tell me?"

Bud didn't respond.

"Are you still there?" growled Ormsby.

"Yes, sir."

"Put Mordecai on the line."

"But—"

"Do it. Now!"

He listened to a brief exchange between the two men, and then Mordecai picked up the phone. "I don't know what happened either. I was—"

"Feeding your face, I know. Has anyone bothered to go looking for our guest?"

"Uh… Oh! You mean him."

Ormsby wondered how much longer his teeth would survive all the grinding to which he was subjecting them. "Yes," he managed to say without unclenching his jaws.

"Bud just left to join the others."

"How long has he been gone?"

"It's hard to say," Mordecai said, still chewing. "For some reason, no one was looking in his direction, and he just slipped out. That couldn't have been more than a few minutes ago."

"So, what are you doing stuffing your mouth when you should be out looking for him?"

"Good point," Mordecai said and hung up.

Ormsby stared at the dead phone in his hand. His grip tightened as his rage grew, and with it grew his desire to blow the jolly fat man's entire operation into pieces so tiny, they'd never be put back together.

~*~

"Where's Tater?" Ray asked as he and Doc checked off the names of the recovered animals. Nearly all of the rosters checked complete. Those of Artemis Maker and Maeve Blessing, however, were still missing members.

"I thought he was with your grandson," Doc said.

Ray slapped his forehead. "Yes. Of course. So, I'm sure he's okay."

The words had barely left his mouth when Skeeter's voice emanated from Ray's compod. "Gramps? Have you seen Tater?"

"I thought he was with you," Ray said.

"He was, but he was actin' real funny, like he needed to go out. I wasn't gonna let him 'cause y'all said not to, but then he started bringin' me his toys, and I figured he just wanted to go out and play fetch."

"Okay, so?"

"Well, we did do that for a while, and then…."

"And then, what?" asked Doc.

"He perked up his ears like he'd heard a siren or somethin', and then he just ran off. I didn't even know he could move that fast. I called him and called him, but he wouldn't come back."

Ray chewed his lower lip. "How long ago did that happen?"

"I dunno. A long time I guess. I've been out lookin' for him. I figured he was after a rabbit or something, but I followed his tracks in the snow and they got mixed up with some others, and then… and then…" His words became lost in tears and sniffles, but he eventually managed to add, "You just gotta find him. You just gotta."

Chapter Thirteen

"He put a ring in the toe of a stocking. On Christmas Eve we opened our stockings, and it was there at the bottom. Then he got down on his knees, and he was shaking." –Kyra Sedgwick

Before she could rest or even think about organizing a search team to look for the missing dogs, Doc's compod signaled yet another alert. She shook her head in surprise and muttered, "Twice in one night? Seriously? This is getting ridiculous."

"Who is it?" Ray asked.

Doc greeted the caller, then put the device to her ear rather than broadcast the conversation. She listened intently to a message sent to all members of the Grand Committee, "The Boss has returned along with the security team dispatched shortly after his disappearance. He asked to speak with a healer. Docquinella, if you're receiving this message please report to the main security office."

"I've got to go," she told Ray.

"What's up?"

"The Boss is back. The security team we sent to New York City found him. He asked to speak with a healer, and the Committee wants me to go see him."

Ray appeared concerned. "Want me to tag along?"

She thought for a moment. "I would, actually. But let me get someone to go after—"

"Art and Maeve's dogs?" Ray grimaced. "Why not send Art and Maeve, assuming they haven't already begun their own search."

Doc contacted them and learned they'd been on the hunt for some time already. She gestured for Ray to follow her. "Let's go!"

~*~

Once again, Ray found himself impressed by the travel options made available to Doc. He assumed such things were likewise available to everyone living in the remote Arctic settlement, an assessment Doc readily acknowledged. "We must often pool our resources since our connection to the outside world is so limited. We try not to import anything, but since the primary objective of almost everyone who lives here is the support of the Boss, we have to. As you know, much of what we deliver comes from your world. And yet, only a tiny, tiny fraction of humanity even knows we exist."

"But that's largely because you want it that way, isn't it?" Ray asked.

She smiled. "Of course. And I realize it sounds like I'm complaining—wanting to eat our cake—"

"And bake it, too," Ray said. "Where are we going, by the way?"

218

"The Central Security Office. It's where the Boss is."

"Is that like your police department?"

Doc shrugged. "It's as close to one as we need. Crime is virtually nonexistent here. For the most part, we all have what we need. And for those who don't, there are ample ways to obtain whatever they're looking for. No one needs to resort to crime."

Ray snorted. "Utopia. Who knew someone actually pulled it off?"

With a quick shake of her head, Doc disagreed. "We have our problems, believe me. If we didn't, there would be no need for the Committee."

"Have you been on it very long?"

"Too long," she said in an aside she made no attempt to soften. "My term runs out soon, and I'll be glad to let go of the responsibilities. I'm a healer; that's what I prefer to focus on, not running a huge organization like ours." She gestured to the buildings, the surrounding woodlands, and everyone in sight.

They rumbled through several neighborhoods, a shopping and entertainment area, and some farmland, which Ray assumed was only possible through the good offices of the wizards. He asked about them.

"We don't actually call them wizards," she said. "That's a pretty archaic term."

"Then, what do you call them?"

She shrugged. "They're just... elders. A very few elves have even longer lifespans than normal. The downside is that they remain old and infirm for a very long time, and their ability to engage with the rest of the population is limited."

"So, what do you do with them?"

"We make them comfortable and give them whatever they need to develop or enhance their capacity to manage enchantments."

"Like the weather," Ray said, observing the fallow, winter fields.

"Among other things," she added.

Eventually they passed through more heavily populated areas and reached a complex near what Ray guessed was the center of the village. "So, this is the capitol?"

She laughed. "I suppose you could call it that. We don't really have a government other than the Boss and the Committee."

Ray frowned. "You make him sound like a dictator instead of a jolly old elf."

"He's neither," Doc said, "elf or dictator. He's as human as you are."

"You mean Chuck Fyfe, right? The Boss? The guy playing Santa Claus?"

"It's Charlie, or Charlemagne, though the only one who ever calls him that is his wife, and then only when he's done something really stupid."

Feeling a bit of kinship with the man, Ray chuckled. "I think that happens to most married guys. I'm glad to hear he's no different."

"He's the most decent human I've ever met," Doc said. "And I've had the good fortune to meet several." She lightly thumped his chest. "You could be one of 'em."

Ray made a face. "Yeah, right." *Nobody, but nobody, will ever believe that!*

"It's time you met him," Doc said as their vehicle came to a stop in front of a small, modest building that could have housed a one-man travel agency or a fortune teller's place.

Ray followed her into the building which, just like her own home, seemed to grow once they were inside.

He spied the Boss surrounded by four robust, male elves, all dressed in dark blue though he could detect no rank or other indication of status. When they stepped away, Ray got a better look at the man they'd rescued and nearly fainted. They could have been twins, although the Boss's face carried quite a few more wrinkles.

"Doc!" the man cried out when Ray's companion strolled into his line of vision. "It's so good to see you!"

The two hugged, and he patted the cushioned seat beside him. Doc quickly lowered herself into it and looked straight into his eyes. "How are you feeling?"

He pulled at his full, white beard. "Tired. Very, very tired. And weary of watching television."

"Anything else? No aches and pains?"

"No new ones, anyway," he said, then lowered his voice. "But I've got stomach troubles. Probably from all the milk and cookies they fed me. One or two of the fellows who had me would sneak real food to me from time to time, but

221

the two guys in charge…." He sighed. "They didn't want me to have anything else."

Doc palmed his face. "I'm so sorry. Nothing like this has ever happened before. Do you have any idea who was responsible?"

"I only recognized one name: Bud. Short for Budforth. He got bullied as a kid."

"He told you that?" Ray asked.

The Boss looked up at him and then back at Doc. "So, this is my doppelganger?"

She nodded, and he looked back at Ray, extended his hand, and smiled. "Charlie Fyfe," he said. "Pleased to meet you."

Ray shook his hand, comforted by the man's firm grip. "Ray Mays," he responded. "I didn't mean to interrupt. It's just… *Budforth?* Who'd hang a name like that on a kid?"

The Boss laughed. "Most likely the same kind of folks who named me Charlemagne. Have you any idea how long it took me to learn how to spell that? I mean, when I was a kid, everyone called me Chuck, or Charlie. Fortunately, nobody bullied me like they did Budforth."

"A couple things puzzle me," Ray said. "First and foremost, why did those guys grab you and treat you like a prisoner? And secondly, why aren't you mad about it?"

"Y'know, I never could understand why they did it, and believe me, I asked. But none of those willing to talk to me gave me a reason. A couple made guesses, but those didn't make sense."

"And being grabbed didn't make you angry?"

"Well, sure it did! But what good would it do to be upset all the time? Instead, I tried to make friends."

Doc's mouth opened in surprise. "Make friends? *With kidnappers?*"

The Boss's shoulders slumped. "It's not like I was going to overpower them. One of those fellows was huge." He squinted as if straining to recall something. "The big one's name is Mort, or Morty. He and Budforth were at odds the whole time. I hoped they'd have a falling out so I could get away."

"Why didn't you use your compod?" Ray asked. He looked at the security team still gathered nearby. "Doc said the Committee sent a team to look for you."

"They took it away from me," the Boss said. "Along with my hat and coat. And the really big guy, he insisted I take my boots off, too. He wasn't very talkative, but he made that much clear."

Doc closed her eyes and nodded knowingly. Ray nudged her. "What'd I miss?"

"He's got his hat and coat, doesn't he? Boots, too?"

Ray acknowledged as much.

The Boss continued, "I told a couple of the guys I wanted to get dressed, one last time, since I'd miss out on my deliveries this year. They took pity on me, I guess, 'cause they gave me everything but my compod. Budforth had that."

Ray's confusion remained. "So? What difference did that make?"

"It's his hat," Doc said. She snickered. "See the white pompom at the end?"

"Yeah. So? It makes him invisible?"

"In a way, yes," the Boss said. "It makes anyone near me turn away. I have no idea how it works."

"You'd have to ask the elders," Doc said, "but I doubt they'd tell you anything you'd understand."

"Santas have been using it for generations," the Boss said. "It solved the problem of people waking up and investigating while a delivery was being made. That's why it hangs down and remains within easy reach. I just press it, and—*Bingo!*—folks ignore me. They either look or turn away. I might as well be invisible."

Ray laughed, too. "So, the kidnappers turned away, and you just walked out?"

"Correct. I hit the streets and went in search of a pay phone." He snorted. "Have you tried to find one of those darn things lately? Oy. But then I realized even if I did find one, I didn't have a dime to make a call."

"I think they charge a quarter these days," Ray said. "Some even allow charge cards."

"Didn't have either of those. I can't remember the last time I carried a wallet. I know what charge cards are, though. Back in the day, I had one, for gas I think. But I haven't needed anything like that for a long time. Now, even when I'm on vacation, I pay cash for everything."

"Sounds a little risky to me," Ray said.

The Boss chuckled. "Try filling out a credit application

and listing *my* job. How far d'ya think that'd go?"

Ray liked the man's gentle laugh and easy manner. "Yep. I get it now."

Turning back toward Doc, the Boss shook his head slowly from side to side. "I hate to say this, but I've never felt more tired than I do right now. I just want to go home, hug my sweet wife, and sleep for a month or three."

Doc patted his cheek and gave him a sympathetic moue. "I understand. We'll have you back home very soon, and I'll fix you some tea that'll help restore some energy."

"I appreciate that," he said. "But I think it's time for me to let someone else take over. I'm way too old for this, and it's not fair to Angelina."

Ray queried Doc with a blank look.

"Angelina is Mrs. Claus," Doc said.

The Boss aimed a thumb in Ray's direction. "Why not let him take over? You trust him, don't you?"

Suddenly, Ray found everyone in the room staring at him. He responded with a massive gulp of air as his heartbeat rose instantly. And dramatically. "*Me?*"

Doc held up her hands. "Let's not rush into anything, okay? The Boss needs rest, and you need time, too. We'll discuss this more tomorrow."

"But tomorrow is Christmas Eve," exclaimed one of the security crewmembers. "We can't wait! We—"

"We'll *discuss* it in the morning," said Doc, laying down the law. "The Committee needs to be involved, too, and

I wouldn't want to be the one to have to wake them up this late at night." She stared at the elf who had raised the objection. "Would you?"

"Uh, no ma'am."

"All right then. Let's get Santa to bed. Everyone else go home."

~*~

"How're you feelin', sport?" Gloria asked.

Skeeter looked up at her from the sofa in Doc's parlor. "Okay, I guess."

"Just okay? Doc says you should be feeling a lot stronger. She says you're eating well and moving around just fine."

He didn't respond other than to stare at a book lying closed in his lap.

Skeeter reading? Something had to be wrong. "Watcha got there? Is that a book? A real, live book?"

"Yeah."

"What's the title?" Gloria asked. "Maybe I've read it. Hey, I know! We could talk about it. Compare notes or something."

"It's a Harry Potter book," he said, his voice depressed enough to lower the room's sea level. "I didn't get real far."

"Worried about Tater, huh?"

"Yeah."

"He'll be fine. Maeve and Artemis are out looking for

him right now, along with a bunch of others. They'll find him."

His eyes teared up as he spoke. "But what if they don't? What if—"

"Hey now," she said, tussling his hair. "Have faith."

"That's easy for you to say. You'll be out tonight delivering toys and stuff. Havin' a great time. The dogs'll be in your lap and licking your face. But not me. I'll be stuck here. All alone." He stared directly into her eyes. "So... Merry Christmas, Mom."

Gloria felt as if someone had stepped on her heart. *How could I have let something like this happen?* "Sweetie, I'm so sorry. I just got caught up in everything, and... You know what? I'm going to tell Maeve and Doc and anyone else I need to tell, that I'm staying here with you tonight. They've gotten along well enough without me all these years; one more isn't going to make a bit of difference."

To prove the point she grabbed her compod, punched the button, and asked for Doc.

The healer responded almost immediately. "Hi, Gloria. Ready for your first flight?"

"Uh, no, actually," Gloria said. "Much as I'd love to go, Skeeter needs me. It's Christmas Eve, and I'm the only family he has. I... I just can't leave him all alone."

She imagined Doc grimacing as she heard the news but was surprised by her response. "Don't give it another thought," Doc said. "Maeve's been hounding me to go with Artemis. They're going to combine what's left of their teams. Have you got Tater with you?"

"No," Gloria said, "But he's got good sense. He'll

come back."

Doc agreed, and they ended the conversation.

Skeeter finally began to perk up. "Maybe you and I could go look for Tater. What d'ya think?"

"I don't see why not," she said. "I just don't want to wear you out."

"You won't," he said. "I promise."

~*~

"C'mon," Doc said once the security team accompanied the Boss back to his house. "You know you want to do it."

"Do what? Jump in a sleigh with Charlie and fly off behind eight tiny reindeer?"

"Will you please stop quoting that annoying poem?"

"Sorry."

"That's better. Now, what's the problem?"

"I don't even know where to begin," he said. "First and foremost, I'm probably the least reliable guy in the world. At the first sign of trouble, I'll probably—"

"What? Give up? You'll be in a flying sled with the Boss, maybe a dog or two, and a great load of packages. There's no telling where in the world you'll be. So, are you going to just abandon ship and go looking for a bar? In the middle of the night? On Christmas Eve? With goodness knows how many children depending on you?"

"You're not being fair."

"I'm being *honest*," Doc said, determined to change the way Ray looked at himself and his place in—for him—a radically new universe. "You can do this. You're not the man you once were. You're so much more."

Ray shook his head, still unconvinced. "That's easy for you to say."

"Is it?" She began to wonder if her tactic was doomed. "Let's move our thinking to a slightly wider platform, okay?"

"What do you mean?"

"Think about everything that's happened to you in the past month or so. How much of that could you have predicted?"

Ray looked at her as if she'd addressed him in Swahili. "Uh…."

"None of it," she answered for him. "Not the first thing."

"Well," he said, "I had my job at the mall."

"Granted. But after that?"

"Gloria called me."

"Why?" asked Doc.

"Because she needed help. She wanted me to go to Leon Farms."

"You never noticed that Leon is Noel spelled backwards, did you?"

He laughed. "Ya got me there. Should that have been a clue?"

Doc gripped him by the upper arms and looked straight

229

at him, their faces mere inches apart. "Do you think any of that just happened by coincidence?"

"Well, yeah, actually. I thought—"

"You've been groomed, Ray. It began the first year you signed up to play Santa. The elders had their eyes on you and a hundred or so other potential candidates. They knew the day would come when Charlie Fyfe would toss in the towel."

"A hundred mall Santas?"

"At least. And they picked you."

Ray looked stunned. "*Me?*"

"Yes."

"But how could they know Skeeter would—"

"With the help of the security team during the slack season, they checked out you *and* your family."

"We weren't actually a family back then," he said. "Because of my—"

"Stop it," she said. "That Raymond Mays no longer exists. Accept it and move on."

As he stared into her eyes, something in his demeanor gradually changed. He sat up straighter and cleared his throat. "You really think I can do this? I've had absolutely no training at all. I don't even know—"

"The Boss will take care of that," she said. "He needs you, and he needs you to be successful. He wouldn't turn the job over to just anyone. It's not just that the elders think you can do it, the Committee is behind you as well."

230

"What if I screw something up?"

"It'll simply prove you're human. Elves make mistakes, too." She smiled at him. "So, are you ready to take the next step in your new life?"

He swallowed hard. "If you think I'm ready."

"I do," she said.

"All right then," he said with a thin note of conviction in his voice. "I'll do it."

~*~

Getting the go-ahead to travel with Art came as a huge relief, and Maeve wasted no time updating Art and assembling her remaining team members.

She struggled to look unconcerned though she certainly didn't feel that way. Art insisted on taking care of the loading chores and left it up to her to settle all the dogs. Fortunately, they all knew where they needed to go, and all Maeve had to do was whistle to get them moving.

Finley, Buck, JJ, and Maggie from Art's original crew took their places beside Cody, Zoe, and Maple. She did a quick mental recap of their assigned functions.

Finley and Buck would haul the larger packages and leave the smaller ones to Cody, a sturdy Jack Russel/beagle mix. When not hauling, the two doodles—one Golden and one Labrador—would provide security and watch over the entire team.

The rest—Maggie, JJ, Zoe, and Maple—would feed and operate the stocking fillers, although Maeve still had some concerns about Zoe's ability to concentrate. The smaller

231

version of Cody was little more than a pup.

"I think we're ready to go," Art said.

Maeve checked to make sure all the dogs had moved to their secure travel beds and settled down for the first leg of the initial voyage. It would be a very long night, and she had more confidence in Art and the canines than she had in herself.

Doc had cautioned her not to push herself too hard. "You're part of a two-elf team. You're simply not capable of performing all the tasks you'll face by yourself. So, be smart. Work together. Do the best you can. And if you run into trouble, use your compod. They work anywhere on Earth."

"I just don't want to let you down," Maeve told Art. "I don't want to be a burden."

He laughed off her concerns. "With two of us working together, this'll be a snap."

Once the two of them were settled in their side-by-side command chairs, Art reached for the "Launch" button, but Maeve abruptly stayed his hand.

"What is it?"

"Peanut!" she said, her voice panicky.

Art slipped his hand under the space between their seats and hauled out the little black cat with bright green eyes. "She looks ready to go far as I can tell." He frowned. "Y'know, we never talked about her much. What job is she trained for?"

"You'll see," Maeve said, finally beginning to relax. "Just you wait."

"Whatever you say." Art pressed the button.

The doors to the loading shed opened quietly revealing a night sky frosted with sparkly stars and a full moon shining bright. Good omens all.

As the sled crept forward and its engine revved to launch speed, Art reached for Maeve's hand and gripped it tight. "Here we go. It's gonna be great!"

Maeve prayed he'd be right.

~*~

"She talked you into it, eh?" the Boss asked.

Ray nodded and tried to appear confident. He hoped his acting skills held out.

"Listen Ray, I think we'll get along better if we use our first names, don't you? It'll seem... I don't know, less formal."

"Thanks, Charlie," Ray said. "This is all so new. Anything that makes it easier is welcome."

The Boss took a moment to examine Ray's outfit. "I see you got a proper hat. That's good. You never know when you'll need it. Have you tried it?"

"Only on my daughter. It worked great, and she didn't realize it was happening. I had lunch with her and my grandson."

"Skeeter, right?"

"Yeah. How'd you—"

The Boss laughed. "I'm Santa Claus, remember? I

know all the kids." He paused. "Actually, I only know the ones who write."

"Skeeter *wrote* you a letter?"

"Last year, I think. Or maybe it was the year before."

Ray threw up his hands. "There's no way I'll be able to remember all that—all the different kid's names, where they live, what they want, or more—what *year* they wanted it in!" He shook his head, defeated before he'd even started.

"Fiddlesticks. There's nothing to worry about," Charlie said. "Doc and the elders will help with that. And if all else fails, there are endless computer files. You should've seen all the printouts I dragged along with me." He thumped a video screen on the sled's dashboard. "Now we've got a direct line." He laughed. "And I'm not kidding, when I first started, I could hardly remember my own name."

You were a useless drunk, too? Ray opted not to inquire.

"Nowadays," Charlie went on, "a lot of this is automated. Some genius on the Committee worked things out with the elders."

"What do you mean?"

"I don't have to drive anymore. I pick the landing spots I like, but that's about it. The computer handles the rest."

"And the elders?"

Charlie's lips twisted. "Yeah, them. Gotta tell ya, sometimes they scare me. When I was a kid, the thought of magic excited me. I even kicked around the idea of becoming a magician. You know, on stage. That never panned out. But here? Magic's everywhere."

"I heard about the weather," Ray said.

"That and communications, healthcare, education, housing, food production—all of it is impacted by magic in one way or another. Without it, none of this would be possible." He spread his arms in a grand gesture.

Ray scratched his beard. "Kinda hard for me to fathom it all."

"Me, too," said Charlie. "You ready to get going?"

"I suppose."

"Good!" Charlie put two fingers in his mouth and let out a whistle Ray found most distracting. In response a very old golden retriever meandered toward them. "This ol' gal is my very best friend," Charlie said. "She's come along on my trips for years. Noël, meet Ray."

The old dog lifted her head, tilted it to one side and appeared to smile.

"She's coming with us?" Ray asked, wondering how all three of them would fit on the bench seat.

"You betcha."

"What does she do?"

Charlie looked from Ray to the dog. "She keeps me company."

When Noël was safely stashed in her travel bed, Charlie reached toward the dashboard and punched the Launch button.

Chapter Fourteen

*"We shall see that at which dogs howl in the dark,
and that at which cats prick up their ears after
midnight."* –H. P. Lovecraft

Gloria spent as much time observing her son as she did looking for his dog. They had begun their search walking on the roads, but Skeeter insisted Tater would be more interested in areas featuring trees and shrubs, a change from his usual choices of lampposts and fire hydrants.

"And besides," he said, "there's snow on the ground. So, all we really need to do is find a set of his tracks and follow 'em."

In the face of such irrefutable logic, Gloria agreed to go off-road, though she wished she could've done it in a cozy, all-terrain vehicle rather than go trekking through the woods and fields in street shoes. Fortunately, the snow wasn't the icy wet version which fell in her native Georgia from time to time. Instead, mother and son walked through a six-inch layer of feathery white fluff.

It didn't take long to find the area where Gloria had

previously encountered the dog pack led by Foster and the charming female she'd christened Brandy. She quickly reminded Skeeter of the encounter with special emphasis on the dog without a collar.

"Did I tell you about her?"

Skeeter paused in his search for Tater tracks. "You mean the hound dog with beautiful brown eyes that just melted your poor widdle heart?" He clasped his hands at his chest as if in prayer and ready to swoon. "That one?"

Gloria scooped up a handful of snow and dumped it on him. "Yeah, that one."

Skeeter immediately retaliated, gathering up a double handful of snow which he tried diligently to pack into a ball. The effort failed, however, and he could do little more than throw the mass of flakes at her. "This snow sucks," he said in disgust.

Gloria frowned. "You know I don't like that kind of language."

"Sorry." He kicked up a cloud of snowflakes with his tennis shoe. "It's true though."

"If so, then shouldn't it stick together?"

"Aw, Mom…" Suddenly stopping, Skeeter pointed at a set of tracks that clearly weren't made by a herd.

"Could've been a rabbit," Gloria said.

Skeeter looked hopeful. "Or it coulda been Tater. C'mon! Let's go."

Gloria hurried to catch up with her son who took off

with a burst of speed and energy she hadn't seen in weeks. And while it did her heart good to see him returning to his normal active self, she worried what could happen if she failed to keep up with him.

"Slow down!" she yelled as he crested a steep hill and disappeared on the other side. "Skeet? Did you hear me? Skeeter!"

Panting heavily, she did her best to slog up the hill though slippery spots seemed to find her no matter where she stepped. She went down hard twice before reaching the top. "Skeet? Where the heck are you?"

"Down here," he said. "In the trees."

"Can you please wait for me? I can't keep up!"

"Okay," he said. "I'm gettin' kinda tired, too."

Gloria half slid and half raced down the other side of the hill and eventually made her way into a clutch of trees that had hidden Skeeter from view. He had settled himself on a stump with one leg crossed over the other. He breathed harder than she did.

"You okay?" Gloria asked.

"Yeah."

"Tired?"

He nodded. "And dizzy."

She put her arm around him. "You pushed yourself too hard."

He didn't respond, and Gloria gazed at the hill they had just traversed. She didn't relish the thought of crossing back over it by herself let alone trying to do it while dragging, or possibly carrying him. She looked back at her son. "Think you can haul yourself back up that hill?"

When he meekly shook his head, Gloria began looking for an alternative route, one which didn't include hills or mountains. What she found looked like a valley which ran alongside the hill they'd just scaled.

With the sun already down and Skeeter moving slowly, Gloria worked her way toward what she hoped would be a settled area. Her sense of direction provided no help at all; she was, in a word, lost.

She reached for her compod in order to call her father, then stopped. Ray was with the Boss. They'd probably already made some deliveries; she couldn't call him. The same applied to Artemis and Maeve. That left Doc as the only resident she actually knew, and she likely had her hands full. Surely, they'd want their best healer standing by in case of emergencies. Gloria put her compod away.

"We've gotta keep going, sweetheart," she said as she helped Skeeter stand.

"I'm gettin' cold," he said. "And I'm tired. And I'm afraid. And Tater's tracks don't go in the direction we're goin'. What if he has to stay out all night? He could freeze!"

"Hey, you!" Gloria said in an effort to cheer him up. "He'll be fine. I wouldn't be surprised if he's already holed up somewhere warm and comfy. And that's what we need, too."

Together, they trudged through the snow which grew less accommodating as the night wore on. Gloria constantly looked ahead and behind in order to maintain a fairly straight path. She would either reach civilization, or they'd find the edge of the settlement and the start of truly arctic weather and terrain.

"I'm tired, Mom," Skeeter said for the umpteenth time.

"I know, babe. But we're making progress. We'll—" She stopped talking when she saw lights in the distance and felt a flicker of hope in her heart. "We'll be okay. I promise."

She forged ahead with a renewed sense of vitality. The lights grew brighter, and she pushed Skeeter to move faster.

In the distance she could make out the silhouette of a female waving her arms at them. Gloria waved back, and when she felt they were within hailing distance, she called out, "Help!"

Mere moments later, Doc arrived in an odd conveyance that looked like a motorcycle with dual sidecars, but instead of wheels, the machine had runners. Gloria wouldn't have cared if it rode on carved, wooden dolphins. It was a ride, and Doc was driving.

"Climb in," she said. "I'll have you back at Healer's House before you know it."

They clambered into the vehicle sitting one on either side of the elf.

"Mom!" Skeeter cried out. "What about Tater? It's gettin' colder and darker."

"I know, darlin'. And if Doc will show me how to drive this thing and loan me a decent coat, I'll go back out and look for him."

~*~

Pleased that their first few stops had gone smoothly, Maeve began to relax. The tension she'd felt eased up, and with it went some of the pain in her back and neck. She couldn't help but wonder why her leg didn't hurt, too, but accepted it as simply good karma.

Thus far, the dogs had done an admirable job, and the two elves had encountered no problems. The dream beam worked perfectly; Finley and Buck were eager to haul packages inside; Cody, Maple, and Maggie performed brilliantly when filling stockings, while Zoe and JJ worked on any milk and cookies left out for Santa. These, unfortunately, they ate. Maeve decided to put an end to that. Either Peanut could keep a feline eye on them and make sure they stayed in line, or Maeve would have to take on the chore herself. That, of course, would require that she climb in and out of the sled which might slow them down.

As if it were still more good karma, Peanut rose to the challenge. If either JJ or Zoe even looked like they intended to eat one of the sugary offerings, Peanut would raise a paw and threaten them. After a couple claw-free swats to the nose, both dogs fell into line. Peanut adopted an even more regal stroll while patrolling.

They eventually worked their way to a home that wasn't as accommodating as those on their earlier stops.

"The dream beam didn't work," Art said. "And the door doesn't have a conventional lock." He shook his head. "I've never seen a lock like this. Have you?"

"No," Maeve said. "It's keyless. There must be some sort of digital gizmo that operates it. Wait while I poke around in the tool box. There may be something in there that'll help."

Art struggled to keep the dogs from trying to knock the door down while Maeve hurriedly dug through their tools. When she couldn't find anything that offered even a hint of a solution, she gave Art a look of defeat.

Finley chose that moment to howl, something neither of the elves had ever heard her do; Cody and Zoe instantly added their two cents, barking as if their lives depended on it. Maeve shook off her surprise and scolded the canines in a harsh whisper, "Hush, you three! You'll wake up the whole neighborhood."

The sound of a window sliding open in the upper story got all their attention. The dogs fell silent.

"Who's there? What're you doing? What d'ya want?" asked a thoroughly annoyed, female voice.

Maeve, Art, and their team went silent.

"Tell me," shouted the aggrieved voice, "or I'm callin' the cops!"

~*~

Doc helped Skeeter into the house and guided him back to bed. Though he complained he needed to find Tater more than he needed rest, Doc knew better. "Your Mom's going to find him," she insisted.

She rejoined Gloria in the parlor and offered her food and something hot to drink. Gloria refused both. "Will Skeeter be okay? I know I shouldn't have let him exert himself so much. This is all on me; I'm a terrible parent. I just—"

Doc delicately touched her lips and tried to give her a reassuring smile. "Your son's going to be fine, I promise. This

242

isn't a set-back, it's merely an indication that his will is stronger than his body. They'll both be in synch very soon; I'd guess no more than a week or two."

"I still think he'd do better if Tater were here with him. I know *I'd* feel better!"

"And what about the other dog you're so fond of?"

"Brandy." Gloria's look of apprehension eased dramatically with the mere mention of the dog's name. "I hope to find them both. If not together, I'll track them down separately."

"Just be sure you don't wear yourself down," Doc cautioned. "There are some heavier coats in the foyer closet. Help yourself."

"And that ski machine thing?" Gloria asked. "I don't even know what it's called. How hard is that to handle?"

"It's a snow rover, and it's incredibly simple; you don't even need to balance—the side seats take care of that. There's a pedal on the left which makes it slow and stop and a pedal on the right that makes it go."

Gloria looked less nervous, then frowned. "I have my driver's license, but—"

Doc laughed. "Don't worry. No one's going to stop you. We don't issue licenses here anyway."

"Good!" She slipped on a heavy coat and buttoned it. "Okay then, I'm on my way."

"Please take along a thermos of tea or coffee. It could be a while before you find the dogs. Hang on, I'll get it for you."

Gloria thanked her profusely for everything and then took her leave. Doc prayed she'd be all right. She also prayed the rover had enough fuel.

~*~

Ray couldn't believe how fast Charlie moved. The guy had at least twenty years on Ray, maybe more, but he hustled like a teenager. Ray's admiration for the man did little for his own confidence. If anything, it bruised it further.

"There's a certain rhythm you get into," Charlie explained. "The goodies come out of the storage area ready to go; the doors are almost always unlocked before I get there, and it's not difficult to slip a package or two under the tree, or wherever, and toss some candy into the stockings."

Charlie engaged the autopilot, and they lifted off toward the next stop.

"You make it look effortless," Ray said.

"And *you're* just tryin' to talk yourself out of the best job in the world. So, listen, I want you to handle the next few stops."

"*Me?* But—"

"You. That's right. I'll be sitting right here if you need me, but you won't."

Charlie's smile of reassurance accomplished little, but Ray didn't want to embarrass himself further by refusing to cooperate. "Okay," he said. "I'll do my best."

Noël offered up a melodious howl, and Charlie scratched her behind the ears. "You tell him, babe."

Gloria had only been gone long enough for Doc to do a little clean up in her kitchen. She had some gentle Gaelic music playing in the background. Christmas music, no matter how sweet or moving, got to her after a while since it played continually in public areas all year long.

She responded to a knock at her door and opened it to greet whomever might need her help. "Come right in," she said, stepping away to make room for her oversized guest. She recognized him instantly. "You're Max, aren't you?"

"Yes," he said. "And you're Docquinella Bright, healer and Grand Committee member."

"That's right," she said, wondering what the giant was up to. When she'd been around him earlier he'd smiled. Now he looked positively sinister. "Are you hurt? Does someone need me?"

"I need you," he said. "Is there anyone else here?"

"Just a child. He's sleeping."

"Where?"

"In his room." She gave him a stern look. "What's this all about?"

"Show me the kid," he said, taking her arm in his massive hand and squeezing.

"That hurts!"

He frowned at her. "Of course it hurts! It's supposed to. Now where's the brat?"

She intended to resist, but his size, weight, and strength

245

overwhelmed her. Though she didn't take him on a tour, he dragged her along as he looked in one patient room after another until he found Skeeter.

"Wake him up. See that he's dressed."

"I don't want to leave him alone," she said.

"You won't. He's coming with us."

"*Us?* What are you talking about?"

His voice had all the charm of a wolf's growl. "You're going to show me where the main computer is. The one that stores all the Boss's data."

"And why would I do that?" she asked.

"Because if you don't, I'm going to hurt the kid. Badly."

Doc sucked in a breath. "You wouldn't dare!"

"Try me."

The look in his eyes spelled maniac as clearly as if it had been painted across his broad forehead. "I don't believe you."

He twisted her arm sharply; the pain arrived instantly, and she shrieked.

"Satisfied?" He reached for the compod hanging from her neck and snatched it so hard the cord snapped. "Now get the kid ready to go. We're wasting time."

~*~

Maeve heard another voice, this one deeper, male, and likely responding to the first voice from the window directly above them. "*The cops?* They won't come here. They know who we are. I'll call Vinny and the boys. They'll take care of it. Nobody's gettin' in here!"

Maeve checked the roster for the name of the letter-writer whose efforts resulted in their current delivery. She cleared her throat and tried to sound like a child, "Is this Mattie's house? I know it's late, but we brought her a gift."

"*Mattie?* Mattie who? There's no Mattie here. Get lost!"

"But… But it's from Santa Claus," she added.

"I'll give you a gift from Santa Claus, ya little snot. You just wait 'til I git downstairs!"

Finley and Buck stood side-by-side on the front stoop, as if waiting for the opportunity to tear the homeowner to shreds. Maeve wasted no time calling them back into the sled where Art punched a button on the console. The engine instantly kicked in.

And then stopped.

A bright light came on over the porch, and an angry man yanked open the front door. He held a gun in one hand and a flashlight in the other.

Maeve and Art were both crushing the bulbs at the tassle-ends of their hats, praying the angry homeowner would look in some other direction. Sadly, there was nowhere else for him to look.

Buck and Finley commenced to growl. Their voices combined in a steady, threatening rumble. Cody and Zoe chimed in and barked frantically, as if their combined weight, though about half of Buck's, would make a difference.

"What *is* that thing?" asked the man with the gun, not

waiting for any answers. "Where'd you get it? Why are you here? And what's with all the dogs? I'm warnin' you, if one o' them gits outta that buggy of yours, I'll shoot 'em dead. And trust me; I never miss."

"We're sorry we disturbed you sir," Art said. "We must've been given the wrong address."

The man kept brandishing the gun at them. "Go on. Get outta here!"

Art punched the starter button again, but got only a brief rumble and some silence for his trouble.

"What'sa matter?" asked the annoyed homeowner.

"Nothing," Art said. "I'll get it going in a moment. It's just a little starter issue."

"I'm a patient man," the homeowner said, "but it's the middle of the night, and my wife needs her sleep. I do, too!"

"We apologize," Maeve said. "Truly. We never meant to disturb you."

"You got that thing runnin' yet?"

Finally, the engine turned over, and Art waved goodbye. The man with the gun watched as they trundled down the street. They had no intention of letting him know they could fly. When they reached the corner and turned to get out of sight, Maeve motioned for Art to stop.

"Why?" he asked, his voice on edge.

"Because I don't see Peanut."

Art reached down to the space below and between their seats, then sat upright. "I can't believe it," he said. "She's gone."

Gloria climbed onto Doc's snow rover and grabbed the grips on the handlebar. She pressed the brake pedal and pushed the button to start the machine. It purred to life quickly, giving her an unaccustomed feeling of power. She wondered if the bikers she'd seen on the highways back home suffered the same delusion.

No tattoos or leather jackets for this babe!

She eased her foot off the brake, and the vehicle inched forward. When she pressed down on the accelerator, however, it leaped forward, and she lurched backwards, barely maintaining her grip on the handlebar.

After a few more herky-jerky attempts, she got the hang of the machine and began her search for Tater and Brandy.

The bright moonlight helped and cast the snowy landscape in shades of luminescent gray bordering on white. The trees still looked dark and forbidding, but there weren't many of them, and those were clustered together as if huddling for warmth. Stars blanketed the sky, and while they seemed to radiate light, they did nothing for the cold which was growing progressively worse. The chill wind in her face didn't help either.

Keep moving, girl.

Though the engine powering the snow rover didn't generate loud noise, it did give off enough to obscure distant sounds. Gloria made frequent stops just to listen and call out. She felt sure if Tater heard her voice, he would respond. For the longest time, he didn't.

After weathering the cold and often bleak terrain for

some time—she guessed hours but it couldn't have been all that long—she heard her first dog sounds: howling.

Or maybe they're wolves.

A lifelong victim of her own imagination, Gloria forced herself to ignore the scarier possibilities and focus on finding Skeeter's dog. If there were others as well, she would consider that a bonus.

While the sounds were clear and distinct, she couldn't tell from which direction they'd come. She did, however, have a clear view in all directions, and there were only a few spots, all clumps of evergreens, which offered any cover. She assumed, therefore, the dogs had holed up in one of them.

She struck paydirt on the third try. Nine canines in various shapes, colors, and sizes all sat up as she approached, their tails wagging furiously. All but one wore a collar, but she recognized Brandy instantly. As the others milled about, she read their names as she picked them up one-by-one and distributed them in the sidecars. The two largest, Augie the boxer, and Brandy the hound sat on opposite sides, the way she and Skeeter had when Doc found them. Getting those two loaded taxed her to the limit. Fortunately, the rest of the herd consisted of much smaller animals.

Foster went in next to Brandy. Gloria balanced the white speedster by putting Spike, a feisty schnauzer and Rascal, a big Pomeranian in the seat with Augie. Other than Tater, that left Rosie, a Maltese, and MacKenzie, a Westie, which she placed in opposite seats, exhausting the available space in both.

She looked down at Tater and smiled. "I guess you're riding up here, with me, big guy."

Tater gave it his best and managed to stand on his one hind leg long enough for Gloria to snatch him up and settle him on what she guessed was the fuel tank which stretched out directly in front of her. Tater turned to face her and barked a friendly greeting.

"I love you, too, kiddo. Now, let's get out of here."

She restarted the snow racer, grateful that none of the dogs seemed bothered by the engine noise. With her cargo settled and seemingly happy, she looked out on the horizon and realized she had no idea which way to go.

Ray's first stop went smoothly—easy access, quick delivery, stockings topped off, milk and cookies consumed—all in very short order.

"I've gotta warn ya," Charlie said as he prepped the sled for the next stop. "Take it easy on the goodies folks leave out. They may look tempting now, but I promise that's only temporary." He coughed. "And don't offer any to me. I had my fill, and then some, in New York."

Charlie glanced at a bit of text that flashed on the sled's little computer screen. "Take Noël with you on the next stop," he said.

"Why? You want me to give her the milk and cookies?"

"No way!" Charlie laughed. "She needs to watch her weight more than I do." He pointed at the video screen on the dashboard. "There's a big watchdog living in the next house. I made a note after I ran into him last year. He's a mean brute, a big rottweiler."

Ray gulped. "Uh… Maybe you should do the next one, seeing as how Noël's your dog and all, and you—"

"Not a chance, Santa," Charlie said. "Get ready. With Noël at your side, there isn't a dog on the planet that'd try anything."

"How do you know that?"

"It's the pheromones. Noël's got 'em; the pets we'll run into don't. You'll see."

Swell. I'll be the first Santa ever eaten by a guard dog. My heirs will read about it in the papers: "Yes, Virginia, there was a Santa Claus, but he's been reduced to a canine stool sample."

All too soon they arrived at their next stop which Ray thought of as his Winter Waterloo. Though he had the mild-mannered and profoundly gentle Noël at his side, he knew a good hundred pounds of muscle and teeth awaited him on the other side of the door.

With gifts in hand, Ray hitched up his pants, straightened his hat, tightened his grip on Noël's collar, and stepped as cautiously as possible toward his next delivery.

Chapter Fifteen

"Owners of dogs will have noticed that, if you provide them with food, water, shelter, and affection, they will think you are God. Whereas owners of cats are compelled to realize that, if you provide them with food, water, and affection, they draw the conclusion that they are God." –Christopher Hitchens

"Where could Peanut be?" Maeve asked, frantically searching for the black cat that should have been lounging in her sheltered bed beneath the center armrest.

"I don't know," Art said. "I thought you were looking after her."

"I was watching the dogs! And… and the knucklehead with the gun."

"We've gotta go find her," Art said.

Maeve frowned. "Shouldn't we at least wait until that guy goes back to bed? And what about the other guy they mentioned?"

"*Vinnie?* Or maybe it was Vito."

"Doesn't matter," Maeve said. "They both sound like gangsters."

"I have no idea," Art said. "But I think I'd rather go a couple rounds with Max the Monster."

"I know it's going to hurt our schedule to go look for her, but we can't leave Peanut behind. We just can't." She gave him a gesture of futility.

"I know, I know." Art's voice all but disappearing as he exhaled. "Do we have any other stops around here?"

Maeve checked the computer screen that plotted all their deliveries. She shook her head. "Not a one. Next stop's one town over. A place called Bloomfield." She squinted. "They must be big on flowers."

"Humans," Art said. "What do you expect?"

"If you'll hop out and sneak back there, you could look around. You could call me when you find her," Maeve said.

Art's lips twisted, then he looked at the massive cast on her leg and sighed. "Yeah. Okay. But you'll owe me for this."

She gave him the brightest smile she could muster. "I promise I'll make it up to you."

"Seriously?"

She responded with an evil grin that had an unsettling effect on him. She loved it.

"Well, then," he said as he hopped out of the sled. "That settles it. I'll call you as soon as I find her."

JJ and Maple jumped out of the sled and ran past him

toward the house they'd just left behind, JJ executing a splendid glissade.

Maeve turned the sled around and prepared for an emergency pick-up followed by an immediate take-off. With any luck, Art would be able to hang onto the cat while he loaded the two little dogs and climbed aboard.

~*~

Gloria and her nine passengers remained in lock-down mode while she tried to figure out what to do next. Her compod call to Doc had gone unanswered, and everyone else she knew was out delivering packages.

MacKenzie, the aging West Highland terrier, and Rascal, the feisty Pomeranian, got her attention with a pair of low whines, almost in harmony.

"I know; I know. We've got to get out of here. I'm just not sure which way to turn."

Rascal and Rosie, the Maltese, made it clear they were losing patience. Tater bumped his head against her forearm.

"Now what?" she asked.

Once again, he bumped his head just above her wrist.

Gloria stared at him "You want me to turn?"

When he barked and wagged his tail, Gloria gave in. With the engine purring, she turned the snow racer in the direction the dog had indicated and pressed the accelerator. The machine took off quickly though its load had more than doubled.

Tater appeared confident and sat with his back pressed

tight against her stomach. Whenever he touched his head to one of her arms she shifted in that direction. In no time at all, they reached Healer's House, and Gloria brought the odd little vehicle to a stop.

As she prepared to usher the canine herd indoors, she noticed the front door stood wide open. A hat like the kind Santa wore hung from the doorknob. Suddenly concerned something was wrong, she raced into the house and called for Skeeter.

He didn't respond.

Tater entered the building behind her along with the other dogs. They all congregated in the parlor while Tater nosed about—first in Skeeter's room, then in the kitchen and dining room. When he reached Gloria's side, he sat in front of her and barked, then proceeded to the front door and barked again.

Gloria felt as if she'd fallen into a very strange edition of a Lassie movie, and she was playing the role of the canine prodigy's adolescent owner. "Where to now?" she asked.

Rosie, a spunky little Maltese, leaped up and down a few times before she was able to yank the Santa hat off the knob. Tater responded with an excited string of barks which the other dogs quickly copied. Before Gloria knew it, they had all raced back outside and settled themselves in the snow racer.

Gloria shook her head. She had no choice but to follow along. After all, Tater had saved them from a night out in the cold. The least she could do was give him a chance to find her son and the healer.

What harm could it do?

Ray almost wished the dream beam *hadn't* worked on little Malik Morrisey whose letter to Santa resulted in this delivery. It wouldn't have been a problem if the tyke shared the address with a hamster instead of a hellhound.

With Noël's collar in one hand, and Malik's gift in the other, Ray nudged the front door open and peeked inside. Though the lighting offered little by way of details, he could easily make out the shape of a large animal lounging directly in front of some stockings suspended from a table. A nearby tree appeared to have been decorated with castoffs and hand-me-downs.

No wonder Malik wrote to Santa.

A low, menacing growl put an end to Ray's reverie. Noël heard it, too, and strained to move closer to the sound. "Are you nuts?" he whispered to her.

As he passed another table, he noticed a small, but carefully crafted gingerbread house sitting in the middle of it. He leaned closer and inhaled, then backed away, overcome by the urge to sneeze.

Oh, Lord. Please don't let me—

Too late.

Ray's sneezes were not quite measurable on the Richter scale, but he felt sure his latest could have been heard several doors away.

The rottweiler stood swiftly and aimed its massive head toward them. Ray prayed Noël had launched a flotilla of pheromones in the beast's direction. He tightened his grip on the dog's collar and stood motionless.

This is taking too long. I should've been in, out, and gone by now. Gingerbread! How stupid of me.

The huge rottweiler backed away slowly, head down, and continued to growl.

Ray managed a partial sigh of relief but then felt another sneeze coming. He let go of Noël's collar in order to pinch his nose and dashed forward to slip Malik's gift under the tree. He dumped goodies into all the stockings since none of them bore names, then made a mad dash to the door.

Noël followed him, walking backwards while maintaining eye contact with the massive guard dog.

Ray closed the door as soon as Charlie's dog cleared the threshold, and they both hopped back aboard the sled. At that point, Ray's need to sneeze had subsided. He took a few shuddering breaths.

"How'd it go?" Charlie asked,

Ray wiped his brow. "Piece of cake."

"Oh, yeah? What kind?"

If looks could kill… "Gingerbread," Ray managed to say and then sneezed even louder than before.

"I figured that foghorn was you," Charlie said. "Next year, when you're doing this on your own, remember to take something before launch."

"Next year? You think I'm going to want to do this *again?*"

Charlie favored him with a wide smile. "Yep. I'm pretty

sure you will." He reached in his pocket, pulled out a package of tablets, and handed them to Ray. "Help yourself. Doc gave 'em to me. I'm allergic to certain fir trees."

~*~

Though Doc had no choice but to do as Max demanded, she was determined to cross him up somehow. Her first opportunity occurred as they were leaving Healer House. She grabbed a Santa hat from a coat rack by the front door and hung it on the knob. She not only didn't lock the front door, she left it wide open. Max was too preoccupied with the boy struggling in his arms to notice.

"Where are you taking us?" she asked as he jammed her into a seat in his vehicle. The question was meant as a distraction; she already had a strong suspicion about his destination.

"Like I said before, take me to the main computer."

Doc threw up her hands and feigned helplessness. "What makes you think I even know where it is?"

"'Cause you're on the Committee. You know all the secrets."

"That's absurd. There's a reason they're called 'secrets.' Few of us know everything, and I'm not one of them."

Max squeezed Skeeter's arm until the boy cried out.

"Leave him alone!" she yelled.

Max grunted. "You gonna get me to where I want to go?"

"I can make an educated guess."

He let go of the boy's arm. "That's a start."

The distance between Healer House and the Boss's office complex wasn't far, and she knew that's where the main data processing equipment was stored and operated. Backup data storage had been set up on the opposite side of the settlement. Max could likely guess where either was located, but he clearly didn't intend to find them on his own.

"Don't bother trying to confuse me or lengthen the trip," he warned. "I know these streets as well as anyone."

Doc exhaled wearily. "Then head for the Boss's office. I imagine what you're looking for is in there somewhere."

"I hope you're ready to unlock doors," he said with a sneer, "or Junior here is gonna be very unhappy."

"Why are you doing this? What do you hope to accomplish?"

He laughed. "You wouldn't understand."

"You don't know that."

"You're an elf; I know that much. And I don't trust elves."

"But—"

"I'm on a mission. That's all you need to know."

"A mission for who?"

Max's face lit up. "For God."

"I don't understand what you're talking about, but if you intend to destroy any—"

"Shut up," he bellowed. "When I want your input, I'll

ask for it."

They continued in relative silence until they reached Santa's quarters. He and Angelina lived in a rustic looking yet comfortably furnished home on a large wooded lot. A series of paths led from that building to others arranged in a semi-circle. The open side faced a horizon that featured a dramatic set of rugged, snow-topped mountains.

"Where's the computer?" Max asked again.

Doc pointed to one of the out-buildings. "Probably in there, but I can't be sure. I've never seen it."

"What a liar," Max muttered as he shoved Skeeter ahead of him. When they got to the locked front door of the unlighted building, he ordered Doc to open it.

"I don't know—"

"I can either twist the kid's arm or just rip it right out of his shoulder. You got a preference?"

"Don't you dare hurt that child," she said.

"Or what? You gonna pinch me?" He lifted the boy by his shoulders. "Open the door, now!"

Doc grudgingly complied by waving the enchantment that sealed it, and all three moved inside. She left the door slightly ajar.

"Where's the computer?"

"We'll have to look for it," Doc said with a straight face. "Like I told you; I've never been near it."

They searched several rooms until they reached the Boss's office. Doc had been careful to restore the locking spell on the rooms Max wasn't interested in. If anyone from Security had any inkling about what was going on, they'd only have to search the unlocked rooms.

"Is that what I think it is?" Max asked, pointing to a huge, antique wooden desk. "Is that where the Boss works?"

"I believe so," she said, noting the piles of paper, overflowing inbox, and a Santa Claus model train.

"And where's the computer? I'm losing my patience." Once again, he threatened to hurt Skeeter, though the boy gamely pretended he wasn't injured or afraid.

"It's in there," Doc said, nodding at a door in the far wall.

Max shoved Skeeter to one side and grabbed Doc's arm instead. With his free hand, he extracted what looked like a brown paper-wrapped brick from a satchel hung over his shoulder. "Open the door," he barked. "Now."

~*~

When her curiosity got the better of her, Maeve cranked up the sled and inched back toward the gunman's house, hoping to spot Peanut and her three companions without being seen by the homeowner. She cruised by the house and came to a stop outside a shed-like building behind it. There she looked from the street through an open door in the shed as a flashlight beam probed the darkness.

Moments later, Art walked through with an old and very worn, toy wagon under his arm. Immediately behind him marched Peanut followed by JJ and Maple. The two dogs stayed so close to each other they appeared to be welded together. The sight made Maeve smile.

"Got Mattie's gift?" Art asked.

She slipped it into Maple's harness. "Right here," she said. "What's with the wagon?"

He turned it so she could read a childish scrawl on the side—Mattie—the name featured purple paint with pink accents. "So, there really is a Mattie living here."

"That's what I think," Art said. "I'm going to leave the present in the wagon on the front porch. Kindly pray I don't get shot in the process."

When the delivery was completed, Art and the dogs climbed back into the sled. Peanut had already resumed her spot beneath the console.

"What made you go inside the shed?" Maeve asked.

"Peanut." He reached down and gently stroked the black cat. "She may be our smallest team member, but she's smart. She led me into the shed and jumped up in the wagon. She wouldn't move until I inspected it. That's when I saw the name painted on it and realized there was something fishy goin' on."

"You did the right thing," Maeve said. "I feel a lot better, especially since we haven't actually lost anyone." She looked down at Peanut, though the cast on her leg made it difficult. "Next time, don't be so secretive."

In response, the cat yawned and curled up on her bed.

"This isn't our last stop by a long shot," Art said. "We need to make up for lost time."

"Then, let's boogey!" Maeve punched the launch button.

Despite his objections, Ray finished most of the deliveries before they had to reload. That process came as a complete surprise. He had no idea Charlie and his elf brethren had figured out how to resupply the sleds in much the same way the U.S. Air Force refueled aircraft in mid-flight.

And when it came time to do it, he found himself all but petrified.

"It has to be this way," Charlie explained. "The sleds are as big as they can be, but they're still not big enough to carry everything we have to distribute. Not in one night." He paused long enough to kiss his fist and thump his heart. "Thank goodness we have the international date line in our favor. It actually gives us almost 48 hours to complete our rounds."

"Ah ha!" Ray said. "That explains why I'm so dang tired."

Charlie laughed. "Suck it up, buttercup. We're just getting started."

Somehow, the much larger aircraft overhead managed to funnel packages into the sled's hold, once there, they sorted themselves into delivery frames as if handled by a pixie-powered postmaster. When finished, the larger craft moved on to connect with other sleds.

"This is all pretty mind-blowing," Ray said.

"I hear ya," Charlie responded. "The only good thing about the so-called 'good old days' was greatly reduced volume. We're going to have to keep an eye on things going forward, or we'll fall behind. And I'd really hate to see that. Despite all the techno-stuff, at heart we're still just a mom 'n pop operation.

"Right," Ray said as his mind wandered toward the "Mom" part of the equation. He'd lost the only woman he'd ever truly loved; if he took over for Charlie, could he ever find someone else, someone who might be able to fill the void in his heart?

"What d'ya think of Doc?" Charlie asked. "She's single, ya know."

And suddenly Ray thought he might have found an answer.

As before, Tater seemed to have a built-in sense of direction and used his head-butting technique to instruct Gloria on how to proceed. She forged ahead, firm in the knowledge that, at this point anyway, any leadership that might reunite her with her son was better than anything she had to offer.

While they zipped down the snow-covered lanes, she attempted to contact the few she knew who lived in Santa's settlement. Ray and Maeve both responded that they were hip-deep in deliveries and had no idea where Doc was or what she might be up to.

"I thought she was standing by in case one of the teams ran into trouble and needed an emergency consultation," Maeve said.

"That's what I thought, too," Gloria responded. "But she's not answering when I call her."

"That's scary," Art said. Gloria heard his voice in the background. "Keep trying!" he said. "It's imperative that she remain on-call."

"Will do," Gloria said, having not the slightest clue how she might carry through on the promise.

Her father offered even less, and it was abundantly clear to her that he was doing his best just to keep up with his mentor. He wouldn't be returning to the settlement any time soon.

Gloria tried Doc's compod one more time, and once again, there was no answer. She looked up at the buildings whizzing by the loaded-to-the-max snow racer. Every last one of the dogs had aimed their noses into the wind, their ears flying. The sight warmed her heart.

The longer it took to reach a destination—any destination—the more active her imagination became. She had no idea how she might find Skeeter. The only thing she did know, was that something was very, very wrong.

Tater went through a number of corrections during their helter-skelter race to wherever it was the little dog had in mind. But eventually they closed on a charming, two-story cottage backed by a half ring of small, industrial-looking buildings.

Santa's house?

She and the dogs piled out of their conveyance and raced toward the nearest building, a cottage ripped from a Currier and Ives lithograph. Gloria pounded on the front door, and an older woman answered. She appeared slightly confused.

"I'm looking for my son," Gloria began. "He's with an elf named Docquinella. Have you seen either of them?"

The woman broke into a smile. "I know Docquinella. She's so sweet. Is she all right?"

"I don't know," Gloria said. "That's what I'm trying to find out. Do you know where she is?"

"Healer House, I imagine," the woman said. "She's really sweet. Did I mention that?"

Gloria couldn't keep from giving her a closer look. "Uh… Right. Well, I'm sorry to bother you. Have a nice night."

"You, too, dear," she said. "Merry Christmas!"

MacKenzie had one of Gloria's pants cuffs in her mouth trying to pull her away. Rosie must have thought that was a great idea and did the same to Gloria's other cuff. The added ten pounds made little difference, but Gloria got the message.

"I'm coming. I'm coming! Jeepers," she muttered.

The dogs, led by Tater, formed a rough phalanx as they grouped together and headed toward one of the nearby buildings. Gloria had to hurry to keep up with them. Though most of the herd consisted of senior dogs, none acted their age.

Bursting through the front entrance, Gloria expected to run into outraged elves with weapons raised and sympathies lowered. Instead she found a deserted building. While most of the dogs milled around aimlessly, Tater began an aroma-based tour of the interior, stopping at each doorway and testing the floor and walls for a familiar scent.

When he howled for attention, the other dogs immediately raced toward him. Tater looked at Gloria, and his appearance shrieked impatience.

"I'm coming," she said. "Hold your horses."

She opened the door, and the dogs poured in like a tidal wave of canines. Gloria followed them, still expecting to run into armed guards of some kind. Much to her surprise, she ran into Doc and Skeeter, both of whom were staring at the milling mass of dogs.

"What the—" began the other occupant of the room.

Barking dogs blotted out whatever else he meant to say. The two largest, Augie and Brandy held the huge man at bay, daring him to make a move while Foster showed his teeth and circled around looking for a quick way in and out.

"What's going on here?" Gloria cried when she saw Doc sheltering her son.

Doc didn't answer.

Meanwhile, the smaller dogs, Rosie, Spike, Rascal and MacKenzie, kept up a steady roar of barks, growls, and nips. They danced back and forth biting whatever body parts they could reach. Brandy and Augie, being much larger, sought more delicate targets. The big man backed away from them, his hands trembling so much he dropped whatever he'd been holding in order to try and protect the more sensitive parts of his anatomy.

The dogs pressed on.

"You okay, Skeet?" Gloria asked.

"Yes'm. But that guy's mean. I hope the dogs eat him!"

"That's a bit extreme," Doc said. "Have you got your compod, Gloria?" She gestured at the giant. "That idiot took ours."

"Got it right here," she said.

"Call Security before he hurts someone."

"Before he hurts Tater!" Skeeter yelled.

The look on the big man's face suggested he would gladly surrender to anyone who might save him from the dogs. "I give up," he groaned. "Just call 'em off. Please! Call 'em off!"

A security team arrived later by which point Max had been reduced to a quivering pile of frightened flesh. Gloria, Doc, and Skeeter got the dogs to calm down and the security team hauled Max to his feet.

Skeeter dashed from his mother's side and managed to land solid kicks to both of the big man's shins before Gloria collared him and dragged him away.

Doc addressed the jumpsuit clad team. "Find someplace to store this moron until the Committee decides what to do with him.

"I demand a lawyer," Max growled.

"You've been here long enough to know we don't have any," Doc said.

One of the four guards reached down and retrieved the brick-like package Max had dropped.

"What's that?" Gloria asked.

"C4, I think," came the reply. "It's an explosive."

Doc had been searching the satchel Max previously carried and held up two small objects. "I suspect these are the timer and detonator." She glared at the prisoner. "What a lovely

Christmas you planned."

"Can I kick him again now?" Skeeter asked. "Please?"

Epilog

Epilog
*"There's nothing sadder in this world than to wake up
on Christmas morning and not be a child."* –Erma
Bombeck

Doc knew most of the residents of Santa's settlement would be asleep during the day after Christmas, so she always planned her post-holiday gatherings in the evening when everyone would be rested. Similar parties were held throughout the area and were all well attended.

She also knew it would be crowded in her parlor and put in a special request to the elders to see if they could expand it a bit for the evening. To her surprise, they agreed without the usual back and forth required of such things. They told her it was the least they could do in light of the circumstances and wished her and her guests well.

The invitees who weren't already staying in Healer House arrived right on time. Maeve and Artemis entered holding hands and exchanging the sorts of looks young lovers everywhere had mastered eons ago.

The guests of honor were Charlie and Angelina Fyfe.

They arrived wearing non-traditional garb.

Ray, also dressed in something that wasn't red and fur-trimmed, sat with his daughter and grandson on the sofa.

Between the fireplace and a well decorated Christmas tree lounged the dogs, Tater and Brandy.

The room bore the aromas of the season, the sounds of a crackling fire, and the bright colors of Christmas.

"Before we sit down for our traditional Day-After-Christmas feast," Doc said, "I'd like to bring everyone up to date on an item or two of interest."

She nodded in Maeve and Art's direction. "My young friends here have announced their plans to handfast in the days to come, and they've asked me to invite all of you to join in the celebration."

Skeeter leaned into his mother and asked, "Is a handfast like a real quick handshake?"

Gloria smiled. "No, sweetheart. It means they're getting married."

"Oh, that's cool," he said. "Must be an elf thing."

Doc continued. "My dear friend, Charlie Fyfe is retiring. He and his charming bride, Angelina, will be going on a cruise somewhere warm as soon as he's rested. I'll be keeping an eye on Noël, their four-legged family member."

At the mention of Charlie's dog, Gloria stood up and walked over to Brandy. She stroked the animal's head and whispered something in her ear. Brandy stood up, shook herself, ambled over to Ray and took a seat with her head in his lap.

Ray looked up in surprise. "I thought you wanted to keep her."

"I'd be happy to," she said. "But from everything I've heard about your flights with Charlie, you'll need her more than I will."

"Thank you," Ray said as he hugged the no-longer-stray mutt. "Thank you, both."

Doc turned her attention to Skeeter as Gloria went back to the sofa. "While I'm sure this has been a Christmas you're not likely to forget, it's been just a tiny bit thin in the gift department."

Skeeter lowered his head and nodded.

Gloria blushed and started to speak, but Doc smiled and waved her off. "I hope we'll be able to fix that today." She walked across the room and ducked into the hallway for just a moment. When she returned, a tall man with a broad smile accompanied her.

Gloria's jaw dropped. "*Jimmy?*" she said, her voice trembling. "Is it really you?"

"*Dad?*" Skeeter said.

When the man nodded and knelt down, Skeeter shot from the couch as if spring-loaded, tore across the room, and wrapped his arms around the man's neck.

Gloria was close behind, and the three of them ended in a pile on the floor. Even Tater climbed in. Eventually the four of them settled themselves on the sofa.

"I wanted to tell you about him earlier, Gloria," Doc confessed, "but the elders thought it best that I wait until Jim had his final treatment. I'm happy to report it worked, and his memory has been totally restored."

"Where have you been?" Gloria asked him.

"I lived on the streets for a long time," he said. "I had no idea who I was or where I came from. It was terribly frustrating, a complete nightmare. And then, one day, Doc came to the shelter where I was staying and convinced me to come here."

"That was a couple years ago," Doc said. "When we began taking a longer look at your father. While we've been working to restore Jim's memory, he's been managing one of the Leon Farm locations."

"I had no idea," Gloria said, still gripping her husband's arm as if to keep him from fading away. "I thought you were—"

"Gloria," Doc said, "if you and Skeeter are agreeable, we thought the three of you could move into our Georgia farm. If you're willing to manage the place in lieu of paying rent, we'll gladly make the deal, and one or both of you will receive a salary. That will also make it easy for Jim and Skeeter to continue to get our produce which will keep them well."

"And finally," she said with yet another smile, "Ray has something he'd like to say."

Ray stood up, walked toward her, and slipped his arm around her waist. "I've been asked to take over for Charlie, although I'm still not sure what made him or the Committee think I'm capable of it."

Doc delivered a playful punch to his shoulder. "We *know* you are."

"Anyway," he said, "I told them I'd agree on one condition." He slowly scanned the room, looking at each face in turn and stopped when he once again looked at Doc.

"Well, Dad," Gloria said, "what's the condition?"

His mouth twisted before he spoke. "Actually, that's still sorta up in the air."

"He told the Committee," Doc said, "brazenly, I might add, that he'd only take the job if I agreed to play the part of Mrs. Claus."

"The thing is," Ray added, "I didn't want her to just pretend. I wanted her to *be* my wife, too."

Charlie chimed in, "All right then Doc, are you gonna keep us in suspense? What'd you say?"

She grinned. "I think it's high time I got hitched, and who better to spend my life with than Santa Claus?" She kissed Ray on the lips. "I love you."

"I love you, too," he said.

"Aw, c'mon guys," Skeeter said. "That's so mushy. Can we go eat now?"

~*~

Ormsby Ivanov sat in his study looking at his twin sons, Mordecai and Maximillian. They sat on a wide sofa under the sobering glare of the Ivanov patriarch whose image had been faithfully rendered in dark colors on a huge canvas.

Ormsby held a note he'd found pinned to Maximillian's clothing. The young man had been left bound and gagged on the front porch. Mordecai had freed him and accompanied him into the house. Once inside, the new arrival described his failure to destroy the Boss's computer.

The twins' father managed to keep both his anger and his disappointment in check, largely because of the contents of the note which he read for the tenth time:

Mr. Ivanov,

Don't be too hard on Max or Mordecai. They may appear fine now, but they will both soon suffer from an ailment that's unavoidable in those born of elf and human couples. Their memories will disappear completely. They won't remember you or anything you've taught them, including your hate.

The change is rapid and irreversible, at least for those living solely in the human world. For those of us who strive to fulfill the dreams of Santa Claus at Christmastime, there is a cure. But we reserve the right to choose who receives it. Those who do not share our desire to bring joy to children on one special night each year, will remain at the very bottom of our list.

Signed,

Docquinella Bright

~ End ~

About the Author

Josh Langston's fiction has been published in a variety of magazines and anthologies, and both his Christmas and Western short story collections have reached the Amazon top 20 for genre fiction. His many novels are split between historical fiction and, with the exception of this title and one other, contemporary fantasy.

Josh also loves to teach. His classes on novel writing, memoir, and independent publishing are filled with students eager to learn and have their work perused by a pro. His textbooks on the craft of fiction, memoir, and novel writing provide a humorous and easy-to-understand approach to the subjects while imparting valuable tips and techniques. **Naked Notes!** is the fourth title in his textbook series and was released in 2018.

Josh loves to chat with book clubs and can be reached via email at: **DruidJosh@gmail.com**. Be sure to visit his website, too: **www.JoshLangston.com**

~*~

Turn the page for an added bonus: Chapter One of **Garden Clubbed!**, a story about mums, mobsters, and mayhem all centered around a garden club trophy in a small Georgia town where the ladies growing the flowers make some outrageous plans....

Garden Clubbed!

Chapter One

"Whatever women do they must do twice as well as men to be thought half as good. Luckily this is not difficult."
– Charlotte Whitton

Everyone agreed, the Hildegard Henderson Horticultural Award had to be the most bizarre, garish, and wholly undesirable trophy ever conceived. Standing just over four feet tall, it was unrivaled for its tasteless use of semi-precious gems, jewelry grade metals, and hand-blown glass from the famed island of Murano in Venice, Italy. How someone had managed to assemble so many lovely things into something so incontestably hideous was a question only the late founder of the St. Charlotte Garden Club could answer.

Sadly, the trophy's namesake had gone on to that horticultural haven in the hereafter before she'd taken the time to explain what her second-in-command daintily referred to as "diddly squat."

Ramona Dorn, newly elevated leader of the middle Georgia club, paced slowly around the alleged prize making little clicking noises with her tongue, just as most of the other club members had. The object of their concern sat on a velvet-clad pedestal near the front of the club's meeting space, the so-called "grand ballroom" of the Charles County Convention Center. The Center, also home to the Kiwanis, the Junior League, and every other social and/or civic club in the county, occupied the remains of the former Dew Come Inn near the edge of town where a fire had conveniently eliminated the motel's rooms. The only structure still standing had been unattached to the main building and thus escaped the conflagration unscathed.

Ramona closed her eyes and uttered a silent prayer, asking the Almighty for enough strength to see her through the rest of her term as Acting President of the club, a job she had never sought and one which could not end soon enough.

"Ramona, dear," breathed Constance DuBois, the club's resident expert on all things gossip worthy, "have all the terms of the contest been finalized? There's a nasty little rumor going 'round about—"

"Please, Connie. Stop. I'm doing the best I can to pull this thing together. I don't need anyone spreading tales about anything right now."

"Well," coughed the matronly club member. "I certainly hope you're not referring to me!"

"I'm speaking in generalities," Ramona said, not wanting to become a target for one of the club's worst verbal manure spreaders. "As far as I can tell, the rules are set in stone."

"But—"

"Make that granite. Titanium, maybe."

Constance bristled. "That's not a stone."

"Right. But you get the idea."

"I s'pose," she said, breathing out in a prolonged hiss. "And once again, Hildegard Henderson gets her way."

Ramona shrugged. "That's one way to look at it. She could have left her money to—"

"The membership?"

"I was going to say 'charity.' An orphanage or something." With her eye on the overly made-up rumor monger at her side, Ramona thought perhaps a clown college would have been a more worthy recipient.

Constance continued, "It just seems like our dear departed leader might have found a better use for her wealth than this ridiculous contest and..." She paused for breath, as if the room's air had been tainted by the presence of the trophy. "That... thing."

"And yet," Ramona said, "a lot of our members intend to compete for it. Especially the younger ones."

Constance limited herself to a soft grunt. What remained unspoken, by them and most of the other garden clubbers, was the other half of the award, the real reason so many wanted the prize.

~*~

Sheila Moran tried not to look too obvious as she stared at the garden club trophy in front of her. All but dripping with jewels, the prize which had drawn so much disdain from the other club members looked like a gift from God to her. She had to have it. Hoping to remain somewhat discreet when taking cell phone snapshots of the prize, she kept her mobile device at hip level throughout the process. With any luck, one or more of the photos would capture the trophy in depth and give her the opportunity to examine it at her leisure.

As one of the newest club members, Sheila had yet to meet many of the others. She'd grown up in a suburb of Atlanta, but most of the club members seemed to be locally grown. Profound Southern accents were the rule rather than the exception. While Atlanta had become more and more cosmopolitan, St. Charlotte retained—and prided itself—on its rural roots.

Though the club considered its primary goals to be garden-oriented, in reality it served a very different function—to provide a social outlet for its many participants. One simply had to join the clique or face the prospect of being a social outcast. Sheila's interests, however, were more fiduciary than floral. Having influential friends, especially those with conspicuous wealth, could provide a multitude of options for someone like her. She had learned early in life that ethics were fine, provided they didn't get in one's way.

Sheila loved the sparkle of all the little gems on the trophy. Though not classically trained, she could spot a valuable stone as well as any jeweler, and this monstrous compilation of Tiffany flotsam offered more than its share. Best of all, if she won it, nobody would expect to see it again before the following year's competition for it began. Her devious little mind whirled with possibilities.

More pragmatist than optimist, Sheila also realized she'd need nothing less than a Herculean effort to create a competitive garden, a task made even more daunting by the fact she knew nothing about plants. Her horticultural knowledge was limited to a corsage from a high school suitor and a few bouquets gleaned from various romantic adventures.

She refused, however, to let that little detail stand in her way. In fact, she had already begun to form a plan.

~*~

William Broome, known as "Bubba" to most townsfolk, held the title of Site Manager for the Charles County Convention Center. The CCCC, while not a huge building, did provide a non-denominational setting for just about anything and anyone other than the annual 4H Club's Livestock Show. Bubba's current job entailed many of the same duties he'd had as the former manager of the Dew Come Inn, plus any required maintenance. No one could prove he had anything to do with the fire, although his uncle, Odell Odum, the town Sheriff, had questioned him soundly, a process which took nearly a half hour, after which the two went out for lunch.

Bubba watched with more than a casual eye as the garden club ladies ambled slowly around the grand prize as if viewing the guest of honor at a circus funeral. Though their expressions appeared suitably dour, many engaged in animated discussions once they ventured near the back of the room. Most of those chats seemed focused on the mental stability of the trophy's creator and/or the woman who had funded it. The chats which garnered most of his attention were those that touched on the materials that went into the award's construction. This included silver and more than a few bits of gold, to say nothing of gemstones. All of which coalesced in his mind as one thing: unburied treasure.

"Just getting by," at the ripe old age of twenty-five, was a lifestyle Bubba struggled to accept. A little treasure could go a long way toward changing that lifestyle into something far more desirable. But dreams of unbridled wealth weren't the only things to occupy his mind as he eyed the procession of females giving the grand prize their critical review. He'd always thought garden clubs were the exclusive province of old ladies, and yet if the parade in the ballroom was any indication, this club had plenty of younger members. Some, no more than a few years his senior, could have held their own in any number of beauty contests. A lifelong fan of bathing suit competitions, he'd never missed one available on his TV screen. More than once he'd thanked God for cable.

Bubba wiped his forehead with a sleeve. He wasn't used to having his imagination fired so acutely.

Once Ramona ended the meeting and disengaged from a gaggle of garden clubbers asking questions she'd already answered a half dozen times, she made her way home and poured herself a queen-sized glass of much-needed wine. It wasn't a great vintage, not that she cared. The selection at the local Piggly Wiggly left something to be desired, but it met her needs. Feet up and glass in hand, she closed her eyes and relaxed for what seemed like the first time since hearing of Hildegard Henderson's passing. Hildie had been in excellent health, but Ramona never asked her about her desire to visit potentially dangerous places. Clearly, that had been a strategic blunder. She now felt she had little choice but to honor her reluctant pledge to serve as the club's primary officer.

"We've needed someone younger for quite a while," Hildie had said. "We need someone with new ideas, new ways of thinking, and new ways of getting things done."

Ramona had serious doubts about the club's

willingness to do *anything* differently, much less new. That included any thinking process which hadn't evolved during the club's century-plus existence. With that in mind, she'd agreed to serve as the organization's Vice President, a position she hoped would carry few, if any, responsibilities.

Ramona didn't regret joining the organization, though her original intent had nothing to do with socializing, much less learning about shrubs and flowers, or—God forbid—vegetables. She simply wanted to help secure new clients for her son's burgeoning landscape business. Young Donny was earnest and kindhearted but lacked the killer instinct Ramona assumed lay at the heart of any commercial venture.

Donny faced stiff competition. St. Charlotte had more landscapers than one might reasonably expect to find in a Southern country town of middling size. Much to her surprise, however, Donny did reasonably well, especially after he brought some of his college pals on board. Muscular and athletic, Donny's crews usually worked bare-chested during the warmer months, and while many of the garden club ladies commented on it, few ever complained.

Ramona had no idea Hildie even knew who Donny was, so it came as a distinct shock when she discovered Hildie had included a paid-up subscription for Donny's services as the other half of the annual award for her namesake competition. In addition to "ownership" of the garish trophy, this amounted to ten hours of landscape-related labor, per week, for a calendar year to be provided by Donny and/or one of his workers. Materials were not included.

The only conclusion Ramona could draw from this was that Hildie had guaranteed her award would be sought after, at least for as long as Donny hired healthy young studs to do the grunt work.

Grunt work. The irony made her laugh. She had to admit, though sneaky, old Hildie was successful, and Ramona admired that. Some of the younger members would be all in for the laborers, and maybe even some of the labor, while the older members would be assured of having plenty to talk about. A win-win if there ever was one.

~*~

Once home, Sheila had the opportunity to examine her snapshots. She took her time with the study.

The trophy, she assumed, was meant to resemble a garden trowel stuck blade-down in a pail, both of which were apparently fashioned from silver. The handle of the over-sized trowel, along with the "topsoil" in the bucket, were littered with sparkly gems. Surrounding the pail and trowel were long, slender stems of gold supporting glass blossoms in various colors. Sheila assumed there was some correlation between the glass blooms and those which occurred in nature, but she couldn't be sure. That was a gardener thing, and she was hardly a gardener.

Given enough time, she figured she could duplicate the entire thing in faux gems and silver plate. With any luck, she'd be long gone before anyone noticed the switch. She'd have the gold and silver melted down and the gemstones neatly separated by size, weight, and clarity. She doubted any were so valuable that they carried identifying marks; those were usually reserved for jewelry grade stones. That didn't mean the ones in the trophy were worthless. On the contrary, due to their volume, she anticipated raking in enough from their sale to cover the last of the cosmetic surgeries she'd endured over the years.

Then, too, there was always the possibility of connecting with a buyer who wouldn't recognize a real diamond if it cut open his heart. She'd sold distinctively cut glass to more than a few such morons who were only too happy to trust her. At least while she hung around and willingly sat in their laps, a situation which wouldn't last too long if she could just win the stupid gardening contest.

At first, she decided she didn't need a crooked jeweler as much as she needed a crooked gardener, preferably a male with deep pockets. Sadly, they didn't tend to advertise. Then she realized her best bet would be to find someone single who already had a spiffy garden. Love, or the semblance of same, could solve a world of problems.

~*~

"There were some babes in there I tell ya. I never woulda guessed." Bubba Broome knocked the water off the coaster formerly under his beer and put it back in place. Odell Odum sat across from him in the town's most colorful if least affluent bar, the Deep Six. Owing to the usual beer-drinking clientele, most locals referred to it as the Six Pack.

"No kidding? Some of the garden club gals *aren't* on Social Security?"

"That's a fact." Bubba took a long sip of his brew. "I ain't sayin' there weren't some granny types there, 'cause there were. Lots of 'em. But there were some really fine-lookin' ladies in there, too."

"Cougars."

"Huh?"

Odell offered up a modest belch. "One of my deputies got a part-time job as a server at the garden club's annual dinner. He claims a couple of those gals hit on him."

Bubba's interest level spiked. "No kidding?"

Odell shrugged. "I've not reason to doubt him."

Bubba sat back in the wooden booth, his mind clearly wandering. "Imagine that. A room full of lonely women."

"So," continued Odell, "tell me about this trophy you called me about. What's so special about it?"

"It's gotta be worth a fortune!" Bubba gushed. "The thing weighs a ton, I swear. I had to lift it up and set it on some kinda pedestal. Thought I'd get a hernia or something."

"Gotta use your legs."

"I *did* use my legs!"

"Okay, so it's heavy. What else?"

Bubba bobbed his head as he talked and waved his hands as if to weave more meaning into his words. "It stands about yay high," he said, with his flattened hand at belt level, "and it looks kinda like a bucket and a shovel. A small one, y'know?"

"You mean a *trowel*? Like a gardener would use?"

"Exactly!"

"Imagine that," said Odell, trying to put a look of wonder on his face. "A gardening tool used in a gardening award. I'm astonished someone could come up with something like that."

Bubba's expression betrayed confusion. "Anyway,

that part—the biggest part—looks like it's made outta silver. But it's got a whole bunch of diamonds, rubies, sapphires, and I dunno what else stuck to it. Gotta be worth... geez, I dunno how much. A lot, that's for sure."

"All that stuff might just be for show, y'know," Odell said. "Most every trophy I've ever seen was made of plastic. But you say this one's heavy?"

"Oh Lord, yes. Plus, it's got gold flower stems stickin' out of it."

"Out of the bucket?"

"Around the edges."

"How do you know they're flower stems?"

"'Cause they've all got pretty glass flowers attached to the ends."

"*Glass* flowers?"

"Yeah."

"Seems a bit much," observed Odell. He accepted the bar tab and set it beside his empty glass. "Y'know, Bubba, your Momma and I were pretty close. And Lord knows I miss her more than anybody, 'cept maybe you."

Bubba's head drooped slightly, but he remained silent.

"And I've prob'ly told you this a thousand times, but I promised her I'd keep an eye on you. Keep you outta trouble."

"More like a million times."

Odell squinted at him. "Don't be a jerk."

"Sorry."

"I'm your uncle, not your daddy. But he ain't around anymore either, so I reckon I'll have to do."

"Why don't you just go ahead and say what's on your mind," Bubba said. "I can't sit here all night."

Odell exhaled heavily. "Just promise me you won't do anything stupid."

"Like what?"

"Like tryin' to steal that ugly old trophy."

"Never said I would."

"You didn't have to."

"But—"

Odell left a twenty on the table and got up to leave. "I may run the jail, son, but I can't keep you out of it if you're bound and determined to spend time in there."

~*~

News about the club's contest, and the visible part of the prize, had circulated for some time. The *Chatter*, St. Charlotte's local newspaper and Ramona's former employer, had carried the story accompanied by photos of the award. Unfortunately, the article hadn't mentioned her son's landscaping company, which would have been a lovely bit of free advertising.

Ramona still had to provide all the details in the club's newsletter, something she'd been editing since she joined the club two years earlier. After the divorce, she found too much free time on her hands, and when the club learned about her work with the *Chatter*, they were only too eager for her to manage their publication, *The Blossom*. Ramona hated the title, and remembered when she suggested to Hildie that it be changed. The response was laughter.

"The name of the newsletter is that big of a deal?"

"I don't care for it either," Hildie said, "but the membership would rebel if we tried to change it. My plan has always been to introduce new ideas and new things to do. If we're smart, we won't have to change any of the old things."

Ramona nodded. "And pray the old habits just die out?"

Hildie smiled. "You got it! They have a name for it in football. Leonard, my husband, is always using it." She tapped her temple lightly as she searched her memory. "Now I remember. He calls it an 'end around.' I'm not sure what that means in football, but it sure sounds like what I had in mind."

Ramona had endured too many fall weekends dominated by televised football and her ex-husband's devotion to it. His unwillingness to step away from a game on the tube for anything, including their anniversary, was but one of the reasons their marriage had fallen apart. "I hate football," she said.

"I don't!" Hildie said with a laugh. "I can get a lot more done when Leonard's glued to the TV. He must have a dozen 'favorite' teams. I don't know how he keeps 'em straight. But the main thing is, when there's a game on, he forgets I'm there."

"And that's a good thing?"

"When you've been married as long as I have," Hildie said, "that's a great thing. Besides, I know what he's really interested in."

"You do?"

"Oh, sure. It's the cheerleaders. But as long as he's drooling over them on television, I don't have to worry about him drooling over them somewhere else." She chuckled. "Not that any self-respecting cheerleader would have anything to do with the old goat."

~*~

Prior to her 55th birthday, Hildie Henderson had never considered her life or any plans for it in terms of phases. That all changed the following day, and her life veered in a completely different direction.

Phase One had largely been completed. It had taken over a year and a great deal more effort than she at first imagined, but it had been worth it. Though she had started slowly with twice weekly yoga classes, she quickly realized that wouldn't be nearly enough to reach her goals. So, she arranged to attend classes daily using three different instructors. When she advanced faster and farther than her classmates, she was forced to find new classes and new instructors.

Her fitness regimen didn't end with yoga, however. She also hired a personal trainer who oversaw her nutrition and weight training programs. And, as if all that weren't enough, she also took classes in self-defense.

The revelation that caused all this had been a long time coming. Hildie's husband, Leonard, had always been a good provider. He ran a local accounting firm, and she was content to be a homemaker. They had never been blessed with children.

Hildie had never given much thought to their financial circumstances, as Leonard took care of everything. Little changed in their first two decades together; Leonard did whatever accountants did, and

Hildie gardened. And then one day, Leonard announced they were moving to a bigger house. Her input toward this decision had not been sought. The deal was done; they were moving.

Losing her beloved garden had been difficult, but Leonard agreed to foot the bill for anything she wanted to do in their new residence. Once she had an opportunity to explore the potential of their new home and expansive lot, her attitude changed. She would create a bigger and better place of beauty than she'd left behind.

Over the next few years, she concentrated not only on her garden, but the gardening needs of the club members with whom she'd become good friends. And while she was certainly aware of some extravagant changes to the lifestyle Leonard provided, she assumed he was merely reaping the rewards of his keen, mathematical mind and matchless attention to detail.

Until shortly after that 55th birthday, she had no idea he was laundering money for a drug cartel, or that he had a girlfriend about half Hildie's age.

~End of Excerpt~

Made in United States
North Haven, CT
10 December 2022

28400785R10170